THE
SPYCHIP
CONSPIRACY

M. S. MITITCH

iUniverse LLC
Bloomington

THE SPYCHIP CONSPIRACY

iUniverse books may be ordered through booksellers or by contacting:

*iUniverse LLC
1663 Liberty Drive
Bloomington, IN 47403
www.iuniverse.com
1-800-Authors (1-800-288-4677)*

*Because of the dynamic nature of the Internet, any Web addresses or
links contained in this book may have changed since publication and may
no longer be valid. The views expressed in this work are solely those of
the author and do not necessarily reflect the views of the publisher, and
the publisher hereby disclaims any responsibility for them.*

*ISBN: 978-1-4502-3909-7 (sc)
ISBN: 978-1-4502-3910-3 (e)*

Library of Congress Control Number: 2010908949

Printed in the United States of America

iUniverse rev. date: 01/21/2014

PROLOGUE

It began early in the new millennium. A marvel of technology, the VerChip would revolutionize the way people lived. The Radio Frequency Identification (RFID) microchip was about the size of a grain of rice and easily implanted into the right hand or other part of the body. It enabled authorities to electronically track the "chipped" individual, twenty-four hours a day. And its VerChip Identification Number gave instant access to the person's official data: date of birth, DNA code, current photograph, residential address, mobile phone number, employment record, bank account, credit report, and medical history comprised just the primary information.

The VerChip offered maximum personal security, rapid assistance in the event of an emergency, and convenience in purchases and financial transactions. A commercial blitz advertised the wonder product. As it was considered imperative to keep up with technology, sales were highly successful. People chipped themselves as a security precaution. Parents chipped their children to keep track of them. Pets were chipped in case they lost their way. But most of all, people chipped themselves so they did not have to carry a wallet. To perform any financial transaction required only a hand-scan. Technology had the solution, efficiency was good, faster was better.

Of course, the use of the VerChip was completely optional—in the beginning. Soon they announced that convicted felons would be chipped "to protect the public." Clearly, convicts posed a threat to society and had to be monitored. Then they declared that foreigners, immigrants, and migrant workers had to be chipped "to defend national security." These people were not citizens, so it was necessary to monitor them. Then they decreed that military and law enforcement personnel had to be chipped "to ensure civil liberties are respected." Those personnel were authorized to carry firearms, so it was necessary to monitor their activities at all times. Then they required workers to be chipped as a condition of employment, since it was a "cost-effective security measure." And then they aligned public services with the VerChip Identification Number "to save the taxpayers money." Before long, a large majority of the population was marked with the device.

Referring to the microchip as the SpyChip, opposition leaders raised their objections. Conscientious elected representatives argued against mandatory chipping regulations, but received little popular support. Religious leaders vehemently denounced the device, but they were labeled fanatics. Civil liberties groups protested, only to be drowned out by mass media propaganda. Making references to national, religious, and legal texts, leaders declared the SpyChip: unconstitutional, sacrilegious, and an assault on human rights. These leaders mysteriously disappeared from public view. Soon thereafter, the World Government came to power, imposing New World Order and disbanding the nations. Global law replaced national legislation: civil liberties were abolished; globalized commerce was mandated; unapproved religions were oppressed; dissenting speech was prohibited; firearm ownership was made illegal.

Paper money, credit cards, and other forms of payment were declared invalid. To buy or sell, to gain employment, to rent an apartment, to collect an entitlement, to perform any financial transaction required the use of the implanted chip. Global law officially mandated the Universal Identification System—the VerChip—for all world citizens.

In the rapidly approaching future. . . .

ONE

Black clouds moved across the midnight sky, obscuring the moonlight and darkening the alleyway. A warm drizzle began to fall. Trooper Victor Ganin charged his M4 assault rifle, flipped down his helmet-mounted night vision goggles and scanned the alley. The goggles depicted the old brick buildings, rough gray pavements, and barrel fires of the Bronx sector in hues of green. Rebel groups were everywhere in the sector. They thrived on illegal activities, including piracy, smuggling, and gunrunning.

Victor was apprehensive. All his years as a World Government trooper hadn't quite prepared him for this night. Red Team, the Global Police Attack Team under his command, was highly experienced and heavily armed. And some of the team members had fought with him through bloody conflicts in other world regions. But the fact they were now in World Region 1-Northeastern Quadrant-New York City Zone was not encouraging. The Bronx had recently been designated a high-threat sector. According to Global Police Force (GPF) intelligence, the Crusaders Rebel Army had set up headquarters from a building further down the alleyway. Their leader, known only as Steele, was lethal. Several attempts to liquidate him had failed. His fighters didn't take prisoners, not even for interrogation, exchange, or ransom.

"Red Leader, immediate area secure, cleared to go into the target building," said the voice in Victor's earpiece. It was the voice of Commander Drake, regional chief in charge of all liquidation operations. Drake rarely participated in field missions, but this one was so important that he had decided to direct it himself from the command helicopter gunship.

"Have rebel leaders been positively identified in the target building?" Victor spoke into his microphone attached to his helmet.

"Affirmative, Red Leader," Drake replied.

"Robot support is in place?" he inquired further.

"Robot-troopers are integrated with Blue and Green Teams as briefed, Red Leader. Your orders are to move on the target at this time. That means you, Ganin!" Drake snapped.

"Command acknowledged," Victor said, scanning the alleyway, his amber eyes reflecting the dim glow of the night vision goggles. A cold sweat ran down his hawkish face. "Blue and Green Teams, confirm you are in backup positions."

"Blue Team, affirmative," Blue Leader replied.

"Green Team, affirmative," Green Leader responded.

"Miller, Toth, Rodriguez, Branson—we're up," he breathed into his microphone.

"Ready," each team member responded in turn.

Victor signaled his team to move out. He took the lead as the black-clad troopers moved down the alley with their M4 assault rifles held in the ready position. They moved swiftly through the rain toward the target building; water splashed beneath their boots. He paused by the structure adjacent to the building, putting his back to the wall and looking around the corner at the building. A narrow pathway led to the side door. Some of the windows were broken, litter was scattered about, and rats scurried to and from the drainpipes. Next to the door stood a dilapidated fire escape that zigzagged its way to the heights of the twelve-story building.

Victor signaled with a wave of his right hand. The attack team moved down the pathway to the side door. He smashed through the door with his left shoulder, and then ran up the winding stairway with speed and stealth. The commander's voice came through the earpiece again: "Terrorists' coordinates confirmed in apartment seventy-seven: three rebel leaders armed with AK-47s, RPGs, grenades. Engage at will." He continued up the stairway like the wind, counting the floors in his head—floor number one . . . two . . . three . . . four . . . five . . . six. . . . He paused at the top of the stairs on the seventh floor. The team members breathed heavily behind him. An eerie silence hung in the air, disrupted only by the sound of water pipes dripping. He peered around the corner. Along the dreary hallway was a line of wooden doors; there were no lights. He identified door 77 as the fourth door from his position. Victor looked back at his men. Miller was closest to him, his eyes sharply focused, his camouflaged face beaded with sweat. The others were dark silhouettes further down the stairway.

With his left hand gripping the grenade launcher mounted underneath his M4, Victor whirled his right forefinger, giving the attack signal. The team moved into position within seconds—with Victor to the left, and Miller, Toth, Rodriguez, and Branson to the right of the door. Victor kicked open the door. He and Miller pointed their assault rifles inside and fired in sweeping motions—*brrrrr, brrrrr, brrrrr*. Then they rushed into the room with the other team members providing cover.

They scanned the apartment. There were three windows in series on the far wall. Centered in front of the windows was a small round table with a book on it. A crucifix hung above the windows. On the right wall, past the bedroom door, was a striped tricolor banner; below the banner stood a couch with a coffee table in front of it. On the left wall, past the kitchen door, was a large map of New York City; below the map stood a long meeting table with several chairs. In the left rear corner was an old television on a stand. Victor moved to his left into the kitchen. Miller moved in the opposite direction into the bedroom. Toth, Rodriguez, and Branson came forward to cover them.

Victor surveyed the kitchen. An inoperative refrigerator stood in the far right corner with its door open; inside it were pots and jars containing leftover foods. Next to it was an electric stove. Dirty plates and silverware lay in the sink. On the counter were a coffeemaker, mugs, and empty glass bottles. He carefully opened the cabinets, checking for booby traps. The shelves were empty except for a few canned rations.

Miller surveyed the bedroom. In the far left corner was a single bed layered with blankets. Next to it was a nightstand with a reading lamp. A dresser stood against the right wall. He quickly proceeded into the bathroom. A cracked mirror was above the sink. Moist towels hung on the bar above the commode. Water dripped in the open shower stall. He turned back into the bedroom, walked to the dresser, and opened its drawers. Inside them were casual clothes, medicines and bandages.

"All clear," Victor shouted.

"Same here," Miller shouted back.

"Lights on!" Branson said, flipping the light switches. The apartment lit with a dim light.

The team assembled by the small table in front of the windows. They flipped their goggles upward to their helmets and took a moment to adapt themselves to the light.

"Damn it! This is a waste. We've got zilch," Toth said angrily.

"We're never going to get this bastard Steele. He's too slick," Rodriguez said.

The team members looked at each other silently. Victor looked down at the table. On the table was a Bible with three tiny objects next to it. On closer examination, he could see the objects were three VerChips, shimmering in the light. He turned his attention to the right side of the room. A long since faded red, white, and blue flag hung on the wall.

"Terrorists were here all right. We're too damn late," Branson exclaimed. Mike Branson was ardent about his job. He believed in WorldGov. He believed in the New World Order. He believed in killing enemies of the state.

"These are cloned VerChips," Miller said.

Toth nodded. "That explains the false identifications."

Crashing sounds came from the kitchen—Rodriguez was smashing bottles and cabinets. Branson began spraying the walls with bullets. Victor eyed the scene warily. He was beginning to lose control of his men. "Keep it together, troopers, the mission's not over," he shouted. "Secure any evidence."

Toth bagged the falsified identification chips. "Let's get out of here," he said.

"Command gunship, we have negative contact. Further orders?" Victor inquired.

"Understand, negative contact?" Commander Drake questioned from the helicopter gunship.

"That's affirmative," he replied. "Nobody's here, nothing's here; all we have are some falsified chips."

"Stand by for an electronic sweep of the area," said the commander.

Victor waited, wiping the sweat from his face. The troopers were restless and frustrated. They had spent weeks preparing and training for the mission and had little to show for it.

"Sweep complete. No further signs of terrorist presence," Drake reported.

"All right, troopers, let's move out," Victor ordered.

With grim looks on their faces, the troopers lowered their goggles and walked toward the door. Victor took the lead as they filed out the door, through the hallway, and down the stairs . . .

Floor number six . . . five . . . four . . . three . . .

"Damn!" said one of the team members.

Victor spun around, pointing his M4 up the stairway with his forefinger hairpin on the trigger. Dark forms darted past the men. Miller was in a defensive stance with one arm shielding his face. The others were grinning. A waving tail disappeared through a hole in the wall.

"Miller's afraid of rats!" Branson's voice came through the earpiece. He was grinning broadly.

Victor loosened his touch on the trigger. Silently, he turned and continued down the stairway . . . two . . . one . . . ground floor. As he went outside, the windswept rain blew across his face. He peered through the goggles, trying to locate the armored vehicle that would provide their ride out of the sector. The low whirring sound of the hovering helicopter gunship came from above. Headlights flashed at the end of the alley, confirming the location of the vehicle. The team began moving toward it.

Suddenly lights appeared from above—showering down from apartment buildings on the opposite side of the alley. Smashing, shattering, crashing sounds filled the air as Molotov cocktails hit the pavement, spreading fire all around them. *Whoosh, whoosh, whoosh*—rocket-propelled grenades flew in—and exploded like rolling thunder, shaking the ground. The alleyway turned into a blazing inferno.

Red Team ran toward the end of the alley. Victor opened fire on the rebel buildings as he ran. *Whoosh, kaboom!*—an RPG exploded in front of him. The force of the explosion threw him into the brick wall of a building; he tumbled to the ground, coming to rest in a sitting position with his back against the wall and his helmet upside down next to him.

The night sky burned brightly with tracers, lasers, and flames. The *rat-tat-tat* of AK-47s coming from the rebel buildings was countered by the *brrr, brrr, brrr* of M4s from Blue and Green Team positions. Miller, Toth, Rodriguez, and Branson fired their grenade launchers. A hail of bullets struck Miller, riveting his body and shattering his skull; he fell to the ground in a pool of blood. Robot-troopers rushed the doors and fire escapes in an attempt to storm the buildings. *Whoosh, kaboom!*—an RPG scored a direct hit on one of the robots. The blast destroyed it; hundreds of flaming pieces shot in every direction, striking and torching other robots around it. The helicopter gunship turned toward the buildings, then launched laser-guided missiles into several windows; the subsequent explosions sent shock waves through the air. Streams of charred rubble came crashing down onto the pavement.

Victor tried to bring his eyes into focus. His vision alternated from blurs of raging fires to bright flashes. "Get up! Move it, trooper!" he said aloud to himself, but his body refused to obey. A warm liquid ran down his left side, soaking his fatigues to the boot. He felt inside his fatigue shirt. Blood flowed from gashes in his left rib area. More explosions—the earth shook violently. He looked up to the sky. A brilliant flare streaked across it. Lights faded into darkness.

TWO

Victor swam in dreams for endless days, tossing and turning as he fought the fever that afflicted him. Visions faded in and out. His mind spiraled into long ago memories of growing up in New York City . . .

Vladimir and Natasha Ganin, Victor's parents, were Russian immigrants.

"Never be afraid to stand up for your rights," his father used to say. "Nor should you stand idly by while the rights of others are trampled upon."

His mother's eyes beamed when she said, "I love you, son. I love you so much." Her smile was heavenly.

He remembered the night the masked men came for his father:

"Vladimir!" his mother screamed with little Victor wrapped in her arms, restrained by two of the men.

"Natasha, stay back!" Vladimir shouted as he fought with the men, throwing flurries of punches. The men struck him with electric shocks from their stun guns. "There is no justice! There is no freedom! There is no democracy! It's all a lie!" were his last words as he was dragged out the door. Victor, though crying and confused, would never forget those words. As for his father, he would never be seen again and the abduction would officially remain an unsolved case.

He remembered his mother in a hospital bed, dying of cancer:

"Victor," she said weakly.

"Yes, Mother," he replied with tears in his ten-year-old eyes.

"Be a righteous man as your father was. Don't let them mark you." The color faded from her eyes.

"Mother!" he screamed. "Don't leave me!"

"I'm sorry, baby. I'm so sorry . . ."

He remembered the orphanage—the fights over food and other scarce necessities. Fights because he was different: fair-haired with amber eyes. His English wasn't like that of the others. He didn't belong and he knew it.

One day, several of the gang-member boys attacked him. Victor fought back like a cornered wolf, but he was hopelessly outnumbered. In the end he was badly beaten, suffering cuts and bruises all over his body. Victor decided to do something about that. Weeks later, in the cafeteria, he confronted the gang member who had led the assault. In the ensuing fight he thrust a fork into the boy's left eye. The boy fell to the floor, screeching like a banshee, blood spurting from the eye. Orphanage staff frantically called for an ambulance. The boy was rushed to a hospital and didn't come back. After that, nobody bothered Victor. Nobody even spoke to him.

Then one day, a blonde girl from the female section brought him flowers. She sat next to him, extending the bouquet: a wild mix of daisies, lilies, and sunflowers. They gazed into each other's eyes. She smiled silently. He returned the smile. For a fleeting moment they were united in mind and spirit; she was a shining light in the darkness, beauty in the midst of misery.

Then came the day they chipped all the children at the orphanage. Staff members escorted them to the infirmary. Victor protested, then resisted. Two security guards held him down while the doctor used a hypodermic injector gun to implant the VerChip into his right hand. He cried for many nights thereafter, remembering his mother's words: "Don't let them mark you."

He recalled the chaos and madness of war. The jet transport aircraft flying him to various world regions. Helicopters whirring like angry bees, taking him from one combat zone to another. The battles—bloody visions in the night—bodies blown to pieces, flesh torn asunder, arms and legs scattered helter-skelter. Troopers incinerated within seconds—friends, reduced to ashes—once there, once not.

"Jesus . . ." he murmured in his disturbed slumber.

Several days passed. Gradually, Victor began to recover, his twenty-nine-year-old body coming back to life. His eyes came into focus on the yellowish ceiling streaked with watermarks above him. He turned his head to the left: in the center of the ceiling was a lone light bulb. Below it stood a wooden table with four chairs. On the wall beyond the table was a door. Across from him, an open window allowed a summer breeze to enter the room. He lay on a rather comfortable bed, still clothed in his tattered black fatigues with his shirt open and boots removed. Next to the bed was a small nightstand with a lamp on it. A heavy glove covered his right hand, which was handcuffed to the bed rail. His ribs were wrapped in bloodied gauze; he felt stitches in his left side. Hanging above his head was a plasma bag with a tube running down into his arm.

Victor stared at the ceiling. He felt as if he were floating through space: peaceful, tranquil, surreal. The hours drifted by unnoticed.

The door creaked open. A slim, dark-haired woman dressed in casual clothes with a stethoscope around her neck, holding a bowl in one hand, entered the room. "You've lost a lot of blood," she said, walking toward him. "Do you feel dizzy?"

"No."

"Are you hungry?"

"No," Victor said, pausing. The serenity he had felt only moments ago hadn't given him time to think of such earthly matters as hunger. But now he was beginning to feel the familiar demands of his stomach. "On second thought," he said, "it might do me good to eat something."

The woman began spoon-feeding him soup from the bowl she'd carried in. Victor found it bland and somewhat bitter. The soup tasted of beans, peas, and carrots, mixed in with wild leaves or weeds. But it really didn't matter, as hunger had set in, and he finished it to the last drop. The woman placed the empty bowl on the stand. Then she silently inspected the intravenous system above his head. As she stood there, her lustrous hair shined under the light. "Everything looks fine," she stated, turning for the door.

Some minutes later, three figures entered the room—a man, a woman, then another man. The first figure walked toward him. The man was tall with the looks of a bullfighter: dark piercing eyes, longish black hair, mustache and beard. He wore a maroon beret and olive-drab fatigues and had a Beretta 9mm handgun strapped to his side; a four-point star pendant hung on his chest. He took one of the chairs from the table, planted it next to the bed, and seated himself without breaking eye contact. The woman stood by the table. She was in her mid-twenties with an athletic shape, medium-length blonde hair, and deep blue eyes that made him feel transparent. She wore fatigues and a bandana around her head and had an AK-47 assault rifle slung on her back. A silver cross around her neck glimmered in the light. To her left was the second man. He was hulking and bald and stood with his beefy arms crossed. He wore fatigues with rolled-up sleeves and had a hunting knife sheathed on his belt. On his right forearm was a skull-and-crossbones tattoo.

The dark eyes of the bearded man remained fixed on him. Not a word was spoken. *Where am I?* Victor wanted to ask. But he withheld the question as the answer was all too obvious. He was in one of the Crusaders Rebel Army buildings. They were Steele's people. He knew that meant his chances of survival were very bleak.

The door opened again. A young man wearing an orange Hawaiian shirt, Bermuda shorts, and blue-mirrored sunglasses entered the room. The man's appearance was comical. Victor wanted to laugh but thought the better of it. *That might worsen my physical condition, especially the ache in my left side.* The man strolled across the room, handed a stack of computer printouts to the woman, then headed for the door.

The sheets unfolded down to the woman's boots as she read aloud: "'Ganin, Victor J., VerChip Identification Number (VIN). . . . DNA code. . . . Date of birth. . . . Place of birth: World Region 1, New York City, the former USA. Current address. . . . Mobile phone number. . . . Occupation: WorldGov trooper. Agency: Global Police Force. Rank: team leader. Combat tours: Meritorious service in World Region 2, the former Europe; World Region 3, the former Australia; World Region 4, the former Asia; World Region 5, the former South America; and World Region 6, the former Africa. Awards received: one Silver Star, two Purple Hearts, four Commendation Medals,' et cetera, et cetera, et cetera. 'The World Government declares confidence in the patriotism, valor, and fidelity of Team Leader Victor J. Ganin in the defense of our government and New World Order.'" The sheet slipped from her fingers and settled onto the dusty floor.

"Quite the warrior, aren't you, bronze?" said the bearded man, using the slang term for WorldGov law enforcement personnel—all of whom, from the GPF or any other agency, carried bronze badges.

Victor looked at him without responding.

"I suppose you're proud of your work?" the man continued.

"Not particularly," he replied frankly.

"Then why do you fight in conflicts, at home and abroad?"

"I just follow orders."

"WorldGov orders? To slaughter civilians?"

"No, to kill criminals and enemy combatants."

"Don't patronize me! You know most victims of war are not criminals or even combatants, but ordinary civilians."

"I don't start the wars."

"No, you prosecute them—you're the triggerman." The man paused, stroking his beard, glaring at his subject. "You think receiving orders relieves you of responsibility?"

"Nobody is innocent." Victor sighed.

"So you admit your guilt?"

"I do. Do you admit yours?"

The man's eyes lit with anger. He looked over his shoulder at the woman and the hulking man. Neither of them spoke; a group of rebel fighters passed by the half-open door behind them, their boots pounding the floor. The man turned back to Victor. "They call us terrorists. Is this your view?"

"You are classified as a terrorist organization," he replied.

"What is your definition of a terrorist, may I ask?"

"A terrorist is a—" Victor's voice faltered.

"Anyone who opposes WorldGov's dictatorship and refuses the mark," the man finished the sentence for him. "Or maybe you were about to give the official definition: 'Those who are against Unity, Progress, and Total Security for Mankind.'" A few seconds of silence graced the room. "'I just follow orders.' That is always the excuse for murder."

"Perhaps we could debate further when I'm in sporting form, maybe over iced vodka?" Victor's Russian-American sense of humor interposed.

"Get to the core of the matter," said the woman.

"All right," the man replied. "What are the size, equipment, and capabilities of your unit?"

"You know I can't answer that question."

"What are your secure radio frequencies?"

"You know I can't answer that either."

"Future attack plans?"

Victor responded with silence.

"He's uncooperative, as you can see," declared the bearded man, turning to the others in the room. "We'll have to do something about that." He stood up and signaled the hulking man.

The muscular figure stepped forward, mashing his right fist into his left palm. The woman raised her hand abruptly, stopping the man in his tracks. She walked toward Victor, set aside her assault rifle, and sat down in the chair. Her blue eyes peered down at him. Despite her hard stare, something about her put him at ease. Her stare softened then her lips opened slightly as if she didn't know exactly what to say. "Victor . . ." she began. "You're marked with the SpyChip. You are not free." After a short pause, she continued. "Victor, we've lost fifteen good people this week, our supplies are dwindling, and we cannot withstand many more attacks. We're on the verge of destruction. Do you understand?"

The men started with surprise. Victor was taken aback. "Why are you telling me this?" he asked. "Is it because you're going to liquidate me?"

"No, it's because I have searched your heart. You're not truly our enemy."

"I am a man of duty."

"Your heart is greater than your duty."

"He is to be executed—that is the rule!" the bearded man shouted, drawing his Beretta and pointing it at Victor's forehead.

"No," the woman said quietly.

"The rules state that bronze are to be liquidated!" he exclaimed.

"Don't lecture me about the rules," she replied.

"He's seen our faces, damn it," the hulking man chimed in.

"Everything will be all right. Put the gun away," she said, looking at the bearded man.

"The bronze is the enemy of the people!" he protested. The gun shook slightly in his hand; a bead of sweat rolled down his temple. Victor could see his finger beginning to squeeze the trigger.

The woman secured the man's wrist and pulled the weapon downward. "Put the gun away," she repeated.

With his eyes still fixed on his intended target, the man slowly withdrew and holstered the weapon. "You never should have brought him here," he said. "You should've left him to die like a dog in the alleyway."

The woman turned back to Victor. "You won't give us away, will you?" she asked in a calm voice.

He looked at her quizzically. "No . . . I couldn't," he responded without understanding why this was his conviction.

"Okay," she said. "Listen to me, Victor. You'll receive a painkiller drug so you feel well enough to get going. Then you'll be blindfolded and escorted out of here. You will find yourself somewhere outside of the Bronx sector. At that time you can remove the lead glove, which blocks the RF signal from the SpyChip in your hand. That will allow them to find you quickly. You understand?"

Victor nodded.

She waved toward the door.

The slim, dark-haired woman reentered the room with a syringe in hand. She walked over to him, removed his intravenous tube, and gave him a shot. The drug flowed into his veins. "All set," she said, heading for the door.

"I'll escort him out," said the hulking man, drawing a set of keys from his belt clip and unlocking Victor's handcuffs from the bed rail.

"Negative. I will," said the woman, throwing on an olive-drab parka and holstering a Beretta underneath it.

The bearded man looked at her intently. "This is not agreed. We can't—"

"Relax, everything's under control," she said, taking the open end of the handcuffs and clasping them on her left wrist.

Victor came to a sitting position and put his boots on. The hulking man blindfolded him.

"Let's go," said the woman, pulling him to his feet with a force he never expected from her. The handcuffed pair moved quickly across the room into the hallway. Victor stumbled in the blackness, trying to balance himself, feeling for obstacles. "Don't worry, I won't let you fall," she said, guiding him into an elevator. She clicked the button. The lift descended steadily, coming to a stop with the doors clanging open. They exited and walked down another hallway through double doors to the outside. After a short jog down the street, they came to a halt. "This way, down the steps," she said. "Keep your head down."

He lowered his head as they descended the stairs into an underground passageway. They began jogging again. "Hey," Victor said. "Hey, hey, hey . . ." repeated the echo of his voice. *We're in an abandoned subway tunnel,* he thought. "What's your name?" he asked, the echo trailing.

"Be quiet and keep moving," said the woman, pulling on the handcuffs. "Don't think because your life's been spared that I wouldn't put a bullet in your head." Victor held his tongue. They moved quickly through the winding tunnel. His breath grew short in the thick air. The woman breathed faster but her pace did not relent. He grunted in pain as his wounded side glanced off a cement wall. They came to an abrupt halt. "Damn it," she said. "Can't you move any faster?"

Victor leaned against the wall, laboring for air. "Sorry, this is my maximum for the moment."

The woman ran her hand across the gauze on his ribs. "The blood's seeping again. You need more medical attention," she said. "All right, catch your breath. Let me know when you're ready."

He breathed deeply, inhaling all the oxygen his lungs could take in. "I'm ready," he said momentarily.

They moved rapidly again. The air became fresher as they approached the end of the tunnel. Victor tripped on the stairs leading up to the exit; the women caught his fall. "Stand up, don't falter," she ordered. They continued to the top of the staircase. The wind swirled around them as they entered the street. With a swish, she removed his blindfold, observing him as his eyes began to focus. People passed by in a hurry. Electric cars hummed along in near silence. Clouds streamed across the pale blue sky.

They jogged several more blocks to the 161st Street subway station. As they descended on the escalator, the woman unlocked the handcuffs that bound them together. Then she led him through the turnstile toward the train. The doors slid open, and she gave him a shove into the carriage. "If you believe in freedom, Victor," she said in a strong voice, "you're on the wrong side." He turned with the doors closing between them. They stared at each other through the window as the train began accelerating down the tracks.

THREE

The black helicopter gunship flew its standard grid pattern of the Manhattan sector. Northbound over Broadway, the helicopter turned smoothly to the right, following the Harlem River to the southeast. It was a routine search-and-liquidate mission. Specialist Brian MacFarlane viewed his computer screen on his console in the back of the gunship, which showed a real-time moving map of the streets below. He looked up from his screen to the backs of the pilots. They were dressed as he was, in standard-issue flight suits and communications helmets.

The flight commander in the right seat turned toward him, his helmet's sun visor drawn down. "Got any targets?" he asked.

"Negative, sir," Specialist MacFarlane replied into his microphone.

"We have less than an hour's worth of fuel remaining. We'll head back to Global Police Headquarters before long."

"Sounds good to me. I'm ready for a cold brew."

The flight commander retracted his visor, exposing an ugly war-scarred face. "You bet," he said with a nod.

The helicopter gunship turned again, following Park Avenue southbound. MacFarlane looked at his console: a red dot flashed on the screen with an alert message above it. "I think we've got one," he said. "The subject is moving along Park Avenue, crossing 119th Street."

The pilot rolled the gunship into a left turn, circling the intersection.

MacFarlane read the information on his screen. "Subject: one Jeffrey Smith, VerChip Identification Number: 4828-9365-1092-3568."

"Continue," said the commander.

"WorldGov Central Databank criminal record #54072180 identifies subject as a certified target," MacFarlane reported. "He has a lengthy rap sheet, including terrorism, anti-civilization and enemy-of-the-state crimes. Convicted and sentenced to death in absentia by the World Tribunal, New York City Zone." He centered the zoom square on the red dot, zoomed in to a close-up image, and pushed the digital-photo button. "VIN number matches, DNA code matches, photo matches. Positive identification."

"Positive identification confirmed," said the commander. "Arm the laser."

MacFarlane engaged the red guarded switch on his console, arming and opening the laser pod underneath the gunship. "Laser armed," he stated.

"Advise when we're within targeting parameters."

The specialist turned his attention from the screen to the optical sight and joystick on his console. He peered through the sight and maneuvered the joystick with his right hand, putting the crosshairs on the subject; laser and range data showed in the upper corners of the scope. Smith was walking down the sidewalk carrying plastic grocery bags, clueless of what was about to happen.

"Stand by . . ." said the specialist. "Target within parameters."

"Target within parameters," the commander repeated. "Fire at will."

MacFarlane squeezed the trigger on the joystick; laser light flashed instantaneously from the pod underneath the gunship. The subject disintegrated—body, clothes, grocery bags and all. A cloud of ashes swirled on the sidewalk where Smith had been just moments ago—a gravestone blowing in the wind.

"Subject liquidated," the specialist reported, disengaging the laser switch.

"Good work. Any collateral damage?" the commander asked.

"We also wasted a homeless person close by."

"Negligible. There's no need to report it to our press link. Register the VIN numbers with the Global Police Force database."

MacFarlane relayed the VIN numbers of the subject and collateral victim to the GPF mainframe database. The gunship proceeded southbound again.

"All right, Specialist, it's almost party time," said the commander.

"Definitely, sir," MacFarlane replied. A green dot flashed on his computer screen with another alert message. "Receiving more info: VerChip Identification Number identifies one Victor J. Ganin, WorldGov trooper; agency: Global Police Force; rank: team leader. Status: missing in action."

"Ganin? He's on the priority list. What are the coordinates?"

MacFarlane read the latitude/longitude. "He's walking south along Lexington Avenue, passing 96th Street."

"Confirm positive identification."

The specialist zoomed in to a close-up image, then pushed the photo button. "VIN number matches, DNA code matches, photo matches. Positive identification."

"Stand by," said the commander as he raised the ground units on the radio. "They're on their way to recover him," he said, minutes later.

Victor wandered down Lexington Avenue, squinting in the bright sunlight. A short time ago he had removed the lead glove from his right hand and discarded it. His VerChip, he thought, would be briefly identified on the sector-control computers; his recovery was imminent. He paused for a moment and looked around. The sun glinted off the tall buildings along the avenue. Traffic flowed by steadily and quietly. He could see the trees of Central Park a few blocks down the cross street. He continued walking. People passed by like ghosts.

A New York Police Department squad car pulled up to the curb alongside him; its electric engine wound down to idle. "Team Leader Ganin?" inquired an NYPD officer, his head protruding from the open window of the squad.

Victor turned, looking at the officer, blinking his eyes. "That's right."

"We're here to recover you. Please come with us," the officer said in a friendly voice.

"Okay, I thought you guys might show up." He entered the back of the squad, closing the door with a snap. "Man, I've been waiting for ages!" he said jokingly.

"Well, we do our best," replied the sergeant behind the wheel. He drove off, merging smoothly with the relatively light traffic. "Looks like you're wounded. We'll take you straight to the nearest hospital if you like."

"No, that won't be necessary. Let's go directly to Global Police Headquarters in Lower Manhattan."

"You're the boss. In this traffic, the ride won't be too long."

"It's smooth sailing then."

The squad continued southbound—through the Upper East Side, Midtown, and Downtown Manhattan . . .

They drove into the Lower Manhattan militarized district. WorldGov Army and Police troopers lined the streets. The towering skyscraper of Global Security Incorporated, producer of the VerChip, appeared in front of them. The GSI headquarters building with its one hundred twenty stories was the tallest in the city; the *GSI* logo above its entrance flashed brightly. They passed by the building and came to a stop at a red light.

"Would you like one?" the sergeant asked Victor, offering him a stick of gum.

"No, thanks," he said with a grin.

The officers began chewing gum. Then the light changed and the squad took off again.

Some minutes later, the Global Police Headquarters complex came into view. Cement walls crowned with barbed wire surrounded the huge hexagonal building. The Global Police HQ complex had six wings with the Command-and-Control Section in the center: A-Wing: Attack Teams Section, to which Victor belonged; B-Wing: Flight Operations Section; C-Wing: Armored Operations Section; D-Wing: Criminal Records Section; E-Wing: Intelligence Information Section; and F-Wing: Interrogation and Holding Section.

The sergeant lowered his window as he pulled up to the guard booth by the main gate. Heavily armed security guards stood on either side of the gate. "I'm Sergeant O'Neil," he said to the chief guard inside the booth. "We're dropping off Team Leader Ganin."

"Hand-scan, please," the chief guard said through speaker holes in the bulletproof glass.

Sergeant O'Neil scanned his right hand across the Radio Frequency Identification reader unit by the guard booth. The other officer and Victor scanned the RFID reader unit by their side of the car. Their VIN numbers, DNA codes, photos, and relevant data scrolled on the computer inside the booth. The chief reviewed the data, then cleared them to enter.

The squad continued into the compound. They drove by the vast aircraft parking area. The sleek forms of black helicopter gunships occupied the front and middle rows. Remote-control attack drones were parked in the rows behind them. Ground crews were arming the drones with missiles.

The squad came to a stop in front of the main entrance.

"Thanks for the ride," Victor said, opening his door.

"Glad to be of assistance," the sergeant responded.

Victor got out of the car, closed the door and walked to the entrance. The mirrored doors opened automatically. Branson stood in the entrance, grinning. "Decided to take an unauthorized vacation?" he quipped.

"That's not exactly the kind of vacation I usually care for," Victor replied.

"I'm sure it wasn't. It's good to have you back in one piece."

"It's good to be in one piece!"

Commander Drake stood behind Branson, poker-faced. "You'd better go to the infirmary for a medical examination, then report to my office for debriefing."

"Yes, sir. I'm on my way."

After a medical examination, new bandages, and a change of fatigues, Victor stopped by the lunch bar for a meal. The place wasn't too busy and looked airy, with plain white walls and modern furniture. He sat down at the counter and ordered a glass of ice water and a steak sandwich plate. On the wall opposite him, a 3D flat-screen television was on.

"Now for the latest news from the Global News Network," said the talking head on the flat screen. "Global

Security Incorporated, creator of the Universal Identification System—the VerChip—has announced record profits this year. The announcement was followed by a corporate statement. Mr. Maximilian Mephisto, President of GSI, addressed the public from his office on the top floor of the GSI building."

The barman slid the glass of ice water and steak sandwich plate across the counter. Victor took a drink from his glass, then picked up the sandwich and began eating.

"We live in a dangerous world," Mr. Mephisto proclaimed, his dark eyes peering into the camera, his black slicked-back hair reflecting the lights. He stood with his arms at his sides, wearing a black suit with a black-and-red barber-pole necktie, and a crimson silk handkerchief in his breast pocket. The World Government slogan, Unity, Progress, and Total Security for Mankind, was in the background. "Terrorists—including nationalists, religious fanatics, anarchists and others—threaten the world community. Fortunately, Global Security Incorporated created the VerChip. It gives authorities the ability to track, apprehend, and bring these criminals to justice. It protects you and your family as well as all law-abiding world citizens. Our technology will ensure the security of mankind for this millennium and beyond. Those who oppose us are against civilization, democracy, and humanity itself."

"All the world's leaders came to confer with Mr. Mephisto," the talking head continued. "As they left the meeting, leaders were quoted as saying: 'Mr. Mephisto is a prophetic luminary.' 'Mr. Mephisto has great compassion for humanity.' 'Mr. Mephisto brings wisdom and inspiration to the world.'" The talking head grinned with sweat-smeared makeup rolling down his face. "Global leadership has reaffirmed the necessity of VerChipping all world citizens to ensure their security, welfare, and liberty," he concluded for the commercial break.

"The VerChip," said the attractive blonde on the screen, holding up a capsule-shaped microchip between her thumb and forefinger, "protects you and your loved ones from terrorists, subversives, and common criminals. It ensures rapid assistance in the event of an emergency; guarantees your right to buy, sell, and do business; facilitates employment, banking, shopping, and virtually every activity you cherish. It secures your right to life, liberty, and the pursuit of happiness as a valued world citizen. The VerChip—it's safe, it's convenient, and it's the law."

Victor finished his meal, then left the lunch bar and proceeded down the brightly lit corridors of the Global Police HQ complex toward Drake's office. His mind raced as he walked along, exchanging salutes with passing troopers. He knew the debriefing could be a mere formality or very extensive, at the commander's discretion. He thought about how he was going to answer questions without breaking his pledge to the rebel woman or incurring further investigation. *I'll have to recount events without speaking of my capture by the Crusaders Rebel Army.* His story would have to be credible. For if the commander thought he wasn't being entirely truthful, he could be subjected to a Brain-scan Lie Detector test. The lie detector computer mapped a subject's cerebral thought patterns in colored detail. It could distinguish the truth from a lie, or anything in between, with total accuracy. Clearly, such an outcome had to be avoided.

Victor was loyal to the Global Police Force, which was not only his career, it was the closest thing to family he'd had since the premature loss of his parents. So he didn't like the prospect of withholding information from his commander. But the deep blue eyes of the rebel woman pursued his conscience. She had searched his heart as no computer could possibly do. She had looked upon him compassionately, as few people had ever done, and spared his life. Her words revolved in his mind: "We're on the verge of destruction."

Giving information to his commander about her and the others would likely cost them their lives. He was duty bound, but had an obligation to her as well.

Gingerly, Victor knocked on the door.

"Come in," Commander Drake said in his usual authoritative voice.

He entered the commander's office, walked across the room, and stopped one meter from the desk.

Square-featured with a buzz cut and pressed fatigues, Drake sat upright in his armchair. On his desk were models of jet fighter planes, helicopter gunships, and attack drones. On the back wall were various gold-framed certificates and awards.

"Team Leader Victor Ganin, reporting as ordered, sir," he said, snapping a salute.

"Stand at ease, trooper," said the commander, returning the salute. Then he leaned back in his chair and eyed his subordinate. "Well . . . the mission was an abject failure. Tell me about it."

Victor recounted the battle sequentially and in precise detail, without mentioning subsequent events.

"So, the last thing you remember is being thrown into a wall in the alleyway?" Drake asked.

Victor knew this was a trap. If he answered yes, the commander would know immediately that he was withholding information. "No, sir," he responded. "I regained consciousness on a living-room sofa in a local house. The residents had apparently collected me from the alleyway."

"What house? What is the address? What are the names of these people?" Drake fired away.

"I don't know, sir. I wasn't able to get this information," he replied to the blitz of questions.

"Why the hell not? It's your duty to question those people; you know the population in that sector isn't chipped or accounted for."

"I was both physically incapacitated and mentally drained. I wasn't prepared to investigate at the time."

"You should always be prepared. Describe this house and where it's located in relation to the rebel buildings."

"It was a run-down brick house, medium size, with very little furniture," Victor began his story. "I couldn't determine its exact location but am reasonably certain it was in the general vicinity of the buildings. However, I'm sure these people who helped me weren't rebels."

"I assumed that. If they'd been rebels, you wouldn't be standing here in front of me, alive and relatively well, now would you?"

"Probably not, sir."

"So who were those people?"

"They were a young Hispanic couple, medium heights, slender, with dark hair. They spoke Spanish to each other and knew almost no English. They're undoubtedly immigrants, and upstanding, as the house had no weapons, ammunition or contraband, nor was there any sign of illegal activities."

"What were their occupations and how were you cared for?"

"The man was a manual laborer of some kind. He left for work wearing overalls, a hard hat and a tool belt. The woman stayed home most of the time, tending to household tasks and watching over me. She brought me water, soups, and medicines. And I received a visit from a doctor, also Spanish-speaking, who checked on my progress. I believe it was he who had stitched and bandaged my wounds when I was out cold. When I was well enough to walk, the couple escorted me to the subway station."

"There are no friendly elements in that sector. Why do you suppose those people assisted you?"

"I'm not sure why. They were kind and pleasant and wore religious symbols."

"An act of goodwill, you think? Is that what you think?"

"Some people have this type of benevolent philosophy."

"Goodwill only demonstrates weakness!" Drake slammed his fists on his desk, rattling the items on the desktop. "You didn't even get their names?"

"I don't understand Spanish and our communications were very limited. Anyway, under the circumstances, my priority was survival," Victor stated plainly.

"We lost your VerChip signal." The commander's eyes narrowed.

"Perhaps, the RF signal was obstructed by the house's brick construction," he said coolly.

"Perhaps it was," Drake replied. Then he eyed him sharply. "Do you have any objection to a Brain-scan Lie Detector test?"

"Of course not," he bluffed, looking straight into the commander's eyes without revealing his inner fear.

Drake pondered momentarily. "All right, Ganin. You're on convalescent leave for now. Then you will be temporarily reassigned for light-duty work until you've fully recovered from your wounds. You'll perform administrative duties. I trust you can handle the assignment," he added sarcastically.

Victor nodded. "Very well, sir."

"Dismissed," the commander ordered.

He saluted, did an about-face, and walked out the door.

FOUR

Victor drove with a light touch on the wheel. His cobalt-blue hybrid SUV purred through the streets of Manhattan. Skyscrapers towered above, countless shop windows glittered, people moved with unimaginable purpose. *It's good to be back in New York City,* he thought. The late afternoon sun flashed intermittently between the buildings. To his front, the Brooklyn Bridge came into view with the East River shimmering below it. He twisted the radio button as he entered the bridge: techno music came from the panel. Then he leaned back in his seat with one hand on the wheel.

An official announcement interrupted the music. "Attention, world citizens! Global News Network, breaking news: In a historic press release, the World Government affirmed that implementation of New World Order has brought unprecedented peace and prosperity to all. The NWO—a world government, global commerce, and a universal religion—has been officially proclaimed mankind's greatest achievement.

"In other developments: WorldGov is continuing the conflicts between our World Armed Forces and rebel terrorists in World Regions 2 and 5. WorldGov representatives have engaged in extensive negotiations with rebel leaders. Despite these efforts, the rebel elements insist on defying the world community. Their crimes include failure to swear allegiance to global authorities, refusing to embrace globalism, and rejecting the Universal Identification System: the VerChip. 'The rebels' demands of nationhood with true democracy, free enterprise, and freedom of religion are unacceptable,' said government representative Mr. Zhou Ming as he left the negotiations. 'They think it is possible to resist civilization.' WorldGov has ordered additional forces to the regions. An unspecified number of army and police trooper brigades, helicopter gunship units, and fighter plane squadrons have been dispatched to eliminate the terrorist threats. In other news—" He turned off the radio as he reached the end of the bridge.

Victor drove onto the Brooklyn-Queens Expressway, paralleling the East River. A light rain began to fall in the gathering twilight; the windshield wipers switched on automatically. He turned his head to the right, viewing a hazy light across the river. The Statue of Liberty's burning torch was faintly visible in the distance. He looked back to his front, depressed the pedal and accelerated. The white lines on the road pulsed. . . . Twilight turned to night as he drove through Brooklyn into the Brighton Beach neighborhood where he grew up and had now returned.

As Victor drove through the streets of Brighton, his thoughts drifted back to times long past.

His father Vladimir, a strong and handsome man, worked on the docks. He left for work every day with an optimistic smile and a kiss for his wife and son. "We live in America," he used to say in his Russian accent. "Things will surely get better." He would come home exhausted from the heavy labor, his face covered with layers of dried-up sweat. Yet he still had that optimistic smile.

His mother worked a kiosk on the commercial strip, selling herbal teas, caviar, and vodkas imported from the motherland. "Victor, your father and I want to see good grades from school this semester," she always said.

"Yes, Mother," he always responded.

Playing soccer with childhood friends, Victor's best friend, Ivan, would chide him, "I'll bet I score more goals than you do this summer." Ivan was very fast. When he rushed the goal, few goalkeepers could stop him from scoring.

"Yeah, you're a good soccer player but I'm a better swimmer," Victor used to retort.

Then one day, his father came home with his usual exhausted look but the smile absent from his face.

"What's the matter?" his mother asked with worried lines on her forehead.

"They signed the Globalization Treaty today. The nations have given up their sovereignty," his father replied.

His mother smiled. "Vladimir, that's just politics. You mustn't be so concerned about these things."

"Natasha, my love; don't you see? The World Government has imposed New World Order, and the nations are disbanded. This means we are no longer in America, Russia, Europe, or anywhere. From this day forward—culturally, economically, constitutionally—we no longer exist."

"Vladimir, you're overreacting," Natasha said naively.

Several weeks later, the World Government presented a list of demands to the New York City Dock Workers Union. These included the VerChipping of all workers, the globalization of the workforce, and the phased dissolution of the union itself. The demands were unanimously rejected by union leaders and members alike. The case went to the World Tribunal . . .

"The legal rights of workers cannot be compromised," union representatives stated. "These include the right to privacy, the right to fair compensation, and the right to union representation."

"What legal rights do you speak of?" WorldGov representatives countered. "The right to disregard security measures? The right to monopolize the job market? The right to blackmail corporate employers? This is simply a power play by the labor unions and workers. In any case, WorldGov Laws and Regulations invalidate all national legislation."

The presiding judge, his pockets full of government and corporate money, proclaimed: "Regarding the VerChip: security measures are fundamental to society and must be complied with. Concerning workers' rights: all world citizens have the right to compete for employment, fairly and without prejudice, anywhere in the world. With respect to the status of labor unions: organizations that block, disrupt, or otherwise impede global commerce are illegal." The judge was hailed as a great visionary and his decisions declared legal precedents for future cases.

Soon the union was ordered to disband. American dock workers were dismissed as shiploads of foreign workers arrived to replace them. Riots followed—explosions rocked the docks. Vladimir tried to stop the violence, leading peaceful demonstrations against global rule. Before long, the movement commanded the great majority of dock workers. This was not well received by the new globalist authorities and others with vested interests. Hard times had begun.

Victor recalled all these vivid memories. But most of all, he remembered the blonde girl at the orphanage giving him flowers: her beautiful eyes, her kind smile, her graceful hand extending the wildflowers. She had come to him in his time of need, when he was really alone, without a friend in the world.

He turned off the main avenue toward his red brick apartment building, coming to a stop next to the RFID reader unit by the garage ramp. A hand-scan opened the garage door. He drove his SUV down the ramp into the underground lot and parked in his space. Then he exited his vehicle, walked to the elevator, and took it to the eighth floor. As he proceeded down the hallway toward his door, a voice came from behind him.

"Victor, is that you? Where have you been?"

He turned to see his next-door neighbor, Mrs. Vera Stravinsky. "Vera, what are you up to?"

"I thought I'd go out for dinner. Want to come along?" Mrs. Stravinsky offered. Her green eyes sparkled, contrasting with her longish gray hair and weathered overcoat. Since her husband had passed away, she'd neglected her appearance.

"No, thank you. I really need to get some sleep," he said.

"Ha! Sleep! Who needs it? At my age, I don't have the time to waste," she said, smiling. "Oh, and, can you go to the supermarket for me tomorrow? My arthritis is acting up again."

"Sure, no problem." He smiled softly.

Victor entered his apartment, closed the door, and flipped the light switch. It was a spacious apartment, with a living room, kitchen, and bedroom. The living room had a white leather armchair and matching sofa in front of a 3D flat-screen television. There were four windows facing the street. In front of the windows were a glass-top table and two padded chairs. On the table was a half-empty bottle of Stolichnaya vodka, the kind his mother used to sell on the commercial strip. Along the left wall, past the kitchen door, was a desk with a widescreen laptop computer on it. Along the right wall, by the bedroom door, was a fifty gallon aquarium.

He walked to the tank and observed the angel fish moving serenely to and fro. "You must be hungry by now," he said, filling the emptied tubes of the automatic feeder. His ribs were beginning to ache again. He continued to the windows, settled into one of the chairs, and poured himself a shot of Stolichnaya. He sipped the vodka, watching the rain trickling down the windows. Airliners, gunships, and executive helicopters crossed the misty sky. The traffic below moved like rivers in the darkness. He downed the rest of his vodka, temporarily killing the pain in his ribs. Then he went into the bedroom, lay down on his bed, and fell into a deep sleep.

Morning sunshine beamed through the windows. Victor slowly opened his eyes. He got out of bed, then removed his clothes and carefully unraveled his bandages; the bandages and stitches still showed traces of seeping blood. He went into the bathroom, started a hot shower, and stepped into the soothing downpour. "Ahhh . . ." he shouted. The steaming water coursed over him, washing his weariness down the drain and rejuvenating his spirit. After some time, he stepped out, dried himself, and wrapped new bandages around his midsection. Then he dressed in black pants and shoes, strapped on his nylon shoulder holster, and put on a loose khaki sport shirt without tucking it in.

Victor proceeded into the kitchen, toasted two slices of bread, and brewed coffee. He ate the toast with butter and jam then poured himself a steaming mug of coffee. With mug in hand he entered the living room, sat down in the armchair, and pushed the remote-control button illuminating the flat screen.

"Change your wrongful ways! Learn to live a life of peace and tranquility!" exclaimed the white-haired television preacher. "The Universal Ministry, the only officially approved religion, will show you how. We have shown that Christianity, and other so-called traditional religions, are myths that don't represent the one true force. There is no God! There is only The Prophet, whose coming will herald an earthly utopia! Be prepared to follow him or face his wrath. The Universal Ministry will guide you to this true spiritual power! Deny the false religions. Join us today. Remember: your career, prosperity, and welfare depend on it."

Victor took a long drink of coffee then changed the channel.

"Welcome to *Sports Today!*" announced the host, adjusting his shiny tie. "We have a special guest for you this morning! That's right, folks. Sports superstar Michael Taylor is with us to explain his team's spectacular victory this past weekend. Mr. Taylor, the masses idolize you and want to know, what is your main objective as a sportsman? How did you win the game and what's your main objective?"

"Well, I'll tell you," said the player. "Winning's easy. I can beat anybody on the field, ain't no problem. Problem is my contract; I don't work cheap."

"So, your salary of ten million credits per year is not enough?"

"Yeah, fact is, they're short-changin' me. I want my workers' rights."

Victor finished his coffee then changed the channel again.

"Hey folks, welcome to *Instant Millionaire!*" stated the dapper game-show host. "Yes, you can become a millionaire instantly! Just send your request to appear on the show to our e-mail address with a short essay explaining why you want to be a millionaire, and you could be our next guest. Remember to include your name, VerChip Identification Number, and contact information," said the game-show host. "Now I'm pleased to present our first guest, from Region 1, Ms. Tiffany Evans. Ms. Evans, how does it feel to be on our show?"

"It's really thrilling. I can just imagine being a millionaire!" said the young woman in a floral dress.

"And what would you do with all your winnings?" the host inquired.

"Well, um, I would travel the world, spreading goodwill and hope. I would let people know the New World Order is good for them!" she said with a twinkle in her eyes.

"Well that's a great vision—and perhaps why our screeners selected you as a contestant. Now for the first question. Are you ready?"

"Ready," she responded enthusiastically.

"How is globalization a great benefit to mankind?"

"It benefits everybody because, well, we can all compete for jobs and opportunities around the world. For example, if a Region 1, former American, wants to live and work in Region 6, the former Africa, he can get a job there!" she said with a giggle.

"Question two," said the host. "Which is the best economic system, global corporatism or the discarded free enterprise system?"

"Why, clearly, it's global corporatism: government and corporations in partnership. It gives everybody a chance to be a millionaire."

"Yet rebel groups claim this is dictatorship."

"That's a lie, of course. Global corporatism merely provides the highest standard of living to all world citizens through global commerce."

"Question three," the host continued. "Why is it important to comply with VerChipping laws?"

"Obviously, it's important to comply with all laws. The VerChip ensures security for all of us. I have nothing to hide so I don't mind being chipped! Only criminals who have something to hide, object to it," Ms. Evans answered.

Balloons fell from the ceiling as the host declared her a winner. Thunderous computer-generated applause accompanied the announcement. "That's all for today, folks! Now stay tuned for *The World's Most Wanted Criminals . . .*"

Victor switched off the screen, remembering his promise to Mrs. Stravinsky. "Arrr . . ." he grunted, rising from the armchair. He clipped his bronze badge to his belt underneath his shirttail, holstered his Glock 9mm handgun inside his shirt, and headed for the door.

A stiff breeze blew through his sandy hair as he walked in the sunlit streets. He thought of the many times he had brushed with death and how good it was to be alive. The subway streaked overhead as he turned onto Brighton Beach Avenue.

"Halt!" said a metallic voice behind him. Victor recognized the voice of a robot-police officer. He turned, facing the machine. The robocop stood several feet from him, its red electronic eyes bulging from a bulky head mounted on a powerful, blue-armored frame. A bronze law enforcement badge was embossed on its left breast plate. "Your identification, please," it said, putting an articulated hand on the grip of its holstered side arm.

"It is my legal right to know why I am being stopped," Victor said. "What is your reason for stopping me?"

"The subject in question is a male, wearing dark clothes, unaccompanied and walking in an area known for unlawful activities," it said. "You fit the profile that requires investigation."

"And you fit the profile of a piece of scrap that belongs in a junkyard," Victor scoffed. He couldn't logically explain his disdain for robocops. The robots were professional, efficient, and incorruptible. And they were considered yet another technological benefit to mankind. Still, this did not quell his desire to reduce them to recycling material.

The robocop's electronic eyes made a humming sound as they zoomed in. It extended a handheld RFID reader toward him. "Identification, or you will be subject to detention and due process."

"No problem, circuit-brain." Victor passed his right hand across the reader.

The robot focused on the reader's display screen. "WorldGov trooper?"

"That's right, Global Police Force," he said, pulling up his shirttail and exposing the badge clipped to his belt.

"You are free to go. I regret any inconvenience this may have caused you."

"Yeah, sure."

Victor proceeded down the commercial strip, passing by kiosks with colorful fruits, vegetables, and meats. The sunlight intensified, quickly but gently heating the breeze.

"Victor . . . Victor . . ." a voice from the past called out of nowhere. Was it a dream? He looked to his left and right. *"Zdrastvuyte,"* said a black-bearded, middle-aged man wearing black robes, standing by one of the kiosks.

"*Zdrastvuyte,* Father Constantine," Victor responded. "It's been a long time."

"Sure has. I remember your parents," said the Russian Orthodox priest.

He nodded. "You were good friends."

The priest eyed him. "Your parents always came to church. And you?"

"Those were different times," he replied.

"Times have changed, but the principles of life remain the same," the priest remarked stoically.

Victor didn't attend church services as this would draw unwanted attention. WorldGov considered religions a security threat and had long since imposed a "belief tax" on all but the officially approved Universal Ministry. Most churches had closed due to bankruptcy or by direct orders from the government. Saint Nicholas Orthodox Christian Church, Father Constantine's parish, remained open only because of strong local solidarity.

"Maybe next Sunday," he said diplomatically.

"We would all love to see you," Father Constantine said, his robes flowing in the breeze.

Victor nodded pensively. Then he continued down the strip to Anton's supermarket. . . . He entered, took a shopping basket, and strolled down the aisles. The shelves were stocked with all kinds of genetically modified foods. He headed to the natural foods section. *Let's see, what does Vera usually want? Ah, yes: fresh broccoli, cabbage, and beans.* He found the items and tossed them into the basket. *Pasta, potatoes, and beef.* He tossed those into the basket as well. Freshly baked bread came to mind. Mrs. Stravinsky insisted on bread fresh from the oven. He moved on to the bakery, selected the loaf, and put it in the basket. Then he went to the checkout lanes.

The line moved slowly. People were mixed in with nearly identical slim, silver robot-servants shopping on behalf of their owners. A young couple held hands in front of him. An old man was at the front of the line, passing his hand across the electronic reader. The register beeped.

"I'm sorry, sir, but you've exceeded your credit limit," said the checkout girl, chewing her gum.

The old man began removing half of the many medicines and half of the food from the counter. The wrinkles on his face deepened with each item removed. He paused, looking at the box of painkillers he no doubt desperately needed. A shaking hand set it aside with the other items.

"Just a moment," Victor said. "I'll cover it." He made his way to the front of the line and passed his hand across the reader. "Just scan the rest of it," he said to the girl.

"Thank you," the man said quietly.

"Don't mention it," he responded.

Some time later, Victor walked out of the supermarket carrying grocery bags in each hand. He went back up the commercial strip and then through the side streets to his apartment building. At the front entrance he scanned his hand, unlocking the door, then entered and took the elevator. Mrs. Stravinsky was waiting for him as the doors opened.

FIVE

Victor enjoyed his convalescent leave. For the first time in his life he was able to find internal peace. He spent his days strolling on the beach by the ocean, cruising the old neighborhood, and walking through Central Park. The park gave him serenity as he hiked through its meandering trails. From time to time, he could hear robins singing, squirrels leaping from tree to tree, lovers whispering to each other. One late afternoon, at the end of a trail, he encountered a long flowing stream. He sat down on a bench alongside it. The water flowed by smoothly and steadily, reflecting sunlight and the surrounding nature. Scores of birds flew in the sky above, flapping and soaring and circling. His mind whirled into thoughts of the rebel woman: how she saw through him, the sharpness of her words, the way her hair blew in the wind. Her deep blue eyes appeared closer and closer to him in his visions and dreams.

Twilight was gathering. *It's time to go home.* Victor took a deep breath and exhaled, then came to his feet, brushed the dust off his black pants, and started back up the trail. He trekked at a steady pace, following the trail into a walkway that wound through the park. The air cooled rapidly as darkness set in. He glanced at his watch, wondering how

the time had gone so quickly, and picked up his pace. Mist
formed in the trees and meadows along the way. A lighted
exit gate appeared in front of him.

Suddenly he heard a howl. He stopped, reflexively putting
his hand on the grip of his Glock handgun holstered inside
his shirt. Turning to his right, he saw two luminous eyes
looking up at him—another howl, this time fainter. Victor
squinted to see a dog lying on the grass by the walkway.
"What's with you? Lost your way?" he said, withdrawing
his hand from the gun. The dog looked back at him quietly,
panting without shifting his gaze. He was relatively large,
with big hazel eyes, golden fur, and a bushy tail that began
to wag slightly. Victor crouched in front of the dog, eyeing
him carefully. Blood came from the canine's muzzle, chest,
and left front leg. "What happened to you?" he said, slowly
extending his hand and stroking the dog's head. The canine
flinched but did not draw back. Victor determined that the
dog was a Chesapeake Bay retriever. On closer examination,
he concluded the blood came from the distinctive bite marks
of a pit bull. "Gambling bastards've been fighting dogs again
in the Queens borough," he noted. "You're not a fighting
breed. How on earth did you survive a match with a pit
bull?" The dog only continued panting, his eyes shifting
downward.

"Come on," Victor said, gently lifting the dog. With the
canine's blood dripping down his clothes, he exited the gate
onto Fifth Avenue, then walked quickly to where his sport-
utility vehicle was parked. He opened the driver's door, slid
into the seat, and put the dog on the passenger seat. "Let's
get you to a doctor," he said, slamming the door shut.

Driving with his left hand, Victor initialized the Global
Positioning System on the panel with his right. On the touch
screen he entered the keywords: Manhattan, veterinarian,
emergency. The screen presented various addresses. He
selected the nearest one and headed for it. The dog's eyes

began to fade. "Hey! Don't you die on me!" he shouted. The dog's eyes opened again, looking up at him. "That's much better," he said, pressing the accelerator, increasing the speed. Distance remaining: 2.3, 2.2, 2.1 miles . . . counted down rapidly on the screen. Soon the veterinary clinic came into view. He gradually applied the brakes, turned into the parking lot, and parked by the entrance. Then he exited the vehicle and jogged over to the passenger side to collect the dog. Cradling the canine, he walked briskly through the automatic front doors to the reception desk.

"Good evening," said the redhead secretary wearing a lavender dress.

"Good evening," Victor breathed. "I need—"

"What have we here?" asked the gray-haired veterinarian in a white lab coat, standing behind the secretary.

"I found this dog in Central Park. He's badly injured. Can you see him immediately?" Victor asked.

"Absolutely. I'll take care of him right away," said the veterinarian. "Come with me."

He followed the man down the hallway, past a waiting room, and into the examination room.

"I've got it from here," the vet assured him.

"All right," he said, placing the dog on the exam table.

Victor sat on a chair in the waiting room, nervously tapping his fingers and shifting his legs. It was not the first time he had waited for one who was wounded. In fact, this was fairly routine in his profession. It was the causal factors that troubled him. The canine had been intentionally mismatched—set up for the slaughter, for a few electronic bytes' worth of credits. In his anxiety, he got up and wandered through the hallway back to the reception desk. He rarely smoked but thought this would be a fitting occasion to do so.

"Hey, can I bum a smoke?" he asked the alluring secretary.

"Of course you can, honey," she responded with an inviting smile, handing him a slim white cigarette and a lighter.

He returned the smile, flicked the lighter and lit the cigarette. "Thanks sweetheart, I appreciate it," he said, giving back the lighter.

"Anytime," she replied, deliberately crossing her legs in front of him.

Victor stepped outside and smoked the cigarette. Then he went back inside the clinic, past the smiling secretary down the hallway to the waiting room. He sat down again, took a pet magazine from the coffee table, and began looking through it.

"Your pet deserves the same protection that you and your family members enjoy," read the advertisement featuring grinning dogs and cats. "The VerChip ensures the safety, health, and well-being of your valued four-legged companion. Have your pet chipped for its own good. After all, man's best friend deserves man's best technology." He shook his head and tossed the magazine back onto the coffee table.

An hour later, the veterinarian exited the examination room. "Well, your new friend has had a rough time of it," he said. "But he'll be all right."

"Yeah? He's okay?" Victor said, relieved.

"Sure, he'll recover. He has multiple lacerations and a slight fracture in his left front leg. I sedated him then sutured the cuts with catgut stitches that'll dissolve on their own, gave him a shot to guard against infection, and bandaged the leg. Now what he really needs is rest. The blood loss has left him very weak," the vet advised. "It looks like he was used as a fight dog; the bite marks are undoubtedly those of a pit bull. It's a miracle he survived."

"Looks that way to me, too."

"Those vile gambling syndicates in Queens will do anything for profits. When they've got no further use for the dogs, they just abandon them. Anyway, I can see you're fond of him. I assume you want to keep him?"

"Yes, I'll keep him. Do you have any special instructions or advice?"

"Just feed him well, keep him company, and let him rest for a few days. After that, make sure he gets exercise regularly. Does he have a name?"

"Name? Guess I'll have to think of one."

"Well now, I'm sure you'll think of something. You can go in and take him home."

"Thanks for everything, Doctor."

"You're very welcome."

Victor entered the room, collected the bandaged canine from the table, and walked to the reception. Then he passed his hand across the electronic reader to pay for the services. The secretary gave him a wink as he turned for the doors.

He drove across the Brooklyn Bridge again on his way home. The dog lay sleeping in the passenger seat. It was a clear night. The stars sparkled on the dark river below. At the end of the bridge, he took the expressway southbound through Brooklyn into the heart of Brighton Beach. He stopped by the supermarket to buy Mrs. Stravinsky's usual groceries as well as dog food and other items he would need to care for his new companion. Then he continued to his apartment building, scanned his hand and entered the underground parking lot.

With each passing day, both Victor and the dog grew stronger. Every morning he changed the dog's bandages, then his own. They went for walks regularly. Short ones at first—once around the block, twice around, three times around—whatever they could manage until the dog began panting from fatigue. Despite his pains the canine remained silent, never growling a complaint. "We're a pair, you and I," Victor would say to him, "both of us broken and useless." The dog only stared in return.

Then one day, as they were consuming their respective breakfasts, Victor realized the dog still had no name. "What should I call you?" he asked. "How about Lucky? You're lucky to be alive, that's for sure!" He laughed heartily. The dog looked up at him with disdain. "All right, all right—that's not such a good name. You're a regal creature; you need a name that suits you." He thought for a moment longer. "How about Duke? What do you think?" The canine raised his head enthusiastically. "That's it! You're the Duke of Brighton!" Duke barked from the depths of his throat as if he were singing.

"Attention, world citizens!" sounded the flat-screen television in the living room as it self-activated. All official announcements automatically activated the flat screens. "Global News Network, breaking news," said the talking head. "The Region 4, rival quadrants' war has restarted after a breakdown in the peace process. Region 4, Southwestern and Southeastern Quadrant representatives cited irreconcilable differences as the reason for resuming their enduring conflict. Mr. Maximilian Mephisto, President of Global Security Incorporated, served as special mediator to the negotiations. He expressed his regrets: 'The situation is unfortunate. However, after extensive negotiations, it has been determined that there is no viable alternative to war . . .'" Victor pushed the off button several times, but it was impossible to switch off the screen. The mandatory announcements continued: "In other developments, our heroic Global Police troopers have arrested numerous suspects in sweeps of the Manhattan, Brooklyn, and Staten Island sectors in ongoing efforts to stop crime and protect the public. Suspects were charged with a range of crimes, including running contraband, accessing illegal news sources, unlawful speech . . ." The reports went on. "And remember to have your loved ones VerChipped. It's safe, it's convenient, and it's the law! This report is brought to you by GNN News, your official source of information." Finally, the obligatory announcements finished and he was able to turn off the screen.

"Let's go out by the ocean," he said to Duke playfully. He changed into a red T-shirt, a pair of khaki shorts, gym shoes and sunglasses. "The beach has lots of sunshine, clear blue skies, and pretty women today!" The dog looked at him curiously. "Anyhow, we both need the exercise."

Victor walked slowly along the beach, his gym shoes picking up sand. Duke followed, limping, his left leg rigid from the bandages. It was a pristine day: hosts of seagulls soared in an azure sky, sailboats skimmed across the glinting water, and slow-rolling waves washed upon the shore. An abrupt thudding sound came from overhead, followed by another and another. He tilted his head backward, putting a cupped hand to his brow and looking to the sky. Three skydivers flew black parachutes in a chevron formation toward the beach, the lead diver streaming the WorldGov black flag with gold stars. Loudspeakers mounted on lampposts blared the Global Anthem: "The glorious New World Order unites the world as one . . ." The rhythmic song went on.

The skydivers set off smoke canisters on their boots, with the lead man trailing gold smoke and the wingmen trailing black smoke. Then they entered a wide spiraling turn over the shore, progressively tightening the turn in the descent. As they closed in on the beach, the anthem finished playing and the smoke ended—then only the fluttering of their canopies could be heard while people watched in silence. The trio rounded their final turn, holding close formation, and came in for simultaneous stand-up landings. Cheers and applause broke out.

Duke began gnawing the bandages on his leg. "What's the matter?" Victor asked as the skydivers pulled in their chutes. "Are you tired of those or is your leg healed? Let's have a look." He knelt on one knee, took the canine's leg, and unraveled the bandages. Then he felt the leg with his hands, checking for any sign of inflammation or weakness, and determined that it was strong and healthy. "All right, it's okay," he said, releasing the leg. Duke's hazel eyes lit with enthusiasm. "Go ahead if you want—run!"

The dog spun almost instantly and began running along the shore, stretching his legs like a race horse. Wind blew through his fur, water splashed beneath his paws and saliva streaked from his mouth as he sped along the coast. People swiveled their heads, one of the skydivers pointed, even the seagulls flew in circles to view his speedy run.

Inspired, Victor disregarded his gauzed ribs and began running after him. He threw off his shirt as he ran, quickening his pace with every stride, but he couldn't keep up. Duke's form grew smaller in the distance. He knew what Duke was trying to tell him: *You're free—free to spread your wings.* He began to feel the essence of liberty: the fresh air filled his lungs, ocean sounds rushed in his ears, and the sun beamed down upon him. Time, mass, gravity—no longer existed. It was only him and the universe. He squinted through the sunlight; far in front of him the dog's form blurred in the heat waves rising from the sands between them.

The form paused and then turned around. Duke began running toward him; Victor was running at his maximum. The distance between them closed rapidly: a half-mile, a quarter-mile, an eighth-mile. They drew closer and closer. Joining like two exhausted gladiators, they spun to the sands, winded and breathing heavily. . . . "Whoa! You've got spirit, Duke! You've really got spirit!" he said, as they lay on the bright, sunny beach.

SIX

The mobile phone rang on the nightstand. Awakening, Victor reached to his right, took it off the stand and pushed the talk button. "Hello."

"Commander Drake speaking."

"Team Leader Ganin. What can I do for you, sir?"

"It's been three weeks. Medical staff thinks you should be sufficiently recovered for light-duty work."

"When would you like me to come in?"

"Tomorrow morning's roll call, six a.m. sharp."

"Yes, sir. I'll be there."

"All right, trooper." Drake terminated the call abruptly.

Victor put the mobile phone back on the nightstand. "Damn," he said aloud. "They couldn't give me more time off than this?" Slowly, he moved to a sitting position on the edge of the bed, loosened the drawstring of his sweat shorts and removed his T-shirt. Then he stood up and started changing his bandages. Duke rose from the mat by the door to an alert stance and began sniffing the surroundings.

"What's the matter, Duke? Thought you'd be used to the place by now," he said.

Duke lowered his muzzle and continued sniffing with the look of a bloodhound on his face. The canine followed an invisible trail across the floor to the nightstand. He nudged the mobile phone repeatedly, causing it to fall from the stand and bounce on the floor.

"Hey! Those are expensive," Victor protested as he secured new bandages around his midsection.

The dog ignored him, pawing the phone and growling aggressively.

"All right, pooch, what's the issue with you today?" Victor walked to the canine, picked up the phone, and observed it both front and back. He looked down at the dog suspiciously; Duke looked back at him in anticipation. Victor noticed the phone was warmer than usual. He looked at the battery level indicator. It showed that the battery was draining at a faster than normal rate. *The phone's bugged!* he thought. *Its microphone has been remotely activated to monitor conversations.* All evidence pointed to a roving bug initiated by his own agency. "Sh!" he said, putting his forefinger to his lips. He removed the back cover and battery, deactivating it, and tossed the items on the bed. Then he dressed in chinos and shoes, strapped on his shoulder holster with handgun inside it, threw on a half-zip pullover, and motioned the dog toward the door.

"Bastards!" Victor exclaimed as he walked down the hallway toward the elevator. Duke walked quietly alongside him. "I've been working for the Global Police Force for nearly ten years now. I've risked my life so many times for them and still they don't trust me?" He pushed the call button and waited. The elevator seemed to be taking twice its usual time to arrive. Finally it thumped to a stop and the doors opened. "Damn! Damn them!" he said, entering the elevator. The dog spun as the doors almost closed on his tail. They descended silently.

As the elevator doors opened, a loud popping sound resonated through the front of the building. Victor dashed to the entrance, swung the doors open and ran in the direction of the noise. Duke ran alongside, stretching to keep up with him. Down the street was a WorldGov supply truck that had been raided. Lying next to it was an NYPD police officer with blood flowing from a bullet hole in his chest. Victor stopped by the officer. He crouched and checked the man's neck for a pulse. There was none. *Rest in peace.* Several other blue-uniformed bodies lay further down the street, some of them alive and screaming for help. *We used to call them New York's Finest, now we call them WorldGov's cannon fodder.* A crowd gathered. He directed a citizen to call emergency services and parted the observers, scanning the area for the shooters. Within seconds he spotted a black Charger sedan, exchanging parting gunshots with officers as it skidded around the corner onto the main avenue.

Victor sprinted toward his cobalt-blue sport-utility vehicle with Duke at his heels. Fortunately, he had parked on the street the night before. As he ran he pulled his keychain remote control from his pocket and pushed the buttons, unlocking the doors, lowering the windows, and starting the engine. He threw open the driver's door and jumped into the seat; the canine leaped over his knees into the passenger seat. Victor slammed the door, fastened his seatbelt, threw the shift into drive and took off down the street. As he turned on the avenue, he sighted the black Charger sedan some distance ahead of him. He stepped on the power pedal. *These hybrid vehicles just don't have the power of the old V-8s.* Still, his sport-utility vehicle raced down the avenue.

The black sedan slowed for the turn on Ocean Parkway. The distance between vehicles closed rapidly. By now, the sedan knew it was being pursued. It blew smoke from its dual exhaust pipes, burning tires into the turn. "Let's dance," Victor breathed, skidding through the turn after it. He accelerated again, weaving between vehicles, maneuvering skillfully through traffic. The sedan maneuvered with equal speed and agility. The distance between them remained the same on the parkway.

The sedan merged into the Prospect Expressway. Victor glanced at the passenger seat: the canine was crouched, viewing the chase intently. As they entered the expressway, the sedan came in and out of view as it changed lanes and accelerated. He saw a break in traffic, depressed the pedal and crossed multiple lanes into the far left lane. There was a clear stretch in front of him. He put the pedal to the metal. The engine wound up to full power and the SUV gained speed, racing past other traffic. Victor sighted the sedan to his right front a short distance ahead of him. He sped down the lane until he was side by side with the vehicle. "Get down, Duke!" he shouted, drawing his Glock and straight-arming it to his right. The canine jumped to the floor. *Pop-pop-pop*—he fired three rounds in rapid succession at the driver's window of the sedan. It swerved then collided with the SUV. The vehicles joined. Victor forced the wheel to the right, dropping his gun. The sedan forced to its left. Tires burned the pavement, leaving a smoke trail behind them. Suddenly the sedan disengaged to the right. Victor spun the wheel in the opposite direction to maintain control; the SUV shuddered and swerved. The sedan pulled ahead again. "Damn it," he said, bringing his vehicle back under control.

Both vehicles accelerated toward the interchange. Traffic grew denser. Tail lights flashed from the black sedan as it veered from side to side, unable to go around the truck in front of it. Victor closed to within inches of its rear bumper and then floored the pedal, ramming it. The sedan jolted forward, swerving violently, nearly out of control. He swung to the right, pressed the accelerator, and pulled alongside it. Then he threw the wheel to the left, broadsiding it. The sedan spun once, then flipped end over end, landing inverted and sliding to rest on the shoulder of the expressway.

Victor leaned on the brakes, skidding to a stop in front of the inverted black sedan. He shifted into park, grabbed his Glock, unbuckled his seatbelt and got out of the SUV; the dog jumped out after him. He approached the sedan with his handgun pointed at it. The mutilated remains of the occupants came into view—two bodies in the front and one in the back of the vehicle. The driver's torso projected from his shattered window; his face was covered in blood, and his arms were spread out. Victor noticed a skull-and-crossbones tattoo on the man's right forearm. *Hercules* was tattooed on his upper arm. He was from the Crusaders Rebel Army, one of Steele's fighters—the hulking man who had participated in his interrogation.

Victor lowered his handgun and leaned against the guardrail on the side of the expressway. *Damn it. Why did they have to be from Steele's group? They don't usually strike in Brooklyn. Now the GPF will go full force against them.* Duke began growling as NYPD squads surrounded them from all directions. "Duke, sit!—stay!" he ordered.

Police officers leaped from their vehicles, aiming their weapons at him. "Hands up! Hands up now!"

Slowly, silently, he raised his hands above his head.

"Drop the weapon! Drop the weapon!"

He opened his right hand, letting the handgun fall to the asphalt.

"Turn around slowly. Keep your hands in the air!"

Victor turned. "*Stay* there, Duke," he ordered again.

The police officers rushed forward, threw him against the guardrail and secured him. Two of the officers began frisking him. "What the—?" said the young officer, who snatched the bronze badge from his belt. "What's this? You're a GPF trooper? Why the hell didn't you say so?" Accompanying officers lowered their weapons.

"Guess it slipped my mind," Victor said, turning to face the officer. "Besides, you boys are so edgy, I doubt you would've heard me anyway."

The officer stared at him uneasily. "Okay," he said, slowly handing back the badge. "You were close to being wasted."

"Yeah," Victor muttered, picking up his handgun and holstering it.

"Your agency's brought us nothing but trouble. The people used to appreciate us, now it's the opposite."

"Sorry about that." He signaled Duke who had been waiting nervously by the guardrail. The dog came to his side, and they began walking toward the heavily damaged sport-utility vehicle.

"What are we supposed to do with this mess you left us?" the officer yelled after him.

"Clean it up," he said over his right shoulder.

They entered the SUV. Victor put on his sunglasses, eyeing the scene in the rearview mirror: squads, fire engines and ambulances with their lights flashing, police diverting traffic around the battered mass of the sedan, firefighters dragging the bodies from the vehicle. A pall of gloom hung over the expressway. Duke gave him a sad look from the passenger seat. He shifted into drive and pulled off.

Victor drove back the way they had come, turning off and then reentering the expressway in the opposite direction. They approached the scene of the overturned sedan from the opposing lanes. The bodies lay in black plastic bags on the side of the road. Police and firefighters were conversing over cups of thermos-bottle coffee. *Times have really changed.* He sighed despairingly as they passed the scene.

The vehicle cruised smoothly along the expressway into the parkway. The engine and drivetrain appeared to be intact. He continued down the parkway into Brighton Beach. Driving through his neighborhood, he thought about how good it was to be home. Brighton was truly home for him; the people in the streets, the architecture of the buildings, even the smell of the air was different from any other place—and always welcoming to a native son.

A warning light illuminated on the panel. The "check engine" light flashed incessantly. Victor glanced at it, disappointed and wondering if his vehicle was about to break down and leave him stranded. He came to a stop behind traffic waiting on a red light. Looking to his right, he saw Saint Nicholas Orthodox Christian Church. He looked at his digital watch. It was Sunday, 10:30 a.m. "I can't believe it!" He laughed aloud, observing the irony of the situation. "All right, you got me. I'll go to church today." He turned the corner and pulled into the parking lot, knowing this would bring trouble if a law enforcement agency downloaded the record of his whereabouts for this date and time.

Victor parked in one of the few remaining spaces. He got out of the vehicle, leaving Duke in the passenger seat, and snapped the door shut. Then he walked toward the church, taking in the beauty of its Byzantine façade and ornate steeple. A celestial chant came from its upper level, filling the air all around him. He approached the heavy oak doors with a feeling of serenity. Slowly, he parted the doors open before him, and then stepped inside, quietly closed the doors, and crossed himself.

A golden cross and holy icon of Jesus Christ adorned the top of the altar. Below it were icons of various saints, all of them handmade mosaics. The saints looked upon the congregation. St. Nicholas was in the center, giving the traditional blessing with his right hand, holding the Bible in his left. St. Michael was to the right, his wings spread for flight, holding his blazing sword. St. George was to the left, riding a white horse, plunging his spear into the mouth of the dragon. Victor looked around him. There were men in suits, women in dresses, children by their sides; all of them were praying, unmindful of the human world. He hadn't been to church since he was a child and didn't know exactly what to do. But he kneeled down, joined his hands, and began to pray. *My Lord, I pray for the souls of my parents and all the faithful who have perished and entered your kingdom. For all who suffer in this world, give them relief. All who struggle, give them strength. All who have strayed, let them find their way home. Amen.* He didn't know where the words came from but those were his thoughts.

Victor rose as the gates of the altar opened. Father Constantine entered with the Bible in his hands, wearing golden robes with silver trim. He placed the book on the podium and looked at his congregation. Most of the people were working class or poor. His gentle dark eyes looked at them as a father would look upon his own children. *"Bog blagoslovit vsekh vas.* God bless all of you," he said, making the sign of the cross. Then he solemnly opened the Bible and began reading from Revelation: "'And he causeth all, both small and great, rich and poor, free and bond, to receive a mark in their right hand, or in their foreheads: And that no man might buy or sell, save he that had the mark, or the name of the beast, or the number of his name. Here is wisdom. Let him that hath understanding count the number of the beast: for it is the number of a man; and his number *is* Six hundred threescore *and* six.'" The priest closed the book. He looked pensively to the upper reaches of the church; the silence was intense. After some time, he looked back at his congregation. He proceeded with steely eyes and a strong voice, "God's followers, brothers and sisters of the faith, be warned: This prophecy has indeed come to pass. The evil is upon us! Yes, the beast's mark is upon us! The VerChip *is* the mark of the beast!—mandated by authorities who run with the devil himself!"

Victor was sure the church was bugged. *What are you doing, Father?—they will come for you.*

Father Constantine continued in a lower tone. "According to Isaiah, the Lord said: 'Fear thou not; for I *am* with thee: be not dismayed; for I *am* thy God: I will strengthen thee; yea, I will help thee; yea, I will uphold thee with the right hand of my righteousness.'" The priest viewed his congregation with a resolute look in his eyes. "So, we will not fear, we will not be dismayed, and we will be strong. We will not give in to the Evil One, his false prophets, or his beasts! Never!" A stark silence filled the place of worship. People looked about anxiously; Victor glanced back at the doors apprehensively. "And so, I too, will uphold you with my righteous right hand! Doctor Petrova!" He beckoned an elegant woman in the front row.

The doctor walked to the altar and stood by his side. The priest extended her his right hand with palm turned upward. "You know what to do," he said.

The doctor took his hand, drew a surgical knife from her pocket, and made an incision into his palm. There was no anesthetic, yet there did not appear to be a need for it: the priest seemed oblivious to pain. After cleaning the cut, she carefully inserted a pair of tweezers, and extracted the VerChip. Then she applied antiseptic and sewed up the hand.

The priest took the microchip from the doctor, tossed it on the floor and crushed it with his heel. Then he raised his hand in the air; a drop of blood trickled from his palm down his wrist and forearm. "Free yourselves! Free yourselves of the evil mark!" he shouted. "Come forth now and free yourselves!"

After a momentary silence followed by whispers and quiet conversations, people began to line up to have their chips removed; others, consumed with fear, quickly headed for the doors.

Victor crossed himself as he stepped backward. Reaching behind him, he pushed open the doors, and went

SEVEN

"Get up, Duke!" Victor said, flipping the light switch; the clock on the living-room wall showed 4:30 a.m. The dog looked up at him rebelliously from the floor rug he had been sleeping on. "Come on, I have to drop off the vehicle at the repair shop and catch the subway. No worries. You'll have the back patio all to yourself." The dog refused to move. He had never put a collar on him. *At this moment that might have been useful—no, I couldn't.* "I can see this is going to be difficult," he said, squatting in front of the canine. "I need to go. I have to report for work today, understand?" He nudged the dog. The canine slowly pulled his muzzle off the rug and stood upright. "That's more like it." He tied his boot laces, then stood up and cinched his narrow tie, holstered his side arm, and put on his dark blue Gore-Tex jacket, completing his uniform. Then he signaled the dog and headed for the door.

The pair started down the hallway. Victor stopped by Mrs. Stravinsky's door and stuck a note on it: "Dear Vera, If for any reason I can't return home on time, please look after Duke who will be in the back patio. He's that Chesapeake Bay retriever you saw me with the other day. You can use the apartment key I gave you to get the dog food or anything else you like. I know I can count on you! Victor." He looked down at the canine as they continued toward the elevator; the dog looked back up at him. A grin appeared on his lips. "Now I know why you're man's best friend. It's because man is his own worst enemy." He smirked as he pushed the call button. They took the elevator to the ground floor, then walked through the hallway to the rear of the building.

As they exited the back door into the patio, Victor motioned toward the far left corner where he had erected a doghouse. It was equipped with a swinging door, blanketed flooring, and food and water bowls. "That's your home during the day," he said, turning back for the door. Duke trotted alongside him, rubbing against his leg. When he opened the door, the dog jumped up, putting his front paws on his chest. "No way! You can't come with me." He pushed the dog back, then entered the building and closed the door behind him. A lonely howl followed him down the stairs to the underground parking lot.

As Victor drove his SUV through the streets in the early morning hours, he saw many law-agency vehicles. There were Supreme Bureau of Investigation (SBI) vehicles, Global Police Force vehicles, Regional Homeland Security vehicles, World Armed Forces vehicles, and NYPD squad cars. *Guess I'd better not be speeding.* The "check engine" light illuminated on the panel again as he turned down the street toward Marco's Garage. The engine shuddered abruptly, then silenced. He coasted to the repair shop and parked in front of it. Then he exited and deposited the keys into the drop-slot. *Wait till Marco sees this wreck!* He took out his grease pencil and scrawled on the windshield, "Fix this heap!"

Victor's thoughts flashed back to his adolescence. He remembered when young Marco, a recent Italian immigrant from Region 2, first attended the public high school. Marco was quiet and reserved, not only because he didn't know a word of English, but for the fact that he didn't trust anybody—nobody, except for Victor. Before long, Victor was spending time after school teaching him English, after which they often played soccer in the schoolyard. The two became the best of friends and remained so thereafter. In his senior year, Marco's exceptional mechanical abilities landed him a job with a local automotive repair shop. Some years later, he opened his own shop and soon earned his reputation as an ace mechanic.

Victor walked briskly down the sidewalks, breathing the cool early morning air. Bright, majestic constellations shined in the sky above. He entered the Kings Highway subway station and descended the stairs with long lines of people. Then he scanned his hand, passed through the turnstile and continued toward the train. The commuters, having noticed his Global Police trooper uniform, maintained a certain distance from him. He felt uncomfortable for a moment. He was there to "protect and serve," so he thought. Still, it was convenient for him to enter the carriage through the parting masses.

He remained standing with his back to a wall. This had been advised to him in training years ago at the WorldGov Police Academy, since terrorists wouldn't hesitate to shoot a trooper in the back. The train pulled off and accelerated, roaring down the tracks with a gentle swaying motion. He looked at the back of the carriage. In the upper corners were surveillance cameras zooming in and out, monitoring the passengers. A robocop stood between the cameras, its red electronic eyes methodically scanning left and right. There were masses of people sitting or standing; they stared straight ahead, without looking at one another. Victor noticed a couple whispering to each other. The conversation stopped as they looked up at him instinctively, then turned away.

Other commuters stirred but said nothing. The silence was masked only by the sound of the subway itself.

A baby began crying. The robocop's head swiveled in that direction. "Hush!" said the mother. The baby cried even louder. "Hush, I said. Be quiet!" she insisted, gently shaking him. The baby quieted, his eyes opening wide with a look of confusion.

A monotone computer voice announced every stop. People shuffled in and out with blank stares on their faces. Victor looked back at the robocop during one of the stops. *We really do create our own monsters.* The train continued toward Manhattan. As it crossed over the East River and Manhattan's shore drew closer, the aurora of city lights grew progressively brighter. The passengers gazed through the windows, watching the great city rise once again. *There's no stopping New York City, it's a grand metropolis.*

"Whitehall Street," announced the computer as the train came to another stop. A crowd of people exited and another crowd entered, including a conspicuous young man. The man had a lean unshaven face, keen gray eyes, and a crew cut. He wore a black leather motorcycle jacket, denim jeans and boots. He paused, surveying the passengers with a look of silent contempt, then gave Victor a cursory glance and turned to grab the handrail; a Maltese cross was embroidered on the back of his jacket. The surveillance cameras immediately zoomed in on him. Yet he seemed unconcerned, almost fearless.

Victor was curious if not suspicious. He made his way to the subject and tapped him on the shoulder.

The young man looked over his shoulder. "What's the problem?"

"Nothing exactly."

"Then why are you tapping my shoulder?"

"Just wondering what you're up to. Are you looking for someone or something?"

The man turned around. He looked up and down at Victor in his trooper uniform and said, "Nothing in particular. But I don't have to look hard to see you're on the road to hell."

Victor was taken aback by the boldness of the response. No one spoke to WorldGov law personnel without an edge of fear in their eyes and words. Perhaps the young man suffered from a psychiatric condition, or he was using mind-altering drugs, or maybe it was only the brashness of his youth. Victor wasn't sure. But something intuitive told him not to take action against the man.

"What is the problem?" said the approaching robocop in a metallic voice.

Victor faced the robot and opened his jacket, exposing the bronze badge clipped to his belt. "I checked him out. Everything's in order."

The robot's electronic eyes zoomed in on Victor, his uniform, and the badge. "Hand-scan, please," it said, extending a handheld RFID reader. He passed his hand across the reader. The robot viewed the screen, then said, "Thank you for your assistance, trooper." And then it moved on down the carriage.

The subway began accelerating again. Victor went back to his original place on the train. *Just one more stop.* He checked his watch. *It's five-thirty; I'll make roll call with time to spare.*

"Rector Street," announced the computer voice.

He walked out of the carriage, went through the turnstile, and up the staircase.

Victor walked through the half-empty streets of the Lower Manhattan militarized district. There were WorldGov Army and Police troopers, and dark-suited agents everywhere. Armored vehicles were parked at the corners with their commanders in the cupolas manning heavy machine guns. Black helicopters circled overhead, beaming spotlights down on the streets. Every block had at least one checkpoint, and all civilians were stopped and hand-scanned.

He arrived at the guard booth by the main gate of the Global Police Headquarters complex. The chief guard recognized him. "I heard you almost crashed taking down suspects in Brooklyn," he said. "I saw the report on the Global News Network—they say you're a hero."

Victor gave a hand-scan. "Well, as the saying goes, don't believe everything you hear on the news." He passed through the gate, went to the main entrance, and entered the complex. Then he proceeded down the corridors to the Attack Teams Section briefing room. As he took his place in the roll call formation, he heard voices behind him.

"Decided to live the easy life for a while?" Mike Branson quipped.

"Been having fun while the rest of us have to work?" Toth joked.

Smiling, Victor looked over his shoulder. "Sure, but I thought I should come back to keep an eye on smart guys like the two of you." Branson and Toth laughed amicably.

"Attention!" Commander Drake stood behind the podium, his square features rigid, looking sternly at the troopers now standing at attention. The WorldGov slogan, Unity, Progress, and Total Security for Mankind, was in the background. "Global Police troopers, you all know what we are up against in this and other world regions," he began. "Terrorists—including nationalists, religious fanatics, anarchists and other scum—threaten our World Government and the glorious New World Order. Our primary mission is to protect WorldGov and the NWO—through total security. What is total security? Need we all be reminded . . . ? I will remind all of you so we are crystal clear about our mission. In the words of Mr. Maximilian Mephisto, President of Global Security Incorporated, creator of the VerChip which has given us omnipotent capabilities: 'Total security means constant surveillance, identification of suspect individuals, and strict enforcement of all laws.'" He waved a forefinger in the air. "Indeed, these are the methods that make us invincible. Nobody can defy us! Subversives will be liquidated! Victory is ours!"

Drake paused, then continued in a lower voice. "Recently, there was a brazen attempt to antagonize the government. Just yesterday a group of terrorists shot and killed law enforcement officers in the Brooklyn sector. But they did not escape retribution; Trooper Victor Ganin pursued and liquidated them." He eyed Victor in the second rank. "We will not tolerate attacks on world authorities or those who represent them. Team Leader Ganin, front and center."

Victor took one step forward, did a right-face, and walked between ranks of troopers . . . then went toward the commander, stopped in front of him and snapped a salute. Drake returned the salute and said, "WorldGov declares confidence in the patriotism, valor, and fidelity of Team Leader Victor J. Ganin in the execution of his duties . . ." He finished his trite recitation, stepped around the podium, and pinned a medal on Victor's chest. "Good work, Ganin," he said with a look of pride.

"Thank you, sir," Victor responded.

"Troopers," Drake bellowed. "Team Leader Ganin is an outstanding service member who all of you can look up to. Be selfless in your duties, sure of your cause, and seize your objectives. To protect and serve, always." He surveyed his audience intently one more time. "Dismissed," he ordered. The troopers proceeded to their assignments. He grabbed Victor by the arm. "We're damn proud of you, Ganin."

"Thank you, sir."

"You've been temporarily reassigned for light-duty work. Report to the Criminal Records Section in D-Wing.

If you need anything, just give me a call, and I'll see that your request is fulfilled."

"Very well, sir."

Victor walked through the Global Police HQ complex following green lines on the floor, which led to D-Wing. As a member of the Attack Teams Section in A-Wing, he had never been there before. One corridor led into another and another. He felt as though he were walking on the moon. Finally he arrived at double doors marked Criminal Records Section. He pushed a door open and entered.

"May I help you?" asked the prim secretary behind the reception desk.

"I'm here to report for light duty," Victor said.

"You're Ganin?"

"Yes, I am."

"You need to report to Mr. Johnson, the section director."

"Where might I find him?"

"In there," she said, pointing to another set of double doors.

He walked through the doors into a vast fluorescent-lighted office area. Across the expanse of shiny white flooring were countless rows of plexiglass cubicles equipped with computers. Hundreds of workers sat in their cubicles looking at the computer screens as they typed away. Throughout the area, large 3D flat screens angled down from the columns and walls.

"You're here for what reason?" inquired a voice from his left.

Victor turned to face a balding, fifty-something man wearing a gray suit and tie. "I was told to report to Mr. Johnson."

"I'm Johnson. I'm in charge around here," said the man. "You must be Ganin."

"That's right, I'm Victor Ganin," he said, extending his hand.

"Follow me, I've got work for you," Johnson said, ignoring the proposed handshake. He walked with a loose stride down several rows of computer workstations, mumbling to himself something about needing a vacation. Then he stopped and pointed at one of the cubicles. "That one's yours. You'll work here for a while."

"All right, Mr. Johnson. Who'll show me what I have to do?"

"Ms. Galloway'll be here shortly."

Victor sat down at his new World Government workstation. A screensaver of the Earth rotating about its axis, with a one-eyed ghost image watching it through a SpyChip, was on the computer. The eye turned and stared at him.

"Ganin?" asked an attractive brunette in a snug outfit, walking toward him.

"Yeah, that's me."

"I'm Ms. Galloway."

"You're more than I expected," he remarked, observing her shapely figure.

"And you're about as cocky as I expected," she countered. Victor could smell a pungent perfume as she sat down in the chair next to him. "Let's get to work, shall we? Pay attention," she said, moving the mouse and eliminating the screensaver. "You're going to work the *persona non grata* files. These are secret records of people who were tried, convicted, sentenced to death, and liquidated—which means they never really existed."

"If they never existed, why are there records of them?"

"You're a clever one. Usually the attack teams' guys are not exactly what you'd call brilliant. Okay, here is what you must do: You'll receive pop-up messages on your screen with criminal records attached to them. Review the records for accuracy and make sure all blocks are filled in correctly. If you get one that has a mistake, send it back to its point of origin. If everything is in order, simply click 'Send to GPF mainframe database,' which makes a permanent copy in our system. Then the record must be forwarded to the WorldGov Central Databank in Region 2's city of Brussels. Click 'Send to WorldGov Central Databank.' And that's it. You got it?"

"Seems easy enough."

"Anything else I can do for you?"

"Sure, how about your number?"

"You can't afford me, buster! The payment for my Porsche alone is more than you make in a month!"

The woman got up and walked away, swaying her hips purposefully.

Victor eyed her with disgust. "Is there any coffee around here?" he grumbled to no one in particular.

"I'll get you one," a voice said from the cubicle to his right. "I'm Camille," said a skinny young blonde in a tan pantsuit, rising from her chair and extending her hand over the glass partition.

"I'm Victor," he replied, joining hands.

"Pleased to meet you," Camille said. "Do you want cream or sweetener?"

"Just plain coffee, please."

She walked to the nearest coffee vending machine and pushed the button, glancing over her shoulder while the dark liquid poured into the cup. The machine stopped. She withdrew the cup and walked back to the cubicles. "There you go," she said, extending the coffee over the partition.

"Thank you," he said, taking the cup.

"It's not so bad around here, once you get used to it."

"I'm not getting used to it at the moment."

"Just don't think too much—they're only statistics. You'll go mad if you do."

"I suppose so . . ." Victor replied, looking back at the computer screen. He remembered the words of his trainers at the police academy: *"You're not paid to think."*

EIGHT

The pop-up messages came in rapidly. Soon, Victor was behind in his work. He clicked on the attachments and focused on the computer screen.

> Global Police Criminal Record #58935146: one Peter Graham, VIN number 4325-5195-9086-2189. Official data follows: Convicted of crimes against humanity, including public discourse subversive to the World Government and New World Order, fomenting dissent against legitimate global authorities, and organizing anti-globalization demonstrations. Sentenced to death by the World Tribunal, New York City Zone, on the date of. . . . Liquidated on the date of. . . . Birth certificate and all other documents of said subject declared invalid. Registered grave denied: *persona non grata.*

> Global Police Criminal Record #58935147: one Mark Schroeder, VIN number 4967-1289-0235-5403. Official data follows: Convicted of crimes against humanity, including leading demonstrations against global corporatism, organizing illegal labor unions,

and disturbing the economic peace. Sentenced to death by the World Tribunal, New York City Zone, on the date of. . . . Liquidated on the date of. . . . Birth certificate and all other documents of said subject declared invalid. Registered grave denied: *persona non grata.*

Global Police Criminal Record #58935148: one Debra O'Donnell, VIN number 5623-3287-4481-8365. Official data follows: Convicted of crimes against humanity, including practicing an unauthorized religion in public, religious recruitment without a license, and disturbing the theological peace. Full confession confirmed by a Brain-scan Lie Detector test. Sentenced to death by the World Tribunal, New York City Zone, on the date of. . . . Liquidated on the date of. . . . Birth certificate and all other documents of said subject declared invalid. Registered grave denied: *persona non grata.*

Victor processed the sea of documents, registering copies with the GPF mainframe database and forwarding the records to the WorldGov Central Databank in Brussels. Document after document appeared on the screen. He could barely keep up with them. *Damn, we're understaffed.* He glanced up at the clock as his fingers tapped the keyboard. *It's eleven o'clock; one more hour till lunchtime. I don't know if I can take this much longer.* "Phew!" he said, leaning back in his chair and loosening his tie.

"What's the matter?" Camille asked, looking through the glass partition.

"There're just too many records to process."

"We're understaffed at the moment. WorldGov simply doesn't have the funds to hire more people."

"Global taxation isn't enough?" Victor inquired.

"Apparently not. I mean, they have to pay for the glorious military campaigns to bring freedom and democracy to people around the world. After all, everyone deserves freedom and democracy just the same as us! Don't you think?"

"Sure they do."

"You *do* believe in worldwide democracy, don't you?"

"Of course I do."

"Somehow, you don't seem like a true believer."

"Look, Camille, I'm just an average guy; I do my job and go home. But on my job, sometimes we go home in a body bag. Understand?"

She looked at him disappointedly, then back to her computer.

Victor sighed, looking at the messages filling the screen. He took a sip of the lukewarm coffee and grimaced. "Ugh! What kind of java do you have in this office?"

Camille looked through the glass. "Sorry, it's artificial. They've been having problems with suppliers in World Region 5. Rebels have disrupted coffee bean production. Can you believe that?"

Victor slid the cup away from him in disgust.

The flat screens came on automatically around the office area, indicating a mandatory announcement. All work stopped as people looked up at the surrounding screens.

"Attention, world citizens!" said the talking head on the screen. "Global News Network, special report: Hail to our leader! Our democratically elected World President speaks from World Government headquarters in London."

"Good day, patriotic world citizens!" said the World President. The president was a youngish, handsome man with zealous eyes and slightly graying hair, wearing a blue suit and tie. He was seated behind a large desk with the WorldGov slogan, Unity, Progress, and Total Security for Mankind, in the background. "As law-abiding citizens, we are appalled at the recent surge of violence in various world regions. This is the work of rebel terrorists who seek to destroy the glorious New World Order and civilization itself. These elements promote war by committing acts of sabotage and terrorism. They create divisiveness by claiming separate national, ethnic, and religious identities. They subvert progress by disrupting production and commerce. Furthermore, to undermine security, avoid capture and evade justice, they reject the Universal Identification System: the VerChip. Clearly, these subversive elements pose a grave danger to the world community. Therefore, I have made the decision, in accordance with our commitment to worldwide freedom and democracy, to escalate the military campaigns against rebel fighters in World Regions 2 and 5. Our heroic World Government forces will triumph! The terrorists will be brought to justice! Victory is ours!"

Appearing behind the World President, placing a hand on his shoulder, was Mr. Mephisto. "Global Security Incorporated expresses its unwavering support for the efforts of WorldGov and global leaders," Mephisto said. "Government and corporations: working together for Unity, Progress, and Total Security for Mankind." He smiled with shiny teeth. The screens changed to images of crowds from around the world applauding and cheering the speech.

"They care so much about us!" Camille exclaimed with tears of admiration.

"Great humanitarians!" chimed in a voice from across the room.

"Death to all subversives!" said another from his glass cubicle.

People sat in a trance, even as GNN signed off and the screens went blank. Victor began tapping his fingers on his desk, observing the workers.

"All right folks, let's get back to work," Mr. Johnson said.

Victor mindlessly processed more documents, hardly noticing the names or circumstances on the records. Lunchtime finally arrived. He left his computer and joined the crowd headed for the cafeteria. The people filed through the two sets of double doors into the corridor. They continued in silent clusters down the D-Wing corridors of the hexagonal structure. Only their footsteps broke up the silence along the way. After some minutes they arrived at glass doors that slid open before them.

The cafeteria was fully automated with robots doing the cooking, serving, and cleaning. The floor gleamed with black-and-gold checkerboard tiles. Victor took a tray, plate, and flatware. He moved along in the line, looking at the menu on the wall: "Today's special: processed beef, genetically modified corn, and artificially flavored ice cream."

"What would you like?" asked the robot-servant behind the service counter.

"Anything but the special," Victor responded.

The robot moved its head in confusion. "My apologies, sir; can you be more specific?"

"That was a joke, circuit-brain. Give me combination one."

"Combo one, immediately, sir."

Victor took his tray full of grayish food to the nearest open table, settled into a chair, and began eating.

Camille wandered over like a stray cat, set her tray on the table, and sat down across from him. "The World President was impressive, don't you think?" she asked.

"Sure he was."

"I mean, really, the speech was inspiring!"

Victor chewed the tasteless food without responding.

"Don't you think he was spectacular?" she pressed, poking his arm with her finger.

"Please leave!" Victor said. Camille pursed her lips, looking back at him incredulously. "Go away," he said firmly. Left speechless, the woman stood up, lifted her tray, and walked to another table some distance away. He stayed alone at the table. The herd of people did not interest him. They were so many sheep in a pen.

The flat screens in the cafeteria were playing a soap opera.

"Fernando, I love you so!" the actress declared.

"We will always be as one!" the actor proclaimed.

"Yes, yes. We will be as one, forever!"

"Let's go to the land of milk and honey together."

"Yes, let's."

Victor swallowed the last of what was on his plate. Then he got up and started walking toward the back doors that let out into an indoor atrium.

"Would you like dessert, sir?" asked a robot's voice behind him.

"No thanks," he said over his shoulder, "I've had enough of the food around here."

The doors slid open and he went into the spacious atrium. There were plastic palm trees around the area, audio speakers emitted bird-chirping sounds, and a water-jet fountain whirled over a circular pool. He sat down in one of the chairs at an aluminum table, putting an elbow on the armrest and his chin in his palm. His thoughts drifted back over recent weeks. The vision of the rebel woman haunted him again, her deep blue eyes peering through him as she said, "If you believe in freedom, Victor—you're on the wrong side."

"Mind if I join you?" said a familiar voice.

Victor turned to see Robert Rodriguez from his attack team. "Hey man, what are you doing here?"

"Light-duty assignment for a while." Rodriguez pointed at the cast on his right arm as he sat down.

"Combat?"

"Not exactly; I fell on my front steps in the early morning. Can you believe it?"

Victor cracked a half-grin. "It happens. Where did they assign you?"

"I'm working in the Intelligence Information Section in E-Wing, adjacent to your wing."

"Is there any intelligence there?" Victor quipped.

"Not much. Most of the workers are pretty dense," Rodriguez said.

"These people too. I fear I'll go mad here."

"I know. You don't like bureaucrats or desk work."

"How's everyone in A-Wing? Any news?"

"Everyone's okay. The word is they're gearing up for a hot mission."

"It's business as usual then. What do they have you doing in the Intelligence Information Section?"

"Processing transcripts. The mainframe computer intercepts and records citizens' electronic and telephonic communications on the basis of keywords," Rodriguez explained. "For example, 'Steele' automatically triggers an intercept in this zone. The conversations are then reviewed and classified. Those that are deemed possible security threats are forwarded to specialists who perform conclusive analyses and determine what actions must be taken."

"Doesn't it disturb you, reading transcripts of private conversations?"

"No, actually it's quite amusing. Today I read a transcript of a woman complaining about her relationship. The conversation was intercepted because of the word 'explosion.' It turns out that she has an 'explosion' of feelings about her boyfriend who frustrates her in various ways. Not the least of which is the lack of sex. Apparently, twice a week is not enough for her. I almost wrote down her number in case I need a date on Friday night!"

Victor laughed. "Be careful. She could turn out to be your worst nightmare!"

"My luck with women? Probably so. Anyway, I'm looking for something meaningful: a wife, children, that sort of thing. I come from a family of eight. You know—a traditional family."

"Yes, I know. They procreate like crazy."

"You're such an insensitive prick!"

"Sure, that's one of my better qualities!"

Rodriguez chuckled, rising from his chair. "See you, Victor."

"Later, Robert."

Victor returned to his workstation and initialized the computer. Camille was already in her cubicle, eagerly processing e-documents for her WorldGov employer. The afternoon hours dragged on endlessly. He was not adapted to sedentary work. Frequently, he left his station to stretch or pace. Sometimes he went into the corridor to do jumping jacks or to run in place. Finally the shift bell rang. Breathing a sigh of relief, Victor rose from his chair and began walking briskly toward the doors.

"Where're you going in such a hurry? Got a hot date or something?" Mr. Johnson asked.

"Something like that," he replied as he continued walking.

The fresh air blew across Victor's face, bringing welcome relief. Even the blank faces of pedestrians and bustling traffic were better than the false atmosphere of the office. He walked at a good clip toward the Canal Street subway station. Along the way, he grew hungry and stopped by a hot dog stand.

"A Chicago-style dog, please," he said to the brawny vendor.

"One Chicago dog, coming up," the vendor replied, picking up a poppy-seed bun. With his tongs he took a frankfurter from one of his steaming metal containers and placed it in the bun. Then he took various other ingredients, piled them on top, added yellow mustard, and handed over the jumbo dog.

Victor took a big bite of the hot dog filled with onions, pickles, relish, and every kind of pepper imaginable. He looked around the streets, chewing and swallowing, then looked back at the vendor. "How many people do you serve every day?" he asked.

The vender eyed him sarcastically. "What's it to you, pal?"

"I'm just curious."

"I figure two hundred or so. Everybody loves hot dogs."

"Do you love them?"

The vendor grinned. "After looking at them all day long, the last thing I'd eat is a hot dog. Anyway, I prefer gyros."

"Thanks for your sincerity."

He finished the hot dog then wiped his hands with a napkin and tossed it in the trash can.

"Food for the homeless?" said a weak female voice. An elderly woman dressed in a gray overcoat with a worn-out sweater and faded pants was leaning against the wall next to the stand.

Victor had grown weary of the ever-increasing numbers of homeless beggars on the streets. Nevertheless, he scanned twenty credits to the stand's electronic reader. "Give her whatever she wants," he said to the vendor.

"God will surely reward you," said the woman.

He continued through busy sidewalks to the subway station. Dark clouds were gathering overhead. *We're in for a raging thunderstorm.* He descended the staircase with the masses. . . .

The train pulsed down the tracks. Victor gripped the handrail above his head, periodically looking at the subway maps posted on the walls to check his progress toward his destination. Stop after stop, crowds of people moved in and out of the public transport.

"DeKalb Avenue," announced the computer voice as the train came to another stop.

As usual, a robocop stood at the back of the carriage, surveying the passengers. As the train began moving again, it made its way through the crowd with a handheld RFID reader, checking identifications. "Hand-scan, please. Hand-scan, please. Hand-scan, please," said the robot repeatedly. Commuters passively passed their hands across the reader.

"Brighton Beach Station," announced the computer many stops later.

Finally, I'm home, he thought, exiting the carriage.

Victor walked from the subway station through the streets of Brighton; a storefront's digital clock showed 6:30 p.m. The streets were relatively tranquil and the air was dead calm. A few children still played on the sidewalks. People watched through their windows.

He continued walking. Loud voices drew closer as he approached St. Nicholas Orthodox Christian Church. Protestors were confronting police lines blockading the house of worship. Supreme Bureau of Investigation agents chained the front entrance; above the doors, the cross hung upside down as it was being dismantled. Iron bells hung silently in the steeple. The protesters shouted with increasing anger, then surged forward. Police lines pushed them back with long plastic shields. Tactical police units moved into backup positions, pointing their heat-ray weapons at the demonstrators.

Victor made his way through the crowd, presented his bronze badge, and crossed police lines to the doors of the church. "What's going on here?" he asked the agent in charge.

"SBI business," replied the stone-faced, dark-suited agent.

He insisted. "Speak, man. What's going on here?"

The agent looked away briefly, then said, "All right, it's like this: the place is shut down, direct orders straight from the top."

His amber eyes narrowed. "The priest, Father Constantine. Where is he?"

"Look . . . There is no Father Constantine, there never was such a person, *persona non grata*, understand?" said the agent. Victor's eyes lit with anger. The man looked back at him coldly. "Listen, I know this establishment was popular with the locals. However, my agency ranks over yours; so I advise you to move on or you will be subject to detention and due process."

Victor held back his words. He looked at St. Nicholas's Byzantine façade, then up to the steeple pointing toward the darkening sky, and walked on.

NINE

The storm was building with a vengeance. Dark clouds billowed on top of dark clouds as evening set in. Hard rain drops began to fall, sporadically at first, then with increasing frequency. Victor quickened his pace, pulling his jacket over his head. The wind howled and the rain intensified. He leaned forward against the force of the wind and rain. Lightning flashed, thunder rolled, and the rain poured down as he turned onto his street toward his apartment building. *I hope Vera has taken Duke inside,* he thought as he approached the building.

Victor hurried past the front entrance, went to the rear of the building and verified the doghouse was unoccupied. Then he turned to the back door, scanned his hand and twisted the knob; stepping forward, he bumped his head on the door. He put his hand on his forehead. *That hurts.* The door hadn't unlocked. The rain was interfering with the RF frequency of his VerChip. *The technology isn't perfect.* He wiped his hand dry inside his jacket and scanned again. This time the door opened.

The rear entrance had no elevator, only a stairway. Victor climbed the winding flights of stairs to the eighth floor, and paused to catch his breath. Then he proceeded down the hallway to his apartment door and took out his keys. A familiar barking came from inside the door. It opened before he could insert the key. Mrs. Vera Stravinsky stood in the doorway, running a hand through her gray hair, wearing a green dress that matched her eyes. "Oh, my! What are you doing out on a night like this?"

"I got delayed coming back from work," Victor replied as he entered. Duke jumped about him, barking again and wagging his tail excitedly. "Hey, pooch," he said, gently tousling the dog's furry head.

"You'd better get out of those wet clothes," Mrs. Stravinsky advised, pushing the door closed.

"I guess so. If I catch a cold, I might have to call in sick for work—that would break my heart." Victor replied sarcastically. He went into the bedroom and changed into a polo shirt, chinos, and casual shoes. Then he came back into the living room. Mrs. Stravinsky was seated at the table with a melancholy look on her face, staring through the window at the storm, taking a drag from her cigarette. Her emptied glass sat next to the uncapped bottle of Stolichnaya vodka on the table.

"Vera, I think I'll join you for a drink. It seems we both need to lift our spirits," he noted. "Would you like an iced glass?"

"Sure, Victor," she responded quietly, still looking through the window.

"All right, I'll get a couple of glasses from the fridge."

"Sounds good, kid," she said with a glance.

Victor went into the kitchen and took two iced glasses from the refrigerator and then walked back into the living room, nearly tripping over Duke, lying on the rug. "You'll have to excuse the mess in my apartment," he said, putting the glasses on the table.

"I had a husband and raised two boys. I'm used to messes!"

"Well okay, but try not to trip over anything, especially a dog!"

"Yeah, sure," she said with a grin, putting out her cigarette in the ashtray and pouring two vodkas.

As he lowered himself into a chair, a splendid array of multicolored lightning bolts flashed outside the windows. They smiled, watching the light show.

Victor lifted his glass. *"Na Zdarovye!"*

"Na Zdarovye!" Mrs. Stravinsky echoed, raising her glass.

They clinked their glasses and downed the fiery liquid.

A single white lightning bolt flashed very close to the windows, blinding them momentarily. Thunder shook the building and the lights flickered. Duke jumped up and barked.

"Wow! Can you believe that?" Victor exclaimed.

"That was a close one," Mrs. Stravinsky replied.

Looking at his desk behind him, he noticed his widescreen laptop blinking then initializing.

"Your computer's turned on by itself," she remarked with a surprised look.

"It's never done that before," Victor said, rising from his chair and walking toward it. The screen materialized as he sat down in front of it. Another bolt streaked by the windows as the tempest continued to rage. The computer opened many stored files in succession. Finally, it stopped on one photo. The photo matched an image ingrained in his memory.

"This is the one photo I have of the orphanage," he said. "I'm always trying to forget about those days."

Mrs. Stravinsky, still half-blinded by the flashes, moved next to him. She focused on the screen. "Who's that in the center, standing next to you?"

"A girl I used to know. She was my only friend in that place." He thought of the wildflowers she had brought him when he was so alone.

"She's a beautiful girl."

"Yes, she is."

"There's something unusual about her."

"What do you mean?" Victor asked.

"She has the deepest blue eyes," Mrs. Stravinsky noted. "Can you zoom in?"

Victor centered the zoom square on the girl's face and clicked the zoom button. Her face enlarged to a close-up. He tilted his head quizzically. *No, that's impossible.* Shaking his head, he applied the age-progression program to the image. The girl's face transformed into that of a woman in her mid-twenties. "What! No, it can't be!" he exclaimed.

"What's the matter, Victor? You look like you've seen a ghost!"

"It can't be . . . It can't be . . ." he repeated in disbelief.

The photo closely resembled the blonde woman of the Crusaders Rebel Army.

"What can't be?" Mrs. Stravinsky asked as more lightning flashed outside the windows. Victor looked back at her, stunned. "Speak, Victor!"

"Vera, I'm sorry but I have to ask you to leave."

She gave him a concerned look for a moment. "All right, dear," she said, patting him on the shoulder. "If you need anything, just knock on my door."

"Thank you kindly."

She gave him another worried look, then walked out the door.

Victor stared at the computer screen in a stupor. Duke came to his side, sat down on the floor and looked up at the screen. *This simply can't be!* He rose from his chair and began pacing back and forth; with every turn, he looked at the screen. It was her, beyond a shadow of a doubt. The rebel woman and the girl he had known at the orphanage were the same person. *What was her name?* He searched his memory extensively. *Tara Anderson, that's her name . . . I have to see her again—but how?*

The storm outside was beginning to move out of the area. A few more lightning bolts shattered the night sky, followed by waning thunder. The rain slowed and the windows began to clear. Victor walked to the windows and folded his arms. He looked down at the table: next to the vodka bottle was a pack of cigarettes with a box of matches on top of it. Mrs. Stravinsky had forgotten her cigarettes. She was the only person he knew who used matches instead of a lighter. He took one of the smokes from the pack, flicked a match, lit the smoke, and took a long drag; then he put his forearm on the window frame and watched the now distant flashes. *The storm must be over the Bronx by now.*

Victor could barely tolerate his work in the Criminal Records Section. The week passed slowly: minute by minute, hour by hour, day by day. It was perhaps the slowest week of his life. By the end of the week time was imperceptible. His mind drifted as he sat in his cubicle processing the endless stream of records. The keyboard rattled as he typed. He glanced up at the clock for maybe the tenth time in as many minutes. It was almost quitting time for his now extended shift. *Thank God it's Friday,* he thought. The shift bell rang. He sprang from his chair and headed for the doors.

"Where're you going? Got a hot date again?" Mr. Johnson asked.

"Sure, I'm looking forward to the weekend."

"That's obvious."

Victor rushed out of the doors as if he were being chased by phantoms. *How many dead souls did I process this week?* He proceeded to his locker and changed into civilian clothes, putting on brown cargo pants, a hooded gray sweatshirt, his shoulder holster with Glock inside it, and his black leather jacket. Then he exited the complex and headed for the subway station, barely noticing the gleaming skyscrapers, which usually drew his attention. Along the way, his stomach began growling. He stopped at a sandwich stand.

"Roast beef on rye, please," he said to the portly vendor.

"Coming your way," the vendor replied.

The stand's radio was on. "Global News Network, breaking news: The Region 4, rival quadrants' war has intensified. Southwestern Quadrant forces clashed with their Southeastern Quadrant rivals in a major confrontation. Fighter planes, armored formations, and infantry fought in one of the bloodiest battles in regional history. Thanks to smart-bomb technology, civilian casualties were nonexistent . . ."

"Would you turn that down, please?" Victor asked, taking out his mobile phone.

"No problem," said the vendor, handing him the sandwich.

Victor took a bite of the sandwich and called the repair shop.

"Hello, Marco's Garage."

"Hi, this is Victor."

"Yeah—owner of the blue SUV that resembles a train wreck."

"Very funny, Marco."

"Listen, Victor, for you I'll do most anything but something like this, I give no guarantees. That mess you dropped off has half my staff tied up. This time you've gone too far."

"Oh, come on now, quit your complaining. How much more time do you need to repair it?"

"Don't you want to know the cost? I mean, it needs engine, electrical, and body work."

"Don't change the subject. How much time?"

"If I didn't consider you like family, I'd tell you to get your heap off my lot. But okay, a few more days."

"A few more days only?" Victor asked in surprise.

"Sure, the work's halfway done already!" Marco snickered.

"Wise guy! You had me going."

"Hey, you know you can count on me. You'll get your wheels back in no time; and when you do, it'll be better than ever."

"That sounds great to me."

"I'll send you the bill. For you, it's at cost; just don't pass out when you see it!"

"I'll try not to! Okay, see you soon, Marco."

"See you, Victor."

He turned off the phone, finished eating the sandwich, then continued through crowded sidewalks to the subway station. *A few more days without my wheels.* Victor descended the staircase, scanned his hand and passed through the turnstile. He was dragging from the office work but it didn't matter. He was determined to catch the train northbound, into the Bronx sector.

It was standing room only in the subway. Victor gripped the handrail above his head, leaning against the back wall as the train went through the city. "103rd Street. . . . 125th Street. . . . 149th Street. . . ." announced the computer voice. The crowd grew thinner with each successive stop until only a small number of people remained in the carriage. He walked to the doors as the train came to its last stop. "161st Street—end of the line. All passengers exit, please." Subway lines beyond 161st Street had long since been decommissioned. He walked out of the carriage, passed through the turnstile and took the escalator. Then he exited the station, pausing to check his watch; it was still early evening.

Victor began his trek into the Bronx. He knew he was entering the most dangerous area in the most dangerous sector of New York City. This did not concern him. He was armed and obsessed with his quest. *I have to see her again.* The streets were dimly lit, mostly from starlight and smoldering barrel fires that filled the cool air with smoke. Few people were out and about, passing each other in silence, or speaking in low voices. The walls were painted with murals of Jesus Christ and the holy saints. No law enforcement vehicles could be seen. This was the land of the desperate, the hopeless, the forgotten. This was rebel territory. As he went further into the sector the streets grew darker and the smoke thickened. He drew his hood over his head to block some of the smoke. At a lighted crossing, he turned the corner and paused to look down the street. Some of the vendors were still selling their goods: guns, ammunition, drugs, clothes, canned foods, bottled water, and other items.

"Lookin' for something?" said a woman vendor selling bottles of whiskey by the corner.

"Some information," he replied.

"Information'll cost you."

"How much?"

"Depends on what you want to know."

"Where can I get an unregistered mobile phone?"

"A dozen bullets."

"What?"

"Bullets are the best payment, if you got 'em. If not, water filters, food or clothes will do; whatever I can use or barter."

Victor looked around him, scanning for a possible setup.

"Don't worry, I'm on the level. If you've got the payment, I've got the information," she said.

He reached into his left cargo-pant pocket and took out one of his spare ammunition magazines. "That's fifteen rounds; keep the extras."

"Go there," she said, taking the magazine and pointing to one of the dilapidated shops down the street.

"Thanks," he said earnestly.

He walked to the shop, then slowly opened the door and entered. A dusty haze hung in the air. Behind the counter was a gray-bearded old man, wearing wire-rimmed glasses and a moth-eaten cardigan.

"Word is, you've got unregistered mobile phones," Victor said, drawing back his hood.

"You heard wrong," said the old man, looking up at him over his glasses. "Everything's legit in this shop."

"Sure, mister." He approached the counter. "Just tell me how much you want."

The man stared at him. "The payment's got to be valuable, understand?"

Victor took out another spare magazine. "Will this cover the cost?"

The man took the magazine in his hand. "Who sent you here?"

"The woman whiskey vendor just up the street."

The man nodded. "If she thinks you're all right, so do I. You say you want a secure mobile phone?"

"That's right."

"Take this one." He slid an old phone across the counter.

Victor picked it up and removed the back cover and battery. It had no serial number. He reinserted the battery, put on the back cover, and called a number to test it. "Great, everything checks out. It's a done deal," he affirmed, turning for the door.

As he continued further into the Bronx, the shadowy streets brightened with the neon signs of the nightclub strip. On the strip a person could find anything, anybody, any destiny. The safe houses of rebel groups were mixed in with fight clubs, gambling bars, and drug houses. Victor knew what he was looking for: according to GPF intelligence, the Gaslight nightclub was a hangout for Crusaders Rebel Army members and other enemies of the state. He kept on walking . . .

Amber neon letters scrawled across an opaque window marked the nightclub. He opened the doors and stepped into the crowded, smoke-filled, former concert hall. The patrons ranged from rebels to outlaws and outcasts; nationalists, libertarians, anarchists, mobsters, and exiles socialized in their respective groups. The club itself was owned by a musician turned businessman.

Victor sat down at a table in the rear of the club, discreetly putting his Glock in his boot. He tapped his fingers on the table as the band began playing a modern version of "New York, New York."

"What'll it be, honey?" asked the peppy waitress, taking a pencil from behind her ear.

"Vodka on the rocks, please," he replied.

"You got it." She scribbled on her notepad, and went away.

A few minutes later the waitress returned with a serving tray. "There you go," she said, placing the iced vodka with a slice of lemon in front of him. "Anything else, sweetheart?"

"Nothing for now, thanks."

Victor took a long drink. . . .

Three black men approached the table. They were stout and wore black suits, and two of them had white ties. The man in the center had a red tie. "What's your business here?" demanded the man with a red tie, exposing a gold tooth as he spoke.

"What's it to you?" Victor said, drawing his Glock under the table.

"You're bronze, ain't you?"

"You're delusional."

"Is that right?" The man's eyes narrowed.

"You can bet on it," Victor said, pointing his left forefinger at him.

The two bodyguards reached inside their suit jackets.

Victor stood up in a flash, pointing his handgun at the forehead of his inquisitor.

The man grimaced and his associates froze. In a composed voice he said, "That doesn't answer the question: what's your business here?"

"Relaxation. This is my kind of joint," Victor replied.

"Ha! All right then!" said the man, extending his hand. "Name's Luther. I own this place."

Victor tossed the gun to his left hand and shook the man's hand with his right. The bodyguards removed their hands from inside their jackets. He followed suit and holstered his weapon.

A tall figure appeared in the shadows behind Luther, observing silently. His silhouette revealed a bearded face, longish hair and a beret on his head. The bulge underneath his parka suggested that he was packing a side arm.

Luther looked over his shoulder. "Got an issue with him?"

"Depends," the figure responded in a low voice.

"Ain't my business, Rafael—so long as there's no trouble in my place."

The three men left, but the figure remained in the shadows.

Victor sat down again, took a drink of his vodka, and pretended not to notice the uninvited guest.

Alternating spotlights swept the stage. The musicians rolled with their music: the lead guitarist jammed, the keyboardist tapped the keys, the bass guitarist plucked away, and the drummer slowed the beat as the singer went into the finale.

"What do you want here, bronze?" the figure demanded.

"What makes you think I'm the bronze?"

"I know the likes of you when I see them."

"It's up to you, New York, Neew Yooork!" finished the band. A scattered applause broke out. "Thank you, people. Thank you very much!" said the singer. The band took a breather, wiping sweat from their faces and drinking from their glasses.

"Great song," Victor said.

"Yes, it is," the figure replied.

"So we meet again."

The figure drew back. "You know who I am?"

Victor shrugged. "I never forget a face or a voice."

The man moved forward into the bluish light. His face became visible: dark piercing eyes, longish black hair, mustache and beard; a four-point star pendant hung on his chest. It was the rebel man who had interrogated him. "I see that you've recovered enough to go back to your foul work," he said caustically.

"I'm recovering," Victor affirmed, downing the rest of his vodka. "Sit down, Rafael—please."

"If it were up to me, I would've wasted you then. I should waste you now, bronze."

Victor eyed the man. "I should waste you, but it would make a mess in this fine establishment."

The band began playing a smooth melody . . .

Rafael sat down at the table, glaring at him. "I suppose you're here as a spy."

"You suppose wrongly. I'm not a spy, only a fighter like you."

"I'm nothing like you—"

"Tara Anderson," Victor said, cutting to the chase.

Rafael leaned forward, looking at him intently.

"Tara," he repeated. "We both know her, don't we? Where may I find her?"

"What's your business with her?"

"I just want to talk to her."

"For what reason?"

"She was my only friend once."

"What are you getting at?"

"See, we knew each other long ago. I was—"

"We know all about you . . . now."

So they know. And most likely Rafael is under orders to discover and report back my intentions. He's only looking for an excuse to be a spoiler. "Then maybe you understand why I'd like to speak with her," Victor said.

"I'll relay a message for you, nothing more," Rafael replied, nervously stroking his beard.

"Tell her to contact me at this number," he said, sliding a piece of paper across the table. "It rings this secure mobile phone I bought on the black market." He reached into his inside jacket pocket, took out the phone and held it in front of him.

"All right . . . I'll do it. But if you bring harm to her, I swear—I'll kill you."

"Understood."

The rebel fighter took the note and left. The band played on, and Victor hummed to the music.

TEN

"How much is it to Brooklyn?" Victor asked the taxi driver parked outside the nightclub.

"Depends on what you've got," replied the grizzled driver with a checkered hat.

"How many credits will it cost?"

The man cracked a dry grin. "Sorry, pal. I need something I can trade, and I need it up front."

"How about a digital watch?" he said, holding up his left wrist.

"It's worth the ride."

Victor removed his watch and handed it to the driver.

"Hop in," said the man.

The neon lights faded behind them as the old taxi rumbled through the dark streets. The figures of gun merchants, drug dealers and prostitutes lined the sidewalks. As a precaution, Victor put his hand on the grip of his side arm. The driver didn't stop for anything, not even for the few functional traffic lights along the way. *Good man.* Bright expressway lights appeared in front of them.

Victor withdrew his hand from the gun. "Tough job you've got," he said to the driver.

"Yeah."

"Is that all you've got to say?"

"Yeah."

"All right." *Why should he have anything to say? There's nothing he can do to change things.*

The car accelerated up the entrance ramp into the expressway. Traffic was light at that time of night. A few luxury vehicles cruised by them. WorldGov black flags with gold stars waved in the wind from the lampposts. The following day was Globalism Day, a universal holiday. The taxi driver looked briefly in the rearview mirror; Victor was looking through his window with a distant stare in his eyes.

"Exactly where in Brooklyn are you headed?" the driver asked.

He slowly turned to the man. "Brighton. I'll direct you when we get there."

The driver smiled slightly. "I had a fiancée there once."

"Ah, yes?—must stir a memory."

"Sure does."

Victor was curious, but he didn't inquire further.

The taxi wound through the vast urban landscape, passing by forests of crystalline skyscrapers, glass-box office buildings, and high-rise hotels, as well as sprawling residential areas. The great metropolis twinkled in the night, like an earthly galaxy with smoke and noise and corruption, but no horizon. Expressway lights pulsed across the windshield. The driver adjusted his hat. "She was beautiful," he said quietly.

"Whatever happened?" Victor asked.

"We were in a bad traffic accident. I was driving with her in the passenger seat. A car ran a red light and slammed into us. She was killed instantly. I survived with minor injuries. I never saw that car coming . . ."

"This was long ago?"

"Yeah, that's right."

"Have you been married since?"

"No . . . she was the only one for me," said the man, sadness trailing his words.

Victor fell silent for a moment, then said, "The accident wasn't your fault. It was just fate."

The driver glanced in the rearview mirror but gave no response. He merged into the parkway and continued to Brighton. Victor gave a few directions, which left them in front of his building. Then he opened the car door and put his right foot on the curb.

"Hey pal . . ." said the driver.

"Yes?" He turned.

"Here's your watch. The ride's on me—thanks," the man said with tears in his eyes.

"No, you keep it," Victor said with a nod. He exited the taxi, closed the door and walked toward his building.

A note was taped on his apartment door: "Dear Victor, Duke's in my apartment. I intend to keep him unless you're willing to draw swords! Vera." Victor chuckled as he went over to Mrs. Stravinsky's adjacent apartment, pausing by her door.

"You want this drumstick, huh?" Mrs. Stravinsky's voice came through the door. Duke began barking. "Well, you can't have it!" The barking turned into howling. "Oh, all right you big baby, there you go." She laughed. The sound of crunching bones followed.

Victor grinned as he knocked on the door.

"Who's there?"

"It's me."

Footsteps moved toward the door. The sound of a bolt sliding open was followed by various chains being removed and the turn of a key. Mrs. Stravinsky opened the door, her green eyes beaming. "Well, our canine friend is engaging. But he has no manners whatever!"

"That's part of his charm!" Victor quipped. Duke was already jumping about him, licking his face and smearing saliva on his jacket.

"Come in, Victor," she said, observing him. He entered, removed his jacket and hung it on the coat rack. "You look like you've got something heavy on your mind."

"Vera, you're one of the few people who can read me," he replied.

"I'm listening . . ." she offered, closing the door.

"Well, it's complicated," Victor began, taking a seat at the dining-room table. Mrs. Stravinsky sat down across from him. "It's like this: I have a conflict of interests."

"A conflict of interests? That's an interesting way of putting it, but at least it's a start."

"There's a woman I can't get out of my mind."

"Oh, I get it—you're in love!"

"I'm not sure how I feel."

"Then you're in love!"

"Maybe, but it's more complicated than that."

"What do you mean?"

"You're a lousy hostess. You haven't even offered me a drink yet."

"My goodness, you're right." Mrs. Stravinsky got up and jogged into the kitchen. She returned with an unlabelled bottle of clear liquid and two glasses, sat down again, and poured two drinks. "There you are," she said, handing him a glass.

Victor eyed the glass suspiciously. "What kind of concoction is this?"

"It's the best homemade vodka from the motherland! I received it just this week from relatives in St. Petersburg."

He took a cautious sip. "It's quite good."

"Told you so," she said, taking a drink from her glass. "Now what's on your mind?"

"All right . . . the woman I'm talking about—"

"Does this have anything to do with the photo we saw the night of the storm?"

"You're very perceptive," he noted.

"Usually," she responded.

Victor took a long drink. "Let me explain it this way: she and I are opposites; maybe not in the usual sense of the word, but we find ourselves on opposite ends of life's spectrum."

"Now, that does sound complicated, at least the way you describe it. Let me ask you this: what does your heart tell you?"

"My heart tells me one thing, my mind another."

"That is one of the greatest dilemmas in life," Mrs. Stravinsky said thoughtfully. "The mind is usually right; and when it is followed, you can avoid many misfortunes. But when the heart is right and you follow it, you gain eternal happiness."

Victor smiled slightly, stroking Duke's head and scratching him behind the ears. He looked at the photographs on the wall: faded photos of Vera and her husband when they were young—strolling arm in arm down sunny boulevards, scenic avenues, and dreamy city streets. She wore long dresses and ribbons in her hair. He wore sport coats, white shirts and wool ties. They were charming together.

"How did the two of you meet?" Victor asked, finishing his drink.

Mrs. Stravinsky smiled and finished hers. "I hit Stephen with my Harley-Davidson."

"You what?"

"I hit him with my Harley as he was crossing the street!"

"I didn't know you rode a motorcycle!"

"Sure did. I had a Sportster."

"I always wanted to have one of those. So you actually tried to kill him?"

Mrs. Stravinsky laughed. "I wasn't trying to kill him. My front brakes failed; it was a cracked brake line, I think. Anyhow, I couldn't stop at the traffic light."

"So you hit an innocent pedestrian."

"Who turned out to be my future husband."

"Then what happened?"

"Well, as a recent immigrant, I knew very little English; so I kept saying I'm sorry. Despite his pain from the accident, he asked if I was all right and helped me lift my bike. He was a true gentleman. I was shaking so badly, I could hardly grasp the note with his phone number when he offered it to me."

"Sounds like you were a wild child," Victor mused.

"You bet," Mrs. Stravinsky replied as she bared her right upper arm, revealing a tattoo of a heart with crossed swords.

"And what does that signify?"

"The fact that true love conquers all."

"Well, the next time I need a thrilling ride to work, I'll call you."

"Ahh, I don't ride motorcycles anymore, just the subway. Besides, when I got married I sold my bike."

"Why's that?"

"Because I was always with Stephen and he preferred to drive a car. We were inseparable and did everything together. A day without seeing each other was like a day without sunshine. Anyway, meeting my husband was the best thing that ever happened to me; for together we found true love, which is sacred, joyful, and everlasting."

"So, it's heart over matter?"

"No, it's mind over matter, but in some cases heart over mind."

"Have you ever felt like you're on the wrong track in life? That what you're doing is wrong? And how do we know the right path?"

"You're asking profound questions today, young man," Mrs. Stravinsky said, observing him pensively. "God defines right and wrong. We just have to apply His Word from the Holy Scriptures, which also lives in our conscience, to any given situation. Some situations we may be challenged with are polemic. For example, is it right or wrong to kill someone who is trying to kill you? To steal food when your children are starving and you have no other options? To fight against a government, including your own, which deprives the people of their rights and freedom?"

Victor looked at her quizzically. "You're saying the answers are in the Scriptures and within us as well?"

"I'm saying His Word supersedes that of any government, organization, or individual. Trust in Him and yourself. Let your conscience be your guide. Sometimes doing the right thing is the tough way. It's rarely the easy way."

He looked at the clock on the wall; it was past midnight. Duke was falling asleep. "Well, it has been an experience talking to you, as always. Thanks Vera, but we have to get going."

"Anytime, Victor."

Victor walked over to his adjacent apartment with Duke ambling alongside, half-asleep. As he entered and closed the door, the black-market mobile phone vibrated in his pocket. He stopped. The response was sooner than expected. *What do I say?* He took out the phone and looked at it. It was a text message. With a sigh of relief, he pushed the button and viewed the screen: "Meet me this morning in Central Park." *Where in the park and at what time? Guess I'll have to play it by ear.* He pushed the off button. Then he went into the bedroom, lay down on his bed, and drifted asleep.

"Get off me, dog! Can't you find a place to sleep besides my bed?" Victor said.

Duke awoke, raised his head and squinted at him. Victor was still dressed in his clothes from the day before. He looked back at the dog. *A staring contest—just what I need in the morning.* He went into the bathroom, pulled off his shirt and looked in the mirror: his eyes were red, his hair was disheveled, and a beard was beginning to form. *She'll think I'm a werewolf!* He washed his face, ran wet fingers through his hair, and shaved himself—then went back into the bedroom and put on a white sport shirt. *Okay, now I'm ready.* He walked into the living room and headed for the door. Duke sprang to his side. "No, you're not invited." The dog growled in protest. "Maybe some other time," he said, patting the canine's head.

The subway wound its way to Columbus Circle. Victor exited the subway station at the traffic circle. Globalism Day celebrations were in full swing: fireworks exploded in the sky, crowds sang the Global Anthem, and parades rolled down the streets. Floats went by with statues of WorldGov leaders on top of them. Troopers marched by in close formations with assault rifles slung on their shoulders. Formations of robot-troopers marched behind them in perfect step. Combat veterans passed by in uniforms with shiny medals pinned on their chests, many of them on crutches or in wheelchairs. Fighter planes streaked past overhead, trailing black and gold smoke from their wingtips.

Loudspeakers blared: "World citizens, rejoice! This day we celebrate mankind's greatest achievement, the New World Order: a world government, global commerce, and a universal religion. The old national, economic, and religious institutions have been abolished. Gone are the days of selfish individualism. We are one! We shall advance together toward our glorious destiny!"

Victor crossed the circle and headed for the entrance to Central Park. *She's taking a risk, meeting me in the middle of Manhattan, only a short distance from the militarized district.* He entered the park, which seemed a world apart from the city itself: trees towering above, birds singing, plants and flowers swaying in the breeze. He went up the main walkway, looking to either side for any sign of the woman. He passed by lush green fields, luminous lily ponds, and colorful flower gardens. The gardens were full of couples walking hand in hand. Men played cards on the benches, gambling for cigarettes and other valued goods. Joggers and in-line skaters went past him from both directions. His trek continued along the shore of a sparkling lake. As he approached the far end of the lake, he heard a quiet voice.

"A penny for your thoughts," said the voice.

Victor turned to see a redhead with purple streaks in her hair, sitting alone on a bench by the lake. She wore a lightweight jacket, short blue jeans, striped socks and gym shoes. The woman had lots of mascara and gave the impression of being an adolescent.

He tilted his head quizzically. "Tara?"

"Shh! Come here," she said.

Victor smirked, walked over to the bench, and sat down next to her.

They looked at the lake in front of them. The ducks swam in files, the adults leading their offspring, leaving silent ripples in their wake. Geese waddled around the water's edge. An occasional swan sailed by.

"You knew who I was all along?" he asked.

"I recognized you the moment I found you unconscious in the alleyway," she replied. "How could I forget the lonely boy at the orphanage?"

"And I've never forgotten the girl at that place who was always there for me." After a short pause, he added, "But I never imagined we would cross paths again."

"I've always known we would see each other again one day."

"Really? How could you know such a thing?"

"I don't know how. I just *knew*."

He was silent for some moments, then smiled slightly and said, "You look the same as always. You haven't changed at all!"

Tara covered her mouth as she chuckled. "Sure, I've always been an odd-looking redhead." She handed him a bouquet of assorted wildflowers. "Here, these are for you, Victor."

He smiled. "Thanks. You're the only woman I know who gives flowers instead of expecting them."

"Look, there's a white one," she said, pointing at the lake.

"A white what?"

"A white swan. It will bring good luck."

"I suspect we can both use lots of luck."

The sunshine gradually intensified. He wiped his forehead as sweat began trickling down his face and chest.

"Nervous?" she asked.

"Somewhat," he responded.

"Well, so am I."

"Why?" he inquired with an arched eyebrow.

"I really don't know," she replied with a glance.

"Aren't you hot in that outfit?"

"Yep."

"Then take off your jacket."

"It comes with the territory. The disguise stays on."

They looked at the lake again. A flock of seagulls landed on the shore, the most majestic one gliding to a perfect landing in front of them.

Tara turned back to him, staring until he felt uncomfortable. "The word is you killed Hercules and his team."

Victor looked at her and frowned. "What are you talking about?" Tara continued staring. Then he remembered the tattooed body protruding from the inverted black sedan. "Damn it," he muttered.

"So, it's true?" she said.

"Listen, I was leaving my apartment building when I heard shots—"

"So it's true, you killed them."

"It's not that simple. I gave chase, Duke and I—"

"Who's Duke?"

"My dog," he breathed nervously. "Listen, it's complicated."

"Apparently so."

"Don't judge me. Don't you judge me!" he said angrily.

"That's not my job, Victor. I don't judge. That's someone else's job."

They both looked back at the lake. The water reflected warming rays of sunlight. Before them, the flock of seagulls took flight, climbing out toward the horizon.

"Tara."

"What?"

"I wish things were different."

"So do I. But that's not the way it is, is it?"

"No, it's not." After a long pause, he turned to her and asked, "Why did you agree to see me?"

She looked at him strangely for a moment. "Because, I just had to, and you're an enigma."

Victor laughed under his breath. "An enigma?"

"Yes, I can't figure you out. It bothers me when I can't put things straight in my mind. Why did you want to see me?"

"You haunt my dreams."

"Your dreams? I didn't mean to do that," she said, turning away.

"Well, you do." He looked away briefly, then said, "I need to see you again."

She gazed out in the distance for some time, then smiled faintly. "Do you prefer me as a redhead, blonde, or brunette?"

"I prefer you as you are."

"Now, that could be difficult. I can't exactly show myself in public; some people want me dead."

"That won't happen as long as you're with me."

Tara looked at him and smiled. Victor smiled back at her. Those were the same deep blue eyes he remembered from long ago.

ELEVEN

A warm morning breeze blew through the open window. Victor lay on his sofa, dressed in a black polo shirt and chinos. Duke sat on the floor rug, howling softly. "Yeah, I know you want to go out for a walk. All right, give me a chance to eat something before we go," he said, looking at the aquarium. The angel fish swam gracefully back and forth, some of them weaving their way through plants at the bottom of the tank. The automatic feeder activated, sprinkling food into the water. The angels swam up to the surface to consume it.

He stepped into the kitchen, made a ham and cheese omelet, and began eating. The dog was crunching nuggets from his bowl. The canine looked up at him, wanting a treat. Victor shook his head. "Can't have one now, maybe later."

There was a knock on the door.

"Who is it?" Victor called.

"The servant of apartment eighty-one. I have a small request, sir," said a robot's voice.

He walked to the door and opened it. A domestic robot-servant was standing at the entrance. The robot looked ridiculous with a floppy chef's hat on its head and an apron around its midsection. "Would, sir, kindly sell my keeper some sweetener?" it asked. "Of course, he will pay the appropriate amount of credits."

"Okay, just a minute," Victor replied, the Chesapeake Bay retriever growling behind him. He stepped around the dog, went back to the kitchen, and returned with a cup of sugar. "Sorry, I only have the real stuff."

"That will be adequate," it said, taking the cup. "Would, sir, please give a hand-scan to receive credits for this item?" The robot extended a handheld RFID reader.

"It's on me."

"My humble apologies. Could, sir, please clarify his response?"

"It's for free, no charge, understand? Or do you have a short circuit?"

"My keeper thanks you for your generosity."

He slammed the door shut. The mobile phone rang on the coffee table. He went to the table, picked up the phone and pushed the talk button. "Hello, Victor speaking."

"Hi, this is Marco. Your heap's ready."

"It's a Sunday."

"I know. I thought you might like to have your wheels for the rest of the weekend."

"You're the best, Marco. When can I pick it up?"

"I'll meet you at my shop's front gate in about an hour if you like."

"That'll be fine. I'll see you there."

"See you there. Goodbye."

"Goodbye." He pushed the off button.

The sun shined brightly as Victor and Duke walked down the sidewalks, headed for Marco's Garage. He strolled with his thumbs hooked in his pants pockets, taking in the street scenes, whistling a lively tune. The dog trotted along with his tongue hanging out. On the way, they stopped at a fast-food stand.

"Two plain hamburgers, please," Victor requested.

"Two? You must be hungry," the vendor noted.

"One's for him," he said, pointing at his companion.

"No problem, two burgers coming right up."

The meat sizzled on the grill for a few minutes.

"There you go," said the vendor, handing him the burgers.

"Thanks," he said, giving a hand-scan. He passed one of the burgers down to the dog.

They ate quickly. Then they continued to the garage. . . .

"Victor, good to see you," Marco said, opening the front gate, his wavy hair blowing in the breeze.

"Likewise, Marco," Victor replied, sighting his cobalt-blue SUV in the front of the lot.

"Come on in. Your wheels are ready to roll," Marco said cheerily. "It's almost like it was originally," he added as they walked toward the vehicle.

"What do you mean by almost?" Victor asked suspiciously.

"I'll show you." The mechanic smiled, going around to the rear hatch and opening it.

He looked inside: twin white cylinders were bolted to the floor. "Pray tell, what are those?"

"Well, you know how you're always complaining about the lack of speed in these hybrids?"

"Yes, that's right."

"Now you've got all the power your heart desires!"

"How does it work?" he inquired, unable to conceal the elation in his voice.

"It's a nitrous-oxide system," Marco explained. "When activated, the bottles release the oxidizing agent through lines leading to the engine, and then through the injectors to the intake ports and into the combustion chambers. This significantly increases the fuel-air mixture. In other words, you'll get a bigger bang."

"How much will it increase acceleration and speed?"

"Overall performance will increase by approximately fifty percent."

"Is that the best you can do?" Victor quipped.

"That's the best I can do within your budget, wise guy," Marco replied, closing the hatch. He walked over to the driver's door and opened it. "Time for a driver's education lesson." Duke jumped past him into the passenger seat without permission. "Dog's got no manners," he remarked.

"So tell me more," Victor said, looking at the panel. "How do I use the system?"

"It's user-friendly. Just flip the red toggle switch on the panel to the up position." Marco pointed to a switch above the radio. "Then, as you're accelerating, simultaneously push and hold the two buttons on opposite sides of the steering wheel."

"For how long?"

"No more than ten seconds continuously. More than that and the engine will self-destruct."

"How many boosts do I have available?"

"With the dual system, from a dozen to twenty—depending on the duration of the boosts."

"Excellent. How did you come up with this?"

"It's one of my inspirations. Of course, it's based on race car technology. I thought you would be an ideal test subject."

"You're a genius," Victor said, jumping into the driver's seat. He closed the door and lowered the windows. "Thanks friend, I really appreciate it."

"For you, anytime. Hey, did you see the game yesterday?"

"What game?"

"The Mets baseball game. They won again. They've been going strong all season."

"Well, how about that," he said, engaging the ignition. The engine started up and purred quietly.

"It's hard to believe, but after all these years we've got a winning team."

Victor snickered. "That's long overdue. Okay, see you around, Marco."

"See you, friend."

He shifted into drive, applied the power pedal and drove out of the lot.

Victor drove his SUV through the streets of Brooklyn. It was beautiful late-summer weather. *It's a nice day to tour New York City,* he thought. *I haven't rambled through The Big Apple since I was a kid!* He varied the speed, accelerating and decelerating to check the vehicle's response. It was running normally. He twisted the radio button and tuned in a station: classical music came from the panel. Then he leaned back in his seat with one hand on the wheel, humming to the music. Duke stuck his head out the open window, squinting his eyes, his golden fur blowing in the breeze.

An official announcement interrupted the music. "Attention, world citizens! GNN breaking news: Our heroic World Government forces have achieved great victories! In rapid combat operations, our forces have liberated strategic cities in Regions 2 and 5. With lightning speed our troopers drove deep inside rebel territories, routing enemy fighters, and deposing regional dictators. Cheering crowds greeted them to express their support and gratitude. The World President and Mr. Maximilian Mephisto issued a joint statement affirming the significance of this historical event: 'Our WorldGov forces have blazed the path to freedom and democracy for those who are yet oppressed. Once again we have prevailed in our noble cause. Rebel forces are on the run—'" He turned off the broadcast.

Victor cruised onto the Belt Parkway, going up Brooklyn's western shoreline. To his left, across the bay, were the sands of Staten Island's South Beach. *There must be lots of people relaxing on the beach today.* The triangular shapes of sailboats dotted the island's long, arcing coastline. Large merchant ships went up the bay, crossing paths with ferry boats going to and from the island. A few kilometers further on, as the parkway curved inland, he merged into the Brooklyn-Queens Expressway and headed for the Brooklyn-Battery Tunnel . . .

As he entered the tunnel, Victor determined that it was clear of traffic as far as the eye could see. *This is a Sunday—a perfect opportunity to test the new system.* "Get down, Duke," he said, depressing the accelerator. The SUV gained speed. *All clear.* He flipped up the red toggle switch and then pushed the steering wheel buttons simultaneously. The vehicle surged into high speed; his back glued to the seat, the speedometer and rpm needles raced, and the steering wheel shook in his hands as tunnel lights blurred. Two to three seconds were sufficient to convince him of the engine's optimized power. He released the buttons nearing the end of the tunnel. "Whoa!" he shouted. Duke gave him a terrified look from his crouched position. Victor slowed his vehicle, smoothly applying the brakes to merge with traffic on the other side. The sunlight steadily intensified. He tilted the visor down and put on his sunglasses.

They entered the Lower Manhattan militarized district. Victor drove up Broadway, passing by countless troopers and armored vehicles, and legions of corporate skyscrapers. The Global Security Incorporated skyscraper stood above all of them. He went through Soho's former shopping area, its buildings now converted into VerChip production plants. The production plants were surrounded by high chain-link fences topped with razor wire and were heavily guarded. He slowed his vehicle, entering the storied streets of Greenwich Village. The heat was making him restless and thirsty. He turned into the side streets, spotted a corner cafe, and parked in front of it.

Victor opened the cafe's redwood doors and entered with Duke alongside. The place had a traditional style with a cedar bar and mirrored backdrop. He strolled across the tile floor and sat down on one of the padded stools. The canine sat on the floor next to him.

The goateed waiter looked over his shoulder and cracked a smile. "I had a dog like that when I was a kid! What can I do you for?"

"An iced tea, please."

The waiter poured the tea and slid an icy glass across the bar.

Victor took a long drink. A yellowed poster advertising poetry readings was pasted on a column in the center of the room. "When's the poetry session?" he inquired.

"What?" said the waiter.

"Right there," he said, pointing. "It says poetry on Sunday afternoons."

"You're really out of it, man. That was abolished a long time ago. Poetry is considered subversive, along with most literature. History, philosophy, the classics can only be presented in their officially approved versions—that is, if they aren't forbidden altogether. The sessions have long since been cancelled."

"Forbidden? By what authority?" he asked, taking another drink.

"By the WorldGov Censor Board, of course. Don't you know that?"

"I'm not too familiar with that agency."

"You haven't been around, have you?"

"It's been a while. I thought Greenwich Village was a magnet for artists?"

"*Was*—the real artists left. The only art you'll find around here nowadays is the politically correct variety, approved by the censor board."

"What kind of art do they have?"

"Movies, plays, music—whatever. Most have all manner of violence, sex, and drug use. Just so long as there's no political theme that could be interpreted as subversive. If you're interested, there are lots of officially approved cinemas, theaters and concert halls, uptown."

"That doesn't sound very promising, but I'm headed uptown anyway." He finished the tea and put the glass down on the bar. "Thanks pal," he said, coming to his feet and heading for the door with the dog by his side.

Victor drove up Fifth Avenue; Duke sat upright in the passenger seat. Corporate buildings were mixed in with upscale stores and theaters along the avenue. *Midtown Manhattan is the epicenter of entertainment,* he thought. Before long, Radio City Music Hall came into view. He turned into the cross street, continued down the block and pulled over across from its main entrance. A banner hung on its façade: "For public safety, all shows and events at this facility have been officially reviewed by the WorldGov Censor Board." Large movie posters advertising the premiere of *The Liquidator 2* were on the wall by the entrance. The posters featured a muscular, ruggedly handsome young man with dark hair, holding a large bowie knife in his right fist and an assault rifle in his left fist. Under his image was the subtitle: "He fights for WorldGov and he's invincible!" Droves of people were waiting in line to purchase tickets and enter.

"Get out of my way! Get the hell out of my way!" yelled an obese man with a large soda cup in his hand, shoving his way to the front of the line. "The Liquidator will save us!" he declared. "He will save the world! We're saved!" Security guards tackled the crazed fan by the entrance; the soda cup flew from his hand and splattered on the sidewalk, spraying those at the front of the line. The man's arms and legs flailed as the guards subdued him.

Victor pulled off and headed north again. He drove by Central Park, through the Upper East Side and Harlem. Then he took the 278 Expressway to the east, traversing the South Bronx along its periphery. He viewed the destitute neighborhoods through his window. Few vehicles were taking the poorly maintained exit ramps into the borough; squads especially, stayed out of the sector. He merged into the 678, crossed over the East River, and exited past Citi Field stadium. The expanse of Flushing Meadows Park came into view, its vast green fields covered with sunshine. *Let's go for a leisurely walk.* He turned off the street and into the parking lot.

Victor and his canine companion ambled on a large walkway that circled the center of the park. The walkway was bordered by green fields, flower beds, and sometimes trees. Along the way, greeting the visitors, were occasional musicians, actors and mimes performing for food. Alcoholics and drug addicts lay about many of the benches and picnic tables. Ragged homeless people scavenged through the garbage cans. As they walked down a tree-lined segment of the route, scores of butterflies of every color fluttered in the air all around them. The trees ended and were followed by rows of trimmed hedges and bright flowers. They continued through open fields full of birds. Flocks of geese flew in traffic patterns similar to those of busy airports. Duke's retriever instincts took hold of him as he assumed a ready-to-leap posture.

"Duke, no! This isn't a hunting expedition," Victor said. "Come on."

They rounded into the center of the park. There, in the middle of a large circular pool, surrounded by an array of water-jet fountains, the Unisphere stood on its tripod pedestal. The colossal globe statue—over one hundred feet high and three hundred eighty tons of stainless steel—cast its long shadow across the field. In the foreground of it was a troupe of university actors performing Shakespeare's *Hamlet*. A modest crowd of spectators had gathered around them.

The play was in Act III, Scene I. The lead actor began Hamlet's soliloquy:

"To be, or not to be: that is the question:
"Whether 'tis nobler in the mind to suffer
"The slings and arrows of outrageous fortune,
"Or to take arms against a sea of troubles,
"And by opposing end them? To die: to sleep;
"No more; and by a sleep to say we end
"The heart-ache and the thousand natural shocks
"That flesh is heir to, 'tis a consummation
"Devoutly to be wish'd. To die, to sleep;
"To sleep: perchance to dream: ay, there's the rub;
"For in that sleep of death what dreams may come
"When we have shuffled off this mortal coil,
"Must give us pause: there's the respect
"That makes calamity of so long life;
"For who would bear the whips and scorns of time,
"The oppressor's wrong, the proud man's contumely,"

The actor continued passionately.

Supreme Bureau of Investigation agents in dark suits with sunglasses and earpieces made their way through the spectators. One of them waved his arms in front of the lead actor, signaling him to stop and pulling him aside. The other men assembled the troupe, engaging them in whispered discussions. The crowd grumbled in discontent.

The agent who had been talking to the lead actor moved toward the spectators, holding up a bronze badge. "SBI— this is an unauthorized performance," he said. "Show's over, folks! Move along now!"

The crowd slowly dispersed. Those who dared, eyed the agents with contempt. The university actors quietly gathered their props and left. Victor remembered the words of Marcellus, the officer who guarded the castle of Elsinore, in *Hamlet*: "Something is rotten in the state of Denmark." He signaled his companion, and they began walking toward the parking lot.

Victor headed for home, driving back onto the expressway and continuing through Queens toward Brooklyn. He drove with a soft touch on the wheel, cruising in the right lane, pegging the speed limit. As they passed through a south-side area of the Queens borough, Duke began growling in a way he had never done before: a low-pitched snarl that was vengeful and destructive. *So that's where they smashed your innocence. Did the pit bull rip through your goodness as well as your body?* The dog had a wild look in his eyes, saliva dripped from his clenched fangs, and his paws clawed the seat.

"Hey, it's all right now," Victor said, changing lanes. He flipped up the toggle switch then pushed the steering wheel buttons simultaneously, jarring the vehicle into high speed. They sped past the locale. He released the buttons and smoothly applied the brakes. Duke calmed down gradually. "Don't worry, friend," Victor said with a sidelong glance. "They can't hurt you anymore."

TWELVE

They met wherever they thought it was safe. She was free. He was marked. Their meeting places were outside of the Bronx sector, in case VerChip records were reviewed of his whereabouts. She sent him text messages, never giving him a way of contacting her. They saw each other usually on weekends, sometimes during the week, at art galleries, museums, and other public places. Mostly they walked together; few words were spoken. When they did speak, it was never about the divide between them.

One day, Victor took Tara's hand without warning. "Do you like baseball?" he asked.

"Yeah, sure," she responded with a startled look.

"Then send me a message when you want to go to Citi Field stadium."

"Citi Field?"

"The Mets are playing at home this coming week."

"Okay," she said, smiling.

The weekend flashed by. Time spent by her side seemed to pass at the speed of light.

It was Monday morning again. Victor passed through the double doors of the Criminal Records Section.

"Ganin," called the secretary, "Mr. Johnson wants to see you."

"All right," he replied, continuing through the second set of doors toward Johnson's central cubicle. As he approached the cubicle, the section director was settling in his chair, entering his VerChip Identification Number and password. Victor memorized the number and password. "You wanted to see me?" he asked.

Johnson turned around. "You need to report to the medical ward."

"I'm on my way." He turned and walked toward the doors.

"You're not walking as fast as you do on Friday nights," Johnson called after him.

Victor paused, looking over his shoulder. "I guess not; then again, I'm used to flying with eagles, not sitting with turkeys." Johnson gave him an ugly look as he proceeded through the doors.

He walked down the brightly lit corridors of the Global Police Headquarters complex toward the infirmary. The flat screens on the walls were broadcasting a mandatory announcement. "Global News Network, breaking news: A tentative truce in the Region 4, rival quadrants' war was announced this morning. The truce was confirmed by both Southwestern and Southeastern Quadrant representatives. Active combat has been suspended as of five a.m. today. Initial reports indicate the ceasefire is holding . . ."

Victor entered the infirmary, checked in at the reception, and continued to the examination room.

"How do you feel?" asked the young doctor.

"The gashes have healed but I still have pain, especially when I bend at the waist." Victor was lying. He was tired of combat. *An extended light-duty assignment is fine with me.*

"Let's see you bend," the doctor requested.

It's time to be an actor. "Arrr!" he said, bending like an old man.

"All right, let's have a look."

Victor removed his shoulder holster and uniform shirt and tie, then unwound the remaining bandages.

"Your wounds have healed, but there are still some bruises that are likely causing the pain." The doctor cut and removed the stitches. "I'll give you a light-duty authorization for two more weeks. But it's the last I can give you, understand? We're under a lot of pressure to put the troopers back in the field."

"Understood," he said, putting on his shirt and holster.

"Okay. I'll send the authorization to your section."

"Thanks Doctor, you're the best."

"No, I am an asset to the New World Order."

Victor cinched his tie. "You most certainly are."

He exited the medical ward and walked up the corridors of the Global Police HQ complex. As he passed by the metal door of the Interrogation and Holding Section, muffled screams stopped him in his tracks.

"What's the matter?" said a voice behind him.

Victor turned around. Drake was standing in front of him. "Commander, this is a surprise."

Another muffled scream came from inside the section. Victor looked at the insulated metal door.

Drake eyed him coldly. "Been to this section before?"

"Never had occasion to."

"Well then, that's just a routine interrogation of a suspected rebel terrorist."

"Suspected?"

"That's right. The Brain-scan Lie Detector computer will get what information is required. But it's always a good idea to let them know who's in control."

Victor nodded reservedly. "I'm sure the professionals know their jobs."

"They do. When're you coming back to the Attack Teams Section? We're short-handed; we need experienced team leaders at this time."

A group of clinically dressed interrogators walked out of the metal door. They brushed past Victor disrespectfully. He eyed them angrily as they continued down the corridor.

"They're like royalty," said the commander, noticing his anger.

Victor turned back to Drake. "What does that mean exactly?"

"They have special expertise. WorldGov values their skills and pays them on a higher scale. Sure, that doesn't seem fair, but that's just the way it goes."

"What . . . skills?"

Drake cracked a wry grin. "What do you think?"

Torture. "This isn't my section," Victor replied.

"Of course not," Drake said. "You see, they're experts at extracting information from suspects. The word is they're the best in the world. Often it's information we require to execute our missions, and it might save the lives of our troopers, including yours."

Victor nodded pensively. "Of course."

Drake slapped him on the back. "We're looking forward to your return."

"Thank you, sir," he said, giving a salute.

Victor proceeded up the corridors back to the Criminal Records Section. He entered the section and began walking down rows of computer workstations. Only Mr. Johnson noticed his entry. "Work's been piling up," he commented.

"Don't worry, I've got a handle on it," Victor replied as he continued down the rows. He arrived at his workstation and sat down in his chair. Then he looked in the adjacent cubicle. Camille was tapping the computer keys like a concert pianist, fervently processing e-documents for her

WorldGov employer. He initialized his computer and began processing records.

The week dragged on and on. Victor began to wonder if he should have accepted reassignment back to the Attack Teams Section without delay. On Friday, his black-market mobile phone vibrated in his pocket. The message read: "See you in Citi Field stadium in the right field bleachers, Saturday afternoon."

The New York Mets were scheduled to play the rival Philadelphia Phillies. Victor purchased a ticket at one of the booths and entered Citi Field stadium. The stadium was impressive, with an emerald playing field, a huge flat screen, and numerous rows of bleachers. People shuffled about in colorful clothes and baseball caps. He walked up an aisle into the right field bleachers, looking discretely in every direction.

"What time is it, mister?" said a brunette with dark sunglasses, a Mets baseball cap and a stylish jean ensemble, sitting on a half-empty bleacher.

Victor recognized Tara's voice immediately. He smiled, walked down the row, and sat down next to her. "Tara, you look different in that outfit," he said, unzipping his leather jacket.

"Don't you like brunettes, Victor?" she asked, taking off her sunglasses and putting them in her jacket pocket.

"Usually, brunettes are trying to look like blondes, not the other way around."

Tara chuckled and turned toward the playing field. Without knowing why, Victor put his arm around her waist, holding her as if he were trying to stop her from flying away. To his surprise, she wrapped both arms around his neck and kissed him on the cheek. Then she laid her head on his shoulder. "Who's gonna win?" she asked softly.

"Us, I hope," he replied.

She nudged her head closer to his. Her eyes began closing.

"Tired?" he asked.

"A little," she responded.

A gentle humming sound filled the air as a dragonfly hovered in front of them, its fluorescent wings fluttering with incredible speed.

"Well, as a true-blue New Yorker, I'm rooting for the Mets," he declared.

"Same here. I hope they hit a home run clear across the city," she said sleepily.

Victor gazed at her tranquil face. In that moment his heart beat faster and then his lips moved closer to hers as if an invisible force was drawing him to her. She reached for him. He kissed her for the first time; her lips passionately received his.

The dragonfly flew a quarter-circle and landed on the bleacher seat next to him.

Snap!—a switchblade snapped open. Tara thrust the knife downward—it passed by Victor's temple, nicking his ear and impaling the dragonfly to the seat.

"What the—!" he gasped.

Tara pulled the knife from the seat and held it between them. The skewered insect was still struggling for life, its legs wiggling, wings gyrating, and yellowish liquid oozing from its belly down the protruding blade.

"What the heck did you do that for?" he asked in shock.

She pulled the dragonfly from the blade and squeezed it with her thumb and forefinger, causing yellowish blood to squirt from its belly, killing it.

"You're mad, woman!" Victor exclaimed.

Tara signaled silence. Then she moved the dragonfly closer to him. Implanted in its belly was a micro receiver-transmitter. She tossed the insect to the ground and crushed it with her heel. "That's the work of your employer. Come on, let's go," she said, taking his hand. He followed her in tow across the bleachers. "They monitor conversations with remotely controlled insect-cyborgs."

"I—I didn't know that," he said incredulously.

"You were always naive. Anyway, our intelligence uncovers facts that authorities don't reveal to anyone—not even to their own personnel."

"Apparently so."

They sat down on a bleacher behind home plate. Victor took a deep breath and exhaled. "Well, you're full of surprises," he remarked.

Tara looked at him and smirked. "Let's finish what we started," she said, joining her lips to his. They held each other tightly. Her fingers ran across his nicked ear. "Are you all right, Victor?"

"It's just a slight cut," he replied.

She took a small adhesive bandage from her jacket pocket and gently placed it on his ear. "Sorry Vic, I didn't mean to hurt you."

"It's okay, Tara."

Victor stood up with the crowd as the Global Anthem began to play. People sang with their hands on their hearts. Tara remained seated.

A robocop made its way down the row and stopped in front of them. Its red electronic eyes zoomed in on her. "It is required that you stand and sing the Global Anthem," it said. "If you refuse, you will be subject to detention and due process."

Tara's eyes grew fierce. Victor looked at her then back at the robot. "She's sick," he said quickly. "Her stomach—she can't get up and sing. We're patriotic world citizens, but we cannot fulfill our duties at this time due to health reasons."

"Then I must see a physician's documentation," the robot demanded.

Tara slowly opened the side-zipper of her jeans, putting her hand on the grip of the compact handgun in her thigh holster. Victor placed his hand on her shoulder in a calming gesture. Beads of sweat formed on his brow. The robot's electronic eyes intensified their focus. *Last resort.* Cracking a smile, he opened his jacket, exposing his bronze badge alongside the stun gun on his belt. "Look, there's no problem here, understand?"

"Hand-scan, please," said the robocop, extending a handheld RFID reader. Victor passed his hand across the reader. The robot viewed the screen, then said, "I regret any inconvenience this may have caused you." It turned and went back up the row. He wiped the sweat from his brow and sat down again, wondering what he would have done without his credentials.

The Phillies didn't score in the top of the first inning. Then the Mets came up to bat in the bottom of the first . . .

The pitcher struck out the leadoff batter and retired the second batter on a fly ball to left field.

The third batter stepped up to the plate, assuming his stance, his eyes keenly focused. The pitcher threw a fastball down the middle. The batter swung, contacting the ball with tremendous force, sending it clear across the sky into the grandstands. Fans cheered as the Mets player jogged around the bases to home plate.

"Looks like our team is off to a good start," Tara said, beaming.

Victor returned the smile. "It's a great start."

In the top of the third, the Phillies evened the score with back-to-back singles followed by a run-scoring double. With two outs and two players on base, their power hitter came to the plate. The pitcher eyed him intently. The batter scowled in return. It was apparent that a feud existed between them. The pitcher nodded at his catcher, acknowledging his signals. Then he raised his glove, kicked up his leg and threw a spiraling curve ball. The batter swung, contacting the ball forcefully, sending it across the sky toward the left outfield bleachers. The left fielder sprinted across the outfield past the warning track, making a leaping catch as he slammed into the wall; he tumbled to the ground, coming to his feet with the gloved ball held high. The fans cheered enthusiastically.

In the bottom of the fifth, the Mets scored again. A single up the middle was followed by a double to left field, leaving players on second and third bases. Then a line-drive single to right field scored the runner from third. . . . The Phillies coach came out of his dugout and walked to the mound. He gestured angrily at his pitcher. Then he signaled the bullpen. The relief pitcher jogged out to the mound as the starter vacated it, shaking his head. . . . The reliever closed the inning with no additional runs scored. The score stood at two to one in favor of the Mets.

In the top of the eighth, the Phillies belted a string of singles, loading the bases with two outs. Their power hitter stepped up to the plate again. . . . Nervously, the Mets coach walked out to the mound. He appeared to be having a heated argument with the pitcher.

"The coach should replace him," Victor remarked.

"No way! He'll do the job. You gotta have faith," Tara said, tilting the visor of her baseball cap upward.

After various signals, the coach walked away, leaving his starter in the game.

Play resumed.

The pitcher delivered. The batter swung at the first pitch without making contact. "Strike one!" said the umpire. The batter grimaced, resuming his stance, firmly gripping the bat. The pitcher delivered again. The batter swung mightily at the second pitch, missing it by a fraction of an inch. "Strike two!" said the umpire. The batter grimaced again, resuming his stance and cocking the bat. The pitcher raised his glove, kicked up his leg and hurled a ninety-mile-an-hour fastball that zoomed past the stunned batter. "Strike three! You're out!" the umpire shouted. The Phillies players vacated the bases for their dugout.

"Don't ever give up hope!" Tara said triumphantly. Victor smiled and kissed her.

It was the top of the ninth and the last chance for the visiting team with two outs and no players on base. "Let's get out of here," Victor whispered in Tara's ear.

"Someone once said, 'It ain't over till it's over.'"

"That's for sure."

"Strike three—you're out! Game's over!" declared the umpire. The multitudes cheered wildly.

"We won!" Victor said, taking Tara's hands and pulling her from her seat.

They walked across the bleachers, down the many steps, and out of the stadium. She grabbed his jacket sleeve and drew him close as they walked together to his cobalt-blue vehicle.

"Where're you headed, beautiful?" he asked.

"Wherever you're going," she answered.

Victor drove to Brighton Beach. . . .

Opening his apartment door, he swept her from her feet and carried her past the startled dog into the bedroom, closing the door behind them.

"Where's the dental floss?" Tara's voice came from the bathroom.

It was five in the morning and Victor was barely waking. "I—I don't have any."

"Don't have any? Even bears have dental floss nowadays!"

Victor squinted at the lighted bathroom. Steam came out of the open door from the recently used shower. His love exited, wrapped in a white towel, her wet hair dripping on her shoulders. Duke ran to her, wagging his tail excitedly. "I see you two are acquainted," he said with a hint of jealousy.

"Dogs and I get along very well," Tara said, petting the canine.

"I can see that. Perhaps you like him better than me?"

"Well, he is handsome and has a great personality!"

"Oh, I see!"

She walked into the kitchen. The aroma of eggs and bacon soon filled the apartment.

Victor got up, showered quickly, and dressed himself. When he entered the living room Tara was seated at the table with Duke by her side, patiently waiting for him. Two breakfast plates were on the table and a heaping bowl of bacon was on the floor for the dog. He strolled to the table and sat down opposite her. Tara was still wrapped in the towel.

"Don't you get dressed for breakfast?" he asked.

"Clothes aren't as comfortable, and in some situations, very inconvenient!" she said with a wink.

He snickered. "Well, thanks for the breakfast, my love."

As soon as he touched his fork, the other two dug into the food. Tara began devouring the eggs and bacon. Duke buried his muzzle in the bowl. *This resembles more a medieval feast than a twenty-first century apartment!*

The couple consumed their breakfasts, finished dressing, then left the apartment.

Victor drove Tara to the subway station. She threw her arms around him, hugging him until he was out of breath. "See you, love," she said, pulling back rapidly and exiting the vehicle before he could respond. He watched her jogging to the entrance. She paused by the stairs, turned around and waved. He waved back. Then she descended the steps, disappearing from view.

The days passed like a dream. *What day is it?* "What day is it?" he said aloud, reaching for his coffee cup. The workers in adjacent cubicles looked at him as if he were mad.

"It's Thursday, silly!" Camille said through the partition.

Victor downed his coffee.

The flat screens came on for a mandatory announcement. "Attention, world citizens!" said the talking head. "GNN special report: A great victory has been won for world civilization! Last night, a coordinated assault by our heroic GPF troopers has destroyed the Crusaders Rebel Army. The terrorist leader known as Steele has been captured." Victor focused on a screen. A blonde woman wearing fatigues was handcuffed and being led through a gauntlet of reporters by black-clad troopers. Her face turned toward the cameras. *Lord, have mercy.* Tara's combat-weary face filled the screen.

"Well, I'll be darned, it's a woman!" Mr. Johnson said, staring at the spectacle.

Tara fell to the ground. The troopers dragged her by the handcuffs. Victor slowly rose from his chair in a state of shock. *Tara is Steele. Why didn't she tell me?* He fell back into his chair.

People began shouting and jeering: "We've got her!" "Tear her to pieces!" "Liquidate her!"

"Enemy of the people!" yelled a furious observer. "Now there will be justice!"

"She will be dealt with. She'll confess all right!" said another.

"Thanks to our heroic troopers, that monster is in custody!" Camille screamed. She turned toward her stunned co-worker.

Victor glanced back at her, trying to gather himself. *The first rule in any situation is to keep calm.* "Thanks, we're real heroes," he said, feeling nauseous.

"Such a monster . . . such a monster . . ." she repeated, looking back at the flat screen.

The troopers dragged Tara mercilessly through lines of reporters and film crews, her blood streaking the pavement.

THIRTEEN

The crowd whipped into a frenzy as the flat screens alternated battle scenes with Steele's capture. The spectators exchanged wild cheers with twisted faces and shaking fists, depending on the video clip. Fighter plane airstrikes, armored assaults, and gun battles had left parts of the Bronx in flames.

Victor's thoughts drifted back to his father's abduction, to the SBI agent's cold stare as he declared Father Constantine *persona non grata*, to all the faceless liquidations he had processed in the Criminal Records Section. His memory faded to the image of Tara handing him wildflowers.

A sudden fury gripped his heart. *Snap out of it! Think fast, Victor! They must have taken her to the interrogation section.* Victor sprang to his feet and walked quickly down rows of crazed spectators toward Mr. Johnson's cubicle. Johnson was standing by his cubicle staring up at a flat screen. Victor stopped behind him, looking at the pile of documents and software on his desk. On top of the pile he eyed a red mini-disk marked Top Secret: Global Police Force Monthly Security Codes. He took a closer look. It was dated for the previous month. *Shoot. Where's the current disk?* He surveyed the desk. *Nothing.* Then he moved closer to Johnson, glancing at him; the man was still mesmerized by the images on the screen. Slowly, he reached into the pile and stirred it. A collection of mini-disks marked Top Secret came into view. *The disks are color-coded. What's the color for this month? Think! Teal—it's teal.* He scattered the disks, spotting the current one. Then he instinctively withdrew his hand.

"What's up?" Johnson asked, looking down at the scrambled pile on his desk.

"What's up?" Victor said wildly. "We have just achieved a great victory against the enemies of civilization. That's what's up!"

"Yes, I know that but—"

"But? There's no but about it!" He put his arm around the man's shoulders. "This is the victory we've all been waiting for!"

Johnson frowned. "Get your damn arm off me, man!" he said, pulling away from him. "Have you lost your mind?"

"Sorry, I got carried away. Still, just look at the devastation of the criminal elements!" Victor said, pointing to the screen. "Isn't it spectacular?" As Johnson focused back on the news reports, Victor took the teal mini-disk and slipped it into his pocket. Then he walked up the rows of raging spectators back to his workstation.

Sitting in front of his computer, Victor clicked on the Main Menu button. An *Enter VIN number* window appeared. He entered his VIN number. *Enter Password.* He entered his password. *Access Granted* appeared on the screen. Then he clicked on the Master Control Panel icon. An *Enter Section Director's Data* window presented itself. Victor entered Johnson's VIN number and password, both of which he had previously memorized. *Enter GPF Security Code,* the computer requested. He inserted the mini-disk into the disk drive and activated it. Then he scrolled down to the monthly security code for the section, copied and pasted it into the previous window, and tapped the Enter key. The

Master Control Panel window materialized. Victor armed the nuclear, chemical, biological attack, and fire emergency alarm systems. An *Activate* button flashed on the screen. He clicked the button. *Confirm Command,* the computer requested. He confirmed the command and waited . . .

All hell broke loose. The rooms blacked out, then alarms and sirens activated in various colors and octaves in a flurry of lights and sounds. And the computers and flat screens faded out, reverting to backup power. The previously cheering and jeering workers were now disoriented.

Victor removed the mini-disk from the computer and pocketed it. Then he walked quickly out of the office area into the corridor. People were moving in semi-organized files for the emergency exits of the hexagonal complex. The myriad of flashing lights and wailing sirens heightened his sense of urgency. *Time is critical.* He moved swiftly through multiple corridors to the Command-and-Control Section in the center of the complex, and then charged through its doors and headed for the arms vault . . .

Two burly guards stood on either side of the vault's steel door. Victor approached from their blind side, drawing his stun gun. *Zap! Zap!* Two shots of high-voltage left the guards unconscious on the floor. He took the keycards from the higher ranking guard's key holder and swiped them one by one through the slot on the door's electronic lock. The third card released the bolts.

He entered and surveyed the vault. To his front was a wide variety of firearms: Glocks, Berettas, Colts, Walthers, Rugers and others hung in the racks; explosives were stored on the shelves. Victor put on a double shoulder holster over his holstered Glock, and threw on a black parka. He then slung an M4 assault rifle on his back, holstered two Uzi machine pistols, clipped grenades to his belt, and filled the parka with ammunition and C-4 explosives with detonation cords.

Victor exited the vault, then rushed to the doors and out of the section. Waving his arms, he ran down the F-Wing corridor shouting, "Make way—rescue team! Make way—rescue team!" The dark masses of people moved to the sides.

He came to a sudden halt at the metal door of the Interrogation and Holding Section. *I hope they haven't moved her to another location.* He twisted the doorknob; it was locked. Digging into his parka's left pocket, he withdrew a block of C-4 explosive. He took a small portion, put it on the door lock, and inserted a detonation cord; then he struck a match, lit the cord and dove to the floor. A brief but loud bang followed. Victor looked through the clearing smoke at the door cracking open. He got up quickly, charged through the door, then stopped and scanned the room . . .

A blonde woman in fatigues was strapped into a leather chair. Her face was beaten, her right eye completely closed, the other half-open. Two clinically dressed interrogators stood on either side of her. They froze, surprised by the intrusion. The chief torturer held shock clamps with wires connected to an automotive-type battery. His assistant wore brass knuckles. Victor drew an Uzi, aimed at the chief and fired a burst. The burst removed the man's head, spraying blood and brains across the room; the body fell to the floor with a thump. "Free her! Now!" he shouted, pointing the Uzi at the assistant and stepping forward. Trembling with fear, the assistant unstrapped the woman. "Down on your knees." The man dropped to his knees. Victor kicked him in the jaw, snapping his neck and sending him crashing to the floor, motionless.

"Hey—it's me, love," Victor said, worried. "Please tell me you're all right."

Tara tried to focus her half-open eye. "Is that you, Vic? Or is this a dream?"

"It's me, Tara . . . It's me. Can you walk?"

With shaking hands, Tara gripped the armrests of the chair and rose slowly; blood ran down her face from several cuts and abrasions. Victor put his arm around her waist to stabilize her. He holstered the Uzi, took a towel from the armrest, and gently wiped her face. "When you're ready," he said, "I need you to walk, if not run, understand?"

"I'm as ready as I'm going to get," she replied. "Let's go."

Victor took Tara's hand and led her out the door. The mayhem continued in the complex; lights flashed and sirens blared. They ran toward the emergency exit closest to the main parking lot. He resumed shouting, "Make way—rescue team! Make way—rescue team!"

Nearing the exit, they crashed into three armed figures. Victor was flung to the wall, and Tara fell to the ground, bumping her head against the wall. The figures reeled backward. . . . "Who goes there?" demanded the man in the middle. Victor recognized the voice. He peered through the red-yellow-blue flashing lights, identifying Commander Drake flanked by Branson and Rodriguez. He breathed heavily but gave no response.

"Is that you, Ganin?" Drake shouted.

"Hey, it's us," Rodriguez called.

They turned their attention to Tara, sitting against the wall.

"You've got Steele in custody—good work," Branson said.

Victor swallowed hard. The three men came forward. He drew both Uzis; "Freeze!" he yelled.

They stopped in their tracks. There was confusion on Drake's face, then perfect clarity, as Tara came to her feet by Victor's side. "What do you think you're doing?" he asked.

"Get out of our way," Victor said in an iron voice.

"You're making a mistake, trooper." Drake took a step forward.

Victor fired a burst inches above their heads. Branson and Rodriguez hit the ground. Drake raised his hands but continued speaking. "Think about it: You're throwing away your career. You'll be branded a traitor. You'll be hunted like an animal for the rest of your days." He paused, looking straight into his eyes. "Just give me Steele and walk away. You have my word this will be forgotten. This never happened, understand?"

"It was all a lie, wasn't it?" Victor said. "All that talk about freedom, justice, and democracy. Those were just words used to manipulate the people, so much propaganda to control the masses."

"What are you talking about?"

"You know exactly what I'm talking about, you bastard!"

"Calm down . . ."

From the corner of his eye, Victor saw Branson raising his handgun. Victor fired, hitting him in his shooting arm. Branson screamed in pain and dropped the weapon.

"Man!" Rodriguez exclaimed. "You shot one of our own."

"That's right, Robert. Make no mistake, I'll kill all of you if necessary," he shouted, leveling both Uzis at the commander.

Drake nodded, the flashing lights highlighting the rage on his face. "All right, Ganin, you made your choice. Now you'll live in misery, with them, with the scum. You'll look over your shoulder all your life. Do you think WorldGov will forget about you?"

"No, they won't. Neither will I forget about them," Victor promised. "Now get out of our way. This is the last warning!" he said, beginning to squeeze the triggers. Drake stepped aside warily. The pair darted past him, jumping over the prone Rodriguez toward the exit.

"We'll get you!" Drake yelled after them as they bolted through the doors.

Victor and Tara paused briefly, their eyes adjusting to the sunlight. "This way," Victor said, spotting his SUV. He led Tara between rows of parked vehicles. She stumbled behind him with her limited vision. They came to a stop at his vehicle, and he opened the driver's door. She climbed in and moved over to the passenger seat. He jumped in after her, slammed the door, engaged the ignition, and threw on his seatbelt; then he shifted into gear and began driving slowly through the lot.

The main gate was opening and closing repeatedly as nonessential personnel were being evacuated.

I'll need good timing to race through the exit, Victor thought. He stopped some distance away, observing the gate, waiting for the right moment.

"Do you think we'll make it?" Tara asked in a weak voice, fastening her seatbelt.

"You bet. You gotta have faith!" he said with a wink. She smiled slightly, remembering the ballgame at Citi Field stadium.

The main gate opened to its maximum as an armored column approached it.

"This is our chance, brace yourself!" Victor started accelerating toward the gate.

The chief guard saw the oncoming vehicle and frantically signaled to close the gate. The gate began closing rapidly. Victor flipped up the toggle switch on the panel and then simultaneously pushed the steering wheel buttons. The SUV surged ahead, running through the gears, flames shooting from the exhaust pipes. It streaked through the exit. He released the buttons and smoothly applied the brakes, slowing down in the streets of Lower Manhattan.

"What the heck was that?" Tara asked with her back still glued to the seat.

"Rocket power," Victor replied. *Thanks a million, Marco.*

He maneuvered through the streets, accelerating into the main drive alongside the East River. *It's only a matter of minutes before they discover the false alarms and Steele's escape. They'll home in on my VerChip.* He sped northbound up the drive, bobbing and weaving through city traffic. At the north end of Manhattan he crossed over the Triborough Bridge into the 278 Expressway, headed for the Bronx. "From here on, you need to give me directions," he said.

"Take the 895 into the 95, then exit west of the Bronx Park," she replied.

"Got it," he acknowledged, depressing the accelerator, proceeding along the route.

As they neared the exit, west of the park, a low whirring sound came from the sky above.

"Damn it," Victor said brusquely.

"It's the gunships," Tara said, leaning weakly against the headrest.

"They've caught up to us," he said, "I need you to drive."

"I can't see, Victor! I'm sorry Vic, but I can't see!" she replied desperately.

Victor looked to the passenger side. Blood was coming down Tara's face again, obscuring her left eye, the one that wasn't completely closed. He popped open the glove box, withdrew a hand towel and put it in her palm. She wiped her face, smearing the blood across her forehead and cheeks. He unbuckled their seatbelts.

"Hold the wheel steady," he said, entering the exit ramp.

"Okay," she said, sliding toward him, taking the wheel.

Victor grabbed his M4, moved into the open window and looked to the sky. Two black helicopter gunships were bearing down behind them; the lead gunship's laser pod was opening. *It's a matter of seconds before they liquidate us.* "Keep it steady!" he yelled.

"There's a turn coming up!" Tara shouted.

"Steady! Steady!" Victor yelled, peering through the M4's scope, aiming at the laser pod. He flipped the switch to full automatic and squeezed the trigger—*brrrrrrr*. Fiery flashes resembling blue lightning bolts erupted on the pod. The gunship disengaged with smoke trailing from its underbelly. He emptied the rest of the ammo magazine on the second gunship. It veered off in the same direction as the first.

"Turning right!" Tara shouted.

Victor gripped the window frame through the skidding turn. Then he dropped back into the driver's seat, letting go of the M4 and taking control of the SUV. "You're a risky driver, you know that?" he said with a half-grin.

Tara smiled slightly as her hand slipped from the wheel.

"The second gunship'll be coming around anytime now," he said. "We need to disappear."

Tara focused her half-open eye. "Take the next right then an immediate left."

He turned right then left. The whirring sound returned, drawing closer and closer. Victor glanced upward over his left shoulder: the gunship was closing in rapidly with its laser pod open—seconds away from liquidating them. He made another quick turn. "We have to jump out. On my command . . ." he shouted. He removed a grenade from his belt, pulled the pin with his teeth and tossed it into the backseat. "Jump now!" They pulled their door handles and leaped clear of the doomed vehicle—rolling to opposite sides of the street.

The gunship closed in on its prey . . .

Suddenly the vehicle exploded into a roiling fireball, shooting flames and smoke through the air all around it. The gunship, rocked by the explosion, peeled off with sparks streaking from its belly.

As the smoke began to clear, Victor dashed across the street and joined Tara on the other side. She led him through

FOURTEEN

Tara led Victor into the underground. They trekked through dark interconnecting tunnels that wound their way invisibly into the Bronx.

"I hope you know where you're going, because I'm disoriented," he said, hiking closely behind her.

"Trust me, Victor," she said over her shoulder.

"I trust you, Tara."

They turned a corner, entering a tunnel with a bright light shining in the distance. Several armed figures appeared in front of them. Tara ran to them with Victor trailing. The tallest figure wrapped her in his arms. Victor stopped short.

"Victor." Tara smiled with the man's arm around her shoulder. "This is Captain Rafael Perez."

"We know each other *sure enough*," he said, eyeing the bearded man in fatigues.

Undeterred, she continued. "And this is Captain Sean Flanagan."

Victor recognized the young man from the subway with the crew cut and the Maltese cross on the back of his leather jacket. "We met on the subway," he said, raising an eyebrow, "I suppose you were spying on me at the time." The young man cracked a sly grin.

"And this is Captain George Sebastian and his wife Anna," Tara concluded.

George was medium build with blue eyes and dark hair. His spouse was slender with brown eyes and a long blonde ponytail. Both were dressed in dark casual clothes. They smiled politely. Victor nodded in return.

"The whole world is looking for you, bronze!" Rafael snapped.

"Don't talk to him that way! Understand?" Tara said angrily.

"All right." Rafael's bearded face was stern. "But what are we supposed to do, Commander? His photo is on every television on the planet." He glared at Victor. "He was one of them. They say he's a traitor."

"I did not betray my conscience," Victor said, returning the glare.

Rafael turned back to Tara. "They'll stop at nothing to get him. He'll bring more troubles our way."

"We'll handle it," she replied confidently.

"He's right," Victor said. "My presence here will endanger all of you. Let me have a night's rest and I'll be on my way."

"You'll do nothing of the sort," Tara said.

"We could use a good professional fighter," George interposed. "Most of us are just common citizens, trying to stay free and survive."

Anna gazed softly in his direction. "His heart's in the right place. What more do we need?"

There was a moment of silence, as if the group were telepathically debating whether to admit Victor or send him back into the streets. After a time, they all looked at Rafael. "It's the commander's decision," he said in a subdued voice.

"You know my call. But we always prefer a unanimous decision." Tara stared at him.

Rafael looked at Victor intently. Reluctantly, he said, "All right, I'll make it unanimous."

"Let's go then." Tara motioned toward the light at the end of the tunnel.

Victor and Tara walked arm in arm behind the others. "He's getting on my nerves," he muttered.

"Rafael's one of our best captains. But he can be quick-tempered and headstrong." Tara glanced at Victor with her half-open eye. A quiet smile came to her lips. "Come on," she said, giving his arm a tug. They quickened their steps and joined up with the others.

"The blood's trickling down your face again," Victor remarked.

"We need to get you to a doctor," Victor and Rafael said almost simultaneously.

"We'll get there soon enough," she replied. "Sean, do you still have that Irish music?"

The young man produced a small music player and pushed the play button. Melodic harp chords filled the underground. Tara leaned her head on Victor's shoulder as they walked along, unwinding. They came to the lighted area at the end of the tunnel. Concrete steps led up to the exit.

"Everyone goes up except for Victor," Tara ordered. "Wait here," she said to him.

"I've got nowhere to go," he replied.

The five of them went up the steps, leaving Victor by himself. A few minutes later Tara came back down followed by a white-haired gentleman in a beige coat. "This is Doctor Collins," she said. The man smiled kindly.

"It's a pleasure," Victor said to him.

"He's here to free you from your bonds," she said.

"Let's have a look," said the doctor, taking Victor's right hand and examining it. "You're lucky the SpyChip is only implanted in your palm. The newer versions are embedded in the bone." He drew a surgical knife from his pocket. "This won't be complicated. But I must apologize—we have no anesthetic."

"Do what you have to do, Doctor," he said.

Doc Collins held Victor's hand firmly and made an incision into his palm. Victor grimaced silently. After cleaning the cut, the doctor inserted a pair of tweezers, and extracted the microchip. Then he applied antiseptic, sewed up the hand and wrapped it with gauze. "Congratulations," he said, dropping the microchip to the ground and crushing it with his shoe. "Now, you are free."

"Thank you, Doctor," Victor replied, tearing from the procedure.

"We can go up now," Tara declared.

Victor went up the steps with Tara and the doctor. They continued down the streets to a series of tall brick buildings. Rafael, Sean, George and Anna were waiting for them as they entered the central building.

"Sorry about the rough start," Rafael said, extending his hand in a conciliatory gesture.

Victor accepted and shook hands.

"Come on, Victor, I'll take you to Command Headquarters," Tara said.

"Don't even think about it!" Doc Collins exclaimed. "You're coming with me immediately so those wounds can get proper attention—doctor's orders!" He grabbed her by the elbow, pulling her in tow.

"We'll take you," George said, linking his arm with Anna's.

The group walked up the stairs to the first floor, then down a long hallway into a spacious room. A sign above the room's large window read: "Jesus saves." In the center of the room was an oak table with seven chairs; several maps, two laptop computers, and a compass were on the table. The walls were decked with maps depicting all the sectors of

New York City. On a stand by the window was a command radio. Next to the door was a shelf with a coffeemaker and mugs on it. Rafael, Sean, George and Anna moved to the table.

"This is Crusaders Rebel Army Headquarters?" Victor looked at Rafael. "You're joking."

"I'm not the joking type," Rafael said firmly.

"The way the Global News Network describes this organization, you'd think you were a powerful army with global-strike capabilities," Victor said.

"Don't believe anything you hear from those GNN sons of bitches," Sean said.

"Is that what you thought? That we threaten the world?" Rafael asked.

"Not really," Victor responded. "But this isn't exactly what I expected. You mean to tell me this is the organization that has resisted WorldGov for all this time?"

"That's right."

"That's incredible. That's truly incredible!"

"We have something WorldGov doesn't have."

"What's that?"

"Faith," George interjected.

Victor looked at them doubtfully. "I know what you're saying. It's just that faith only goes so far; you're outgunned and—"

"Faith goes as far as you want it to go," George said.

"Faith is everything," Anna stated.

"Come on, I'll show you around," Rafael proposed.

Victor and Rafael left Command Headquarters and walked through the hallways.

"After the recent attacks, we evacuated to these buildings more than a kilometer from our previous location," Rafael said. "These are some of the oldest buildings in the city. They're brick construction, built in the twentieth century, and almost indestructible. This building has ten floors."

"Tell me the truth, Rafael. Were there many casualties in the latest attacks? I saw the news reports. Do we still have an army?"

"The reports were partially true, mostly false. Fighter planes attacked several of our buildings with missiles and bombs. Fortunately, we were able to evacuate our people prior to the strikes, based on intelligence reports. Our rearguard action was mostly successful."

"Is there a viable army?"

"You ask too many questions."

"Don't be a pain! Just answer the—"

"All right, calm down! It's just that you're asking a lot of difficult questions," Rafael said defensively. "Look, we've taken significant casualties, many more than Global Police troopers. But our fighters are resilient, we've received new volunteers, and our force is largely intact. Our biggest problem is supplies. We're short on everything: water filtration equipment, food, medicines, and ammunition."

Victor nodded. "I'll need to know more details before long. Tara's got a plan?"

"Look, Victor, I've known Tara long enough to tell you that she's very tough—more than you know. But her heart is vulnerable. I see plainly that she's in love with you. So I feel obliged to say this: you mustn't cloud her judgment."

"You're right. Professional decisions should not be mixed with emotions."

"Furthermore, you must address her as Commander Steele in front of the fighters."

"Understood."

"Then let's continue."

They walked up the stairs to the supply room on the second floor. It had scant supplies of bottled water, dried foods, and clothes. Next to it, the medical facility had mostly full beds and empty shelves. Doc Collins was across the room, standing next to Tara, who was lying on one of the beds. He waved briefly. They returned the wave, and then proceeded to the arms room. AK-47s, Berettas, and Colts were neatly aligned in the racks. Ammunition lay about in half-empty boxes. Explosives and RPGs were stacked against the far wall. "This is your assigned workstation. You'll inspect, maintain, and issue the weapons," Rafael said, handing him the door key.

"Okay," Victor said, nodding. "I'm familiar with these weapons."

"That's enough for today. I'll show you where you can turn in. Commander Steele has ordered a private room for you."

They took the elevator to the fifth floor, walked down the hallway, and entered a room with faded paint. There were two windows, a work desk, a single bed, a kitchen, and a small bathroom. Next to the bed was an open locker with a black leather jacket, several pairs of cargo pants and other clothes in it. Boxes of dried foodstuffs and bottled water were stacked in the kitchen.

"This will do just fine," Victor said. "See you in the morning."

"See you then." Rafael turned for the door.

He stowed his weapons in the locker and ate several cereal bars from the kitchen, then took off his boots, lay down on the bed, and drifted asleep.

"Rise and shine, Vic!"

It was near dawn. Victor tried to focus. "What time is it, Tara?"

"What does it matter? We have work to do."

"Aren't you supposed to be resting in the medical facility?"

"Oh, stop arguing and get up." Tara pulled him from the bed. The silver cross around her neck glimmered in the dim light. White bandages were wrapped around her forehead and right eye. She was dressed in a blue sweater, black pants and chukka boots, and had a Beretta strapped to her side. "Let's get going," she said, turning for the door.

He changed into a gray collared shirt and cargo pants and put his boots on. Then he strapped on his shoulder holster with Glock inside it, threw on the leather jacket, and put spare magazines in his cargo-pant pockets.

Victor joined Tara in the hallway. They walked briskly through several long hallways, then stopped by an open window. Tara went out on the ledge. "Stop, come back here!" Victor said, grasping her arm firmly.

"No worries," she said, "follow me."

He looked out of the window. A swing bridge stretched to the adjacent building.

They began walking across the thick wooden panels. Tara moved swiftly. Victor trailed behind, gripping the ropes on either side. "It's very safe, just keep your balance," she called over her shoulder. He glanced up but did not respond, continuing to negotiate the bridge step by step. The sun peeked over the horizon as he reached the end of the span. Tara had already entered the building and was leaning out of the window, extending her hand. Their hands joined and she pulled him inside.

"Where are we headed?" he asked as they walked down the hallways.

"To give you a new look. Rafael is right: the whole world knows your face. You need a cover."

"What do you have in mind?"

"It's not what I have in mind; it's what Alexandria, our specialist in these matters, has in mind."

They walked past various workshops and offices, then entered a brightly lit studio. The room was painted with images of Michelangelo's frescos. An old television was mounted on the right wall.

"Is this the movie star?" asked a curvy, raven-haired woman in an indigo pantsuit.

"The one and only," Tara declared.

"Well, he's too handsome to change anything about him," Alexandria said with a foxy grin.

"I'm afraid we have to, Alexandria. We need your best work."

"I'll take good care of him, rest assured."

"See you later," Tara said to Victor.

"See you," he replied.

"Well, what have we here? You've been on the news around the clock." Alexandria pointed at the television. Images of Victor were being presented during the news reports. "Have a seat," she said, motioning toward a leather recliner.

"All right," Victor said, sitting down in the recliner. "Did you paint the place yourself?"

"Yes, I did."

"It's impressive. It's as if Michelangelo had painted the room with his own hand."

"Thanks. That's the best compliment you could have given me."

"You're not going to turn me into a freak, are you?"

Alexandria laughed. "No, I promise I won't. There's no surgery. The makeup isn't permanent and can be removed at a time when you think it's prudent or necessary. Just lie back and relax, sweetheart."

Victor lay back and watched the television as Alexandria worked on his face. His image was on the screen again.

"Global News Network update," said the talking head. "As previously reported, the vicious criminal Victor J. Ganin has successfully broken free the rebel leader Steele, killing an unspecified number of innocent bystanders in the process. Among the innocents were many women and children. This, of course, is consistent with his record for disdaining civilization. Criminal, terrorist, traitor—these are the words that people who knew him use to describe the wretched man. Stay tuned for more news after the commercial break."

"GNN is to news what snake oil salesmen are to medicine," Alexandria commented.

"It would be too much to expect the truth from the likes of them," Victor responded.

"The truth? To them, the truth is irrelevant. It's only the spin that matters."

"That's a fact."

She ran her fingers through his hair repeatedly, applying a dark hair dye.

"The VerChip," said the seductive brunette on the screen, "protects you and your loved ones from terrorists, subversives, and common criminals. It ensures rapid assistance in the event of an emergency; guarantees your right to buy, sell, and do business; facilitates employment, banking, shopping, and virtually every activity you cherish. It secures your right to life, liberty, and the pursuit of happiness as a valued world citizen. The VerChip—it's safe, it's convenient, and it's the law."

"Lean your head back a little," Alexandria said. "Are you okay?"

"I'm fine," he replied.

She began working around his eyes, applying eyebrow and eyelash enhancement.

"Welcome back to our continuing coverage of breaking news. GNN investigative reporters have learned that the criminal Victor J. Ganin has psychopathic tendencies," said the talking head. "Due to his violent behavior as a child, he was placed in an orphanage at the request of his parents who feared for their lives. There, for no apparent reason, he stabbed another child in the eye with a fork. Many years later, after infiltrating the GPF, he committed heinous war crimes in various world regions. We go now to our in-the-field reporter."

"Good morning, world citizens," said the in-the-field talking head, reporting from the cocktail lounge of a five-star hotel. "Reporting to you live with an interview of the criminal Victor J. Ganin's former chief, Commander Wesley Drake. Commander, what is your assessment of said individual?"

"Ganin is a psychopath," Drake said, "unfit to be a member of the law enforcement community or society itself. I ask all citizens to remain calm. We will apprehend him, as we will all terrorists and wrongdoers of the world. They will be brought to justice."

"And the war crimes he committed?"

"We are investigating every step Ganin has taken. The families of his victims around the world will receive adequate monetary compensation."

"Thank you for your time, Commander. Now back to our anchor for more news."

Victor drifted for what seemed hours.

"That's the final touch," declared the disguise artist, placing an object on his nose. "Stand up and have a look!"

Victor stood up and looked in the mirror. He could barely recognize himself: his sandy hair was now dark and neatly styled; the stubble on his face was also dark, showing a short mustache and beard; a pair of reading glasses hung on his nose. "That's—that's incredible!" he said.

"Can't recognize yourself, can you?"

"I look like a scientist."

"That's right. From now on your public name is Mr. Miles Ambrose, research scientist, New York University." She handed him a bottle of dense liquid. "Now, as your beard grows out, trim it and apply this dye to maintain the color."

He grinned, removing the glasses. "Thanks, Alexandria."

"Don't mention it, darling."

*   *   *

Victor walked down the hallways to the window exit. He negotiated the swing bridge, this time with more agility, back into the headquarters building. Then he took the elevator to the first floor and continued to Command Headquarters.

Tara, Rafael, Sean, and George stood poring over the maps on the table.

Tara looked up from the maps. "Mr. Ambrose, I believe?"

"Good day, Commander Steele."

"Please come in. We're debating strategy."

Victor walked into the room and looked down at the table. There were detailed maps of the surrounding area as well as blueprints of individual buildings.

"Our best defense is to position fighter teams in the buildings, remotely detonated explosives along the avenues of approach, and snipers on rooftops," George said, pointing at one of the maps. "The rest of our fighters should be at strategic locations, ready to fight a rearguard action."

"A wise plan," Sean agreed.

"I disagree," Rafael said. "We need a more aggressive strategy."

"Aggressive? How? We're short on everything, especially ammunition," Tara stated.

Sighs of frustration filled the room. The group looked at their observing guest.

"What? You want my advice?" Victor asked.

Tara removed her bandana and wiped her bandaged forehead. "Why not? We could use a breath of fresh air."

"Well, you've been very successful at defending yourselves. But I think it's time to shift gears."

"What exactly do you have in mind?"

"We have to cut the head off the cobra."

FIFTEEN

"Meeting called to order," Mr. Maximilian Mephisto announced, smashing the gavel onto its stand. "Esteemed members of the Trident Group—we have an extraordinary mission. As the global power elite, it is our right to rule the world. We are the lords of the earth! We decide the fate of all mankind! And we shall lead the world to its glorious destiny!" He paused, surveying the members.

The meeting was taking place in Mephisto's office on the top floor of the Global Security Incorporated headquarters building in Lower Manhattan. The dimly lit office spanned the entire one hundred twentieth floor of the building. Mephisto sat at the head of an expansive conference table with Trident Group members seated equidistant from each other, their faces shaded by the bluish lights of laptop computers. To his left front was a staircase that led to the ceiling. On the wall behind him was a large flat screen with a digital map of the world; designated regions, quadrants, and zones were depicted in multicolored rectangles. Above the digital map was the crest of a golden phoenix spreading its wings, with the slogan Unity, Progress, and Total Security for Mankind arched around its feathered head. On either side of the map were alabaster statues of ancient gods. Jupiter, the ruler of all gods, stood to the right. Mars, the god of war, stood to the left. Ancient paintings lined the walls. There were Blake's *The Great Red Dragon* series, Munch's *The Scream,* and Fuseli's *The Nightmare,* among others. Along the upper right wall ran a strip of mirrors angled down toward the table; behind the mirrors, it was said, were surveillance cameras.

Another smash of the gavel broke the silence. "Roll call . . ." Mephisto declared. "Although we know each other well, according to protocol we'll begin with introductions. Shall I begin?" he asked rhetorically, rising from his chair. "Maximilian Mephisto, President of Global Security Incorporated and Chairman of the Trident Group."

The members announced themselves in turn:

"Gary Griffon, Chief Executive Officer, Victory Weapons Incorporated," stated the bright-eyed man wearing a designer suit.

"Rolfe Blair, Managing Director, World Banking Consortium," declared the stylish man with swept-back hair.

"Ariel Simon, President, Universal Insurance and Financial Services," said the intellectual-looking man with rimless glasses.

"Morgana Walker, Chief Executive Officer, Global News Network," declared the dark-haired woman with oval glasses.

"Yevgeny Koslov, Managing Director, Triumph Armaments Incorporated," stated the sturdy man with a trimmed beard.

"Ho Zeng, President, Universal Manufacturing Conglomerate," said the slender man with a bow tie.

"Raj Singh, Chief Financial Officer, Global Monetary Fund," declared the dark man with jeweled rings on his fingers.

"Caroline Dubois, Chief Executive Officer, Universal Stock Exchange," stated the sculpted blonde wearing a tailored pantsuit.

"Omar Hakim, Managing Director, World Petrol Consortium," said the blue-turbaned man in a strong voice.

"Antonio Ramirez, Chief Financial Officer, Global Foods Conglomerate," stated the sharp-featured man with a mustache.

Mephisto stood at the head of the conference table, his dark eyes surveying the members, his black slicked-back hair reflecting the lights. He cracked a smile and began. "Honored leaders, I thought it would be appropriate to begin this evening with a brief celebratory history of our organization."

He paused, pulling tight his black leather gloves, straightening his black suit jacket and adjusting his black-and-red barber-pole tie. "Centuries ago, individuals who were the best of their respective civilizations—those of greatest wealth and power—decided that it was necessary to form an organization to rule the world. The world needed leadership or it would surely sink into chaos. For it was obvious the human masses were incapable of governing themselves. So these superior individuals grouped within the halls of top universities, business conventions, and government conferences of the strongest nations. And they secretly formed the organization of global power elites: the *Illuminati*—the enlightened ones.

"Through their wealth and power, the Illuminati gained control of the world's banks and financial institutions, thereby taking control of the so-called sovereign states. *Control of the wealth of nations brings control of the nations along with their governments, militaries, and peoples.* The organization became the true power behind the façade of power. They appointed leaders, ran economies, organized social movements, and when necessary, staged revolutions.

Virtually every significant world event bore the mark of the hidden hand.

"There was opposition of course, primarily from the institutions of church and nation-state. Desperately trying to save their archaic institutions, national and religious leaders outlawed the Illuminati. Due to this resistance as well as the basic necessity to operate covertly, the organization often functioned through various front groups.

"In the twenty-first century, we Illuminati founded the Trident Group as our main front group. As superiors, meant to rule the inferior masses and the world itself, we were poised to seize absolute power. And with a masterstroke, we vanquished our opponents and accomplished our mission of establishing the New World Order: a world government, global commerce, and a universal religion. *We are the power behind WorldGov. We are the true force, the hidden hand, as we have been throughout the centuries and will continue to be, forever.*"

Mephisto paused for a moment, then continued. "Yet, during this entire struggle, the unpredictable human factors of *spirit and free will* remained. Now, thanks to the ingenuity of Global Security Incorporated, we have the technology to crush these factors and finalize our objective: *total control of the masses.*" He reached into his right jacket pocket and withdrew a capsule-shaped microchip, which he presented between his thumb and forefinger. The chip shimmered in the dimness of the room. "The VerChip gives us this capacity. With this RFID device implanted in the population, we can electronically track every movement, every activity, and every transaction any individual has made recently or within his lifetime. It, along with other surveillance technologies, puts the individual in an invisible electronic prison. *This is the ultimate power we had been seeking.*"

He slipped the microchip back into his jacket pocket. Then he proceeded with a displeased look on his face.

"However, there are still rebel elements resisting its implementation. These elements are waging illegal wars against NWO authorities. This is particularly true of quadrants in World Regions 2 and 5." He turned to the flat screen with the digital world map. "Here and here are our biggest problems," he said, indicating quadrants in the former Europe and the former South America with his laser pointer. "Alarmingly, we have encountered resistance from here as well." He flashed the pointer to New York City. "A rebel by the name of Steele has wreaked havoc in the zone."

Mephisto's expression gradually became one of satisfaction. "Nevertheless, overall VerChip global-implementation strategy has been a tremendous success. Some ninety percent of the world population is marked and accounted for.

"This brings us to the first issue on our agenda: to make rejecting the VerChip a global capital crime. In other words, individuals who are not chipped will be subject to liquidation without legal processes. This measure will cut through red tape and facilitate the final solution to the rebel problem. I move to authorize the summary liquidation of all those who break the mandatory VerChipping laws. Discussions, opinions, or comments, anyone?" A prolonged silence ensued.

"Excellent. Call to a vote," Mephisto said. "All those in favor of the motion, raise your hands. . . . We have a unanimous vote in favor of reinforcing the VerChipping laws. The motion is approved in accordance with WorldGov Law No. 100, World Security Act, which decrees: 'No world citizen shall perform a financial transaction or any other activity that is not officially registered through the Universal Identification System: the VerChip. Those in violation of this law will be considered *persona non grata*, thereby officially forfeiting their existence.'" He breathed deeply, taking his seat and adjusting his tie.

"The second issue on our agenda: world fiscal policy," Mephisto declared.

"I should like to begin," Blair said.

"You have our undivided attention, Mr. Blair."

"Thank you, Mr. Chairman, honored members," began the stylishly suited man. "On behalf of the World Banking Consortium, I move to increase the global interest rate by five percentage points. The motion is submitted on the following basis: To our benefit, we globalist elites have destroyed free enterprise and replaced it with global corporatism. Clearly, the banking industry is the pillar of global corporatism. Recently however, we have lost billions on failed loans and investments. The higher interest rate will compensate for these losses and ensure lucrative profits. I would also like to quote WorldGov Law No. 251, Banking Management Act, which states: 'The banking industry is crucial to the world economy. Under no circumstances shall its profitability be compromised.'"

"Nevertheless, there are regions that simply cannot afford to pay these rates," Mr. Simon remarked.

"Certain regions are economically mismanaged. Many of them squander resources on unproductive public services and programs. They will have to be restructured. But consider the consequences if we disappoint the oligarchs and moguls that back us. Surely you are not here today on behalf of the common worker?" Blair stated.

"Certainly not," Simon countered. "I'm only saying we cannot completely ignore the needs of the regional populations."

"He has a valid point," Ms. Dubois remarked. "Let me remind you of WorldGov Law No. 944, Minimum Subsistence Act, which states: 'The needs of the regional populations shall be met and kept at a minimum level.' And bear in mind, disregarding their basic needs may result in social upheaval."

"I don't need lessons about the law from you, Ms. Dubois!" Blair snapped.

"Let's remain civil, shall we?" Mr. Ramirez said.

"Perhaps, there is a compromise," Mr. Singh interjected. "As Chief Financial Officer of the Global Monetary Fund, I understand the necessity to maximize interest rates. As you know, our organization has maintained world indebtedness for decades. Just as we controlled the former nations through debt, so we retain control of the regions. A region in debt is a region we can domineer," Singh stated, twisting the rings on his fingers. "Although the monetary fund's interest rates are independently established, we concur with an increase of the global interest rate. This will give us the leverage to hike rates as well. However, the proposed five percent increase could be considered excessive. May I suggest a three percent increase instead?"

"The banking and credit industries already make higher profits than any other industry," Ms. Dubois noted.

"This is indeed a controversial issue," Mephisto said. "Perhaps we can vote on the compromise proposal? Mr. Blair, is that acceptable to you?"

"I find it a reasonable proposal, Mr. Chairman."

"Very well then. Call to a vote. All those in favor . . . ? Opposed . . . ? We have a count of eight in favor, two opposed, with no abstentions. The motion is approved."

"Next on our agenda: authorization of armed conflict," Mephisto stated.

"Mr. Chairman, honored members," Mr. Griffon began. "The world military-industrial complex is nearing financial crisis. The truce in the Region 4, rival quadrants' war has been holding. There's been little active combat, and arms sales are lagging because of this. As CEO of Victory Weapons Incorporated, I can affirm that profits are down and the stockholders are becoming nervous. I move for a resumption of the conflict."

"I second the motion," Mr. Koslov said. "We are experiencing similar difficulties at Triumph Armaments Incorporated. The resumption of combat is essential. While Mr. Griffon's corporation arms one side of the conflict, we will sell weapons to the other. This maintains the appropriate balance."

"How many more civilian casualties should we expect?" Mr. Hakim inquired.

"Our precision-guided munitions ensure that collateral damage will be negligible," Griffon replied.

"There are disagreements to be resolved in the region," Simon stated.

"Perhaps several more years of conflict will resolve these issues," Koslov said.

"The Global Monetary Fund will, of course, provide humanitarian low-interest loans to the warring quadrants," Singh affirmed.

"Does any other member wish to express an opinion on this matter . . . ?" Mephisto asked. "Very well. Call to a vote. All those in favor of restarting the Region 4, rival quadrants' war, raise your hands. . . . All opposed . . . ? The motion passes with nine in favor, one opposed, and no abstentions. The motion is approved in accordance with WorldGov Law No. 325, Authorization of Armed Conflict Act, which states: 'Armed conflict may be authorized under the following conditions: the adversaries have irreconcilable differences, negotiations have been deemed impractical, and the conflict is financially beneficial to the world economy.'"

"Next issue on our agenda: authorization of public information," Mephisto stated.

"If I may," Ms. Walker began. "Mr. Chairman, esteemed members. The Global News Network has encountered increasing resistance from banned or otherwise unauthorized Internet websites. These bandit sites have been contradicting, in fact challenging the veracity of our official news reports.

I will cite you several examples: When we reported that due to smart-bomb technology there were no civilian casualties in the Region 4, rival quadrants' wars, a banned site presented photographs showing some of the countless dead and wounded civilian victims of these wars. When we aired our GNN special report on the 'People's Revolutions' in Region 2, an unauthorized site presented proof that the mass demonstrations, police confrontations, and eventual overthrow of regional leaders were, in fact, funded and orchestrated by global elites. And when we aired a series of reports on the New York City terrorist organization known as the Crusaders Rebel Army, an unlicensed site repeatedly referred to them as freedom fighters rather than terrorists."

Ms. Walker looked up from her laptop, adjusting her glasses. "These Internet criminals are a source of embarrassment and pose a threat to our credibility. I therefore move for strict enforcement of information censorship laws and to direct the Global Police Force to crack down on these bandits."

"I second the motion," Mr. Singh declared. "It is dangerous for the masses to have access to too much information, especially information that has not been properly censored. Knowledge is power and such power may result in anarchy."

"Well said," Mr. Zeng agreed. "Mr. Singh and I both hail from quadrants with very large populations. We must be cautious; a seemingly insignificant piece of information can be the catalyst for chaos."

"Any other opinions . . . ?" Mephisto inquired. "Call to a vote. All those in favor . . . ? Opposed . . . ? Abstentions . . . ? The final count is eight in favor, one opposed, with one abstention. The motion is approved in accordance with WorldGov Law No. 529, Freedom of Authorized Information Act, which decrees: 'Information that poses a threat to the New World Order is strictly prohibited.'"

"Next on our agenda: genetically modified foods," Mephisto stated.

"Mr. Chairman, honored members," Mr. Ramirez began. "On behalf of the Global Foods Conglomerate, I move to enforce the implementation of genetically modified foods. The motion is submitted on the following basis: There is stiff opposition to genetically modified foods from the remaining regional food producers. The lack of a clear directive from world authorities further complicates the situation. The result is that many world regions are still producing natural foods. This is limiting productive output, creating needless competition, and reducing profit margins."

"It is difficult to implement these technologies in some of our yet underdeveloped quadrants," Zeng said.

"We are aware of this," Ramirez responded. "To remedy the situation, our corporation is working through government channels to restructure agricultural lands into more viable entities."

"That will mean displacing farmers. We are concerned about rural unrest."

"We've taken this into consideration. Those farmers who are displaced will be given the opportunity to work for our global corporation or one of our subsidiaries. Progress is inevitable. They simply must accustom themselves to the modern world."

"Then there is the question of food safety," Koslov remarked. "Are we sure these foods, which are created by the process of gene mutation, are healthy products?"

"Our industry has spent millions on research and development," Ramirez said. "And we have sponsored nearly every scientific study on the matter. These studies have invariably drawn positive conclusions. I assure you that genetically modified foods are quite safe for human consumption. May I also quote WorldGov Law No. 812, Advancement of Technology Act, which states: 'Technologies that generate profits shall be implemented through the most expedient means.'"

"Other opinions . . . ?" Mephisto inquired. "Call to a vote. All in favor . . . ? Opposed . . . ? We have a count of seven in favor, three opposed, with no abstentions. The motion is approved."

"Next issue on our agenda: petroleum production and supply," Mephisto stated.

"Mr. Chairman, esteemed members," Mr. Hakim began. "On behalf of the World Petrol Consortium, I thank you for your cooperation with every aspect of energy production and distribution. As you know, there are many vested interests involved, since nearly all corporations have links to the petroleum industry. As such, we have adjusted production schedules according to your needs. However, we think this is the right time to reduce output in order to boost profits. I move for a cutback in petroleum production."

"What is the suggested reduction and how much will it increase the price of petrol?" Ms. Walker asked.

"We are proposing a cutback of five million barrels per day. That should suffice to reduce production costs, moderately increase prices and ensure gainful profits."

"This is a reasonable proposal. We support the motion wholeheartedly," Koslov said.

"Wait just a minute now," Griffon said. "My region is already paying high prices for petrol. How can we be assured that this is the last price hike?"

"Members, let's not allow petty regional issues to obstruct our global vision," Mephisto interjected. "I would also like to call your attention to WorldGov Law No. 431, Common Energy Act, which decrees: 'Petrol and other forms of energy are world resources. No single region shall be considered the sole proprietor. Energies will be managed by global authorities and produced according to world-market demand.' May I suggest a more modest reduction of four million barrels per day?"

After a lengthy reflection, Hakim replied, "I think this is an acceptable compromise, if it will ensure passage of the motion."

"I believe your motion will pass at four million barrels, Mr. Hakim."

"Then let us proceed."

"Very well. Call to a vote. All in favor . . . ? Opposed . . . ? We have a count of eight in favor, two opposed, with no abstentions. The motion is approved."

"The final issue for this evening: industrial production and wages," Mephisto stated.

"Mr. Chairman, honored members," Mr. Zeng began. "The Universal Manufacturing Conglomerate has successfully increased production and reduced labor costs, thus bringing to the world market an abundance of low-priced products. This was accomplished by moving factories from high-labor-cost to low-labor-cost regions."

"An impressive accomplishment," Blair noted.

"Thank you, sir," Zeng said. "Unfortunately, there has recently been a resurgence of labor unions. It was our understanding that these nationalistic organizations had been effectively eliminated. Yet the concept of workers' rights has once again infected our population. At the moment, these movements are in their infancy and mostly at the local level. Still, they present a threat to global corporatism."

"Have the labor leaders been positively identified?" Blair asked.

"That is the difficulty. The groups meet in secret and are hard to monitor, and in some quadrants there is still a lack of surveillance equipment. Additionally, law enforcement authorities do not prioritize these matters."

"Perhaps mercenary contractors would resolve these difficulties," Ramirez suggested.

"More than that is required," Singh said. "It will be most effective to recruit local informers, perhaps from the workforce itself. Pay them well and they will supply the necessary intelligence information. Once you have obtained the names and VIN numbers of the leaders, simply submit the target list to the GPF."

"How reasonable are these leaders? Negotiation may be the best option," Ms. Dubois said.

"Negotiation will only lead to more negotiations," Blair said casually. "Labor unions are illegal organizations. May I quote WorldGov Law No. 685, Global Commerce Act, which states: 'Global marketers have the absolute right to conduct business. Organizations that block, disrupt, or otherwise impede commerce are banned.'"

"Exactly so. I therefore move to allocate funds for the hiring of informants and mercenaries to resolve the labor problems we are experiencing," Zeng concluded.

"Any other opinions . . . ?" Mephisto asked. "Call to a vote. All in favor . . . ? Opposed . . . ? We have a final count of nine in favor, one opposed, with no abstentions. The motion is approved."

"I believe that concludes our agenda this evening," Mephisto said. "I sincerely thank each and every one of you for your participation. Always remember that our meetings are strictly confidential. Members shall not disclose anything to anyone about the meetings—not even to your families, colleagues, or close associates. This meeting of the Trident Group is officially concluded," Mr. Maximilian Mephisto proclaimed with a triple tap of the gavel.

The members rose from their chairs to shake hands, back slap, and exchange congratulations. Mephisto mingled in the center of the gathering. The sound of an approaching fleet of helicopters resonated in the background.

"Sounds like our rides are arriving," Griffon said cheerfully.

"That's what I call good timing," Ramirez said with a smile.

The windows vibrated slightly as the helicopters landed on the rooftop. A team of Supreme Bureau of Investigation agents entered the room, their blazers bulging with concealed weapons. The SBI chief walked to Mr. Mephisto, exchanged salutations, then stood by his side.

"Honored members, please step this way," Mephisto said, motioning toward the staircase that led to the roof. "Chief, would your men kindly escort our members?"

"Right away, sir," replied the SBI chief, signaling the men.

The agents walked alongside group members as they went up the staircase onto the roof. Mephisto and the chief were the last to exit.

The helicopters were of various colors, bearing the logos of their respective corporations. Their rotors were at idle rpm yet they still generated a strong wind. Suits and ties fluttered in the rotor wash. Mephisto shook a gloved hand with each of the members as they made for their transport.

The helicopters wound up to one-hundred-percent rotor rpm, creating a whirlwind on the rooftop. Then, one by one, they took off toward their respective destinations. Mephisto and the SBI chief watched as their flashing lights grew fainter in the distance.

"Which one is Hakim's?" Mephisto asked as a black aircraft streaked past overhead. Only its speed and low whirring sound identified it as a helicopter gunship.

"That one," the chief replied, pointing to the east.

There was a flicker of red light as the pursuing gunship launched an air-to-air missile. Seconds later—in a bright flash that lit up the night sky—the World Petrol Consortium helicopter exploded into a giant fireball and disintegrated.

"Betrayal carries the ultimate penalty," Mephisto said, viewing the thousands of fiery pieces falling over the East River like a fireworks display.

SIXTEEN

Rafael leaned forward on the headquarters table. "Cut the head off the cobra? You're not seriously suggesting that we go on the offensive? World Government forces would crush us in the very first assault."

"Clearly, direct confrontation would be suicidal," Victor said. "I am suggesting a rapid-strike operation to eliminate the head of the SpyChip conspiracy, Mr. Maximilian Mephisto. One highly skilled assault team could accomplish the mission."

"How would that stop them? The WorldGov structure would still be intact," Sean said.

"WorldGov is *an even greater deception* than our governments of the past. The real power is in the hands of global power elites who control the world economy. They are the hidden hand that manipulates the state. Mephisto, Global Security Incorporated, and the Trident Group are in control," Victor affirmed.

"We have little intelligence information about the Trident Group," George noted.

"They are an Illuminati front group and nearly impossible to infiltrate. However, it's clear that their covert activities are conducted from the GSI skyscraper," Victor said.

"Surely we would need several hundred fighters for supporting missions," Tara said, observing him with her left eye, the one that wasn't bandaged.

Victor nodded. "Agreed, Commander. We will require forces for supporting operations to destroy VerChip production plants and to take over the news network. But I believe these will require minimum personnel if we achieve the primary objective."

Rafael looked at him skeptically. "The GSI building is one of the most heavily guarded structures in the world. Just penetrating the militarized district would require a force many times our size."

"Even the gates of Troy were breached with the right plan."

"Sure, we'll need a Trojan horse. I'll get on that right away!"

"Not a horse, but an aircraft. Mephisto arrives and departs the GSI building from his various fortified compounds by helicopter. The building is accessible from the roof."

Tara pulled up her sweater sleeves and folded her arms, pondering the discussion.

"Captain Dante Manzetti, reporting for duty," said a tall man with wavy auburn hair and a black eyepatch over his left eye, wearing fatigues and a weathered leather jacket, walking through the door. He was followed by two fighters, a man and a woman, also in fatigues, and carrying sniper rifles.

"We've been expecting you, Captain," Tara said, observing him curiously. "This is Victor Ganin, also known as Mr. Miles Ambrose. He'll ride shotgun with you on today's mission."

"Mission? Am I missing something?" asked the newly bearded Victor.

"This is New York City. You have to be flexible!" she said.

"That's a fact!" he replied.

"Captain Manzetti will give you all the details."

"Welcome aboard," Dante said, extending his hand. Victor clasped a gauzed hand with his. "Don't sweat it—the mission's routine. Can you shoot with that hand, just in case?"

"Not a problem," Victor responded.

"Excellent; then we're in business. Are you hungry?"

"Starved."

"Let's go to the canteen. I'll brief you over lunch."

Dante, Victor, and the two fighters headed for the door.

"Oh, Ganin," Tara called. "We'll want to hear more about Trojan horses."

He paused, looking over his shoulder. "Of course. You can count on it."

The group walked out of the room, through the hallway, and down the stairs. Then they continued down another hallway to the canteen. The room had long wooden tables arranged in rows, a series of windows facing the main street, and steaming pots of food on a line of stoves by the far wall. A sign above the stoves read, "Take only one ladleful per item, please."

"I hope you like rice and soybeans. That's all we have at the moment," Dante said, unzipping his leather jacket.

"I'm not particular," Victor replied.

The group served themselves, sat down at a table, and began eating.

"If our mission is successful, we'll have meat, vegetables, and dried fruits," Dante declared.

"Details, please?" Victor asked.

"We're short on supplies, as usual. Our mission is to trade pirated software for basic goods on the black market. It's a routine assignment. Just stay cool but be ready to take action if necessary."

"Absolutely," Victor said, reaching inside his black leather jacket and drawing his Glock. He charged the handgun and holstered it back inside his jacket, then verified that spare magazines were in his cargo-pant pockets.

Dante, Victor, and the fighters finished their meals. Then they left the room, went to the elevator, and took it down to the underground garage. Dante led the way to a row of classic muscle cars: Chevelles, Javelins, and Thunderbirds. Modern hybrid and electric vehicles were parked in the rows behind them.

"I didn't know there were any of these dinosaurs left," Victor remarked.

Dante grinned. "Very few remain; I think we have most of them in this city. We'll take this one," he said, pointing at a green Chevelle with a blower projecting from the hood. "Supercharged V-8—this beast will outrun anything on wheels. Hopefully, we won't need the speed." He opened the driver's door and entered. Victor entered the passenger's side. The fighters entered the back of the vehicle.

The Chevelle rumbled out of the garage into the sunlit streets. Dante continued briefing as he drove, cracking open his window, allowing a cool autumn breeze to enter. "Here's the deal: In the trunk we have thousands of recently produced computer software disks. We're to swap the goods for a truckload of water filtration equipment, food, medicines, and ammunition. We'll meet with Mafia boss Don Sergio Romano. He runs most of the black-market activities in the South Bronx. He's a fair guy, but he doesn't hesitate to gain the upper hand."

"No problem," Victor said. "It sounds clear cut."

"It should be, just keep your eyes open."

They cruised through the rebel area. The streets were bustling with people bartering for goods. There were groups of children playing on the sidewalks. Rebel guards patrolled on motorcycles with assault rifles slung on their backs. Dante accelerated as they left the area. He continued through desolate streets around the Bronx Park toward their destination.

"Want a swig?" Dante extended a whiskey flask.

"No thanks, Captain," Victor replied, waving it off.

"Your loss," he said, taking a drink.

Suddenly a low buzzing sound came from the sky above. "Damn it!" Dante exclaimed as he spun the wheel and hit the gas, turning into the side streets. He turned several more times, coming to a stop in a narrow street with brick-walled structures on either side. "Everyone out!" he yelled. The group jumped out of the vehicle and put their backs to the wall of a building; the fighters pointed their rifles toward the sky. The buzzing sound drew closer. A white aircraft flew by overhead, then rolled into a turn and circled the locale.

Dante took out a pair of binoculars from inside his jacket and scanned above. "It's a hunter-killer drone, armed with missiles."

"It's only filming for now," Victor said.

"For now," Dante echoed. "But it could strike at any moment."

"Just stay calm—don't shoot," he said, looking at the fighters. They nodded silently.

The drone passed again and launched a missile. Seconds later a bright explosion engulfed an apartment building on the adjacent block; the blast demolished it, spewing rubble and debris in every direction.

"That was close," breathed the female fighter.

"We're lucky it wasn't closer," Dante said warily.

The buzzing faded as the drone disappeared beyond the skyline.

"Let's get out of here," said the male fighter.

"Come on," Dante said.

The group ran back to the Chevelle, opened the doors and jumped in.

*   *   *

It was mid-afternoon when they rolled into the South Bronx. Dante pulled over momentarily and the two fighters got out and assumed sniper positions overlooking the rendezvous site. Then he drove down the street, turned into an empty lot, and backed into a parking space.

Almost immediately two burly men with submachine guns, dressed in three-piece suits and silk ties, approached the vehicle. "State your business," demanded one of them.

"We're here for an exchange with Don Romano. Name's Dante; I'm one of Steele's people."

"Wait here." The man put a mobile phone to his ear.

Before long, a bulletproof sedan pulled into the lot and parked close by. A large figure wearing a fedora hat, a tailored suit, and an overcoat stepped out of the right rear door.

"Dante, it's been a while," Romano said in a deep voice.

"A while, depends on one's perspective of time, Sergio." Dante grinned.

Romano signaled his associates. Several more men came out of the vehicle.

"Are you armed?" asked one of the men.

"I've got nothing," Dante replied.

"How about you?" he asked Victor.

"You bet."

"At least this one speaks the truth."

A late model truck pulled in front of the Chevelle, boxing them into the parking space.

"Okay, you made your point. You're in charge," Dante said to Romano.

"You can't be too careful," Romano stated. "Pop the trunk. We'll check out your delivery. You can check out ours if you want. By the way, don't think your two snipers could be of any assistance to you—my men have them in their scopes."

Dante cracked a deceptive grin. "Two? We have four! The other two have your men in their sights!"

"You prick, Manzetti. No way!" The Mafia boss glared at him, neither deceived nor amused.

"Come on, lighten up! You know we're on the level," Dante said, pulling the trunk release lever.

Romano's men went to the back of the Chevelle to inspect the software.

"I'll check out their delivery," Victor said. He exited the vehicle and walked over to the rear of the truck. It was stacked with boxes of water filters, food, medicines, and ammunition. He pulled out several of the boxes and opened them. The items were legitimate and in the correct quantities. "Everything's all right," he called, walking back toward the car.

"Okay Romano, we have a deal," Dante said.

"*Sure* we do. You're still behind on payment," Romano said. "More than two grand as I recall."

"Is that all you care about? The profits?" Victor asked.

The Mafia boss eyed the newcomer. "What's it to you, smart guy?"

"I just thought a man like you might want his legacy to be more than just a truckload of contraband."

"Take it easy," Dante interjected. "We're not here for philosophical discussions."

Romano moved face to face with Victor. "Take care of your business and I'll take care of mine, got it?"

"Sure, you're the boss," Victor answered, opening the car door.

Romano's men transferred the goods between vehicles; the trunk, backseat, and cargo nets strapped on top of the Chevelle were filled to capacity. Then the truck pulled off, clearing their exit.

"See you soon, Sergio." Dante waved briefly.

"Yeah, sure," Romano said.

Dante put the car in gear and applied the gas. The muscle car, heavily laden, moved sluggishly out of the lot and down the streets. "You did good," he said, driving back toward the location where they had dropped off the fighters.

"I doubt that," Victor replied. "I might have chosen my words more carefully."

"Don't let him give you the wrong impression. He likes people who talk straight. Trust me, I know better than anybody."

"How so?"

"Sergio's my uncle!"

"Yeah? Well, you didn't tell me that."

"It slipped my mind. Besides, we had a falling out, long ago."

Dante pulled over at the pick-up point. The fighters sprinted to the vehicle, then entered the back alongside boxes of supplies and shut the doors.

"We're homeward bound," Dante declared, driving off.

"Well, they outdid us this time around," said the male fighter. "They had the jump on us: their snipers were behind us the whole time. But it was good practice!"

Dante drove northbound through the streets then back around the park toward the rebel area. As they approached the area, motorcycle guards manning a checkpoint signaled them to stop. He applied the brakes, coming to a stop behind three pickup trucks returning with fifty-five-gallon drums full of gasoline.

A heavily armed guard walked toward them. "Is that you, Manzetti?"

"The one and only," he replied. "How's it going, Logan?"

"Hanging in there, friend."

The guard waved the vehicles through.

Dante followed the pickups toward the buildings. "We're arriving in five minutes," he reported into the microphone clipped to his jacket.

"Roger that," Tara responded from Command Headquarters.

They cruised down the main street and pulled over by the garage ramp of the headquarters building. A group of men with bandanas around their heads awaited them. Dante, Victor, and the fighters got out of the car. The two groups formed a chain from the vehicle to the garage door. They began unloading the cargo. The boxes were heavy, and they broke a sweat. Victor unzipped his jacket as he worked.

"Alarm!" a motorcycle guard shouted.

Work stopped as the group viewed the scene. In the distance, a cloud of dust spun into the air behind a rapidly approaching figure. Tara leaned out of the headquarters window with the command-radio microphone in her hand. "On guard!" she ordered into the microphone. The guards pointed their AK-47s down the street. Dante looked through his binoculars. Victor moved next to him and squinted.

"Don't shoot! Don't shoot!" Victor yelled as he ran off toward the approaching figure.

"Hold your fire!" Tara said.

A familiar barking came from the charging figure. Victor recognized the sound immediately. *Duke! My stars, it's you!* The two slowed down . . . then stopped in front of each other. Duke, covered with dust, settled on his haunches. Victor noticed a collar around the canine's neck. He knelt on one knee, gently stroked the dog's head, and removed the collar. On the inside of the band was a zipper. He opened it and removed a hidden note that read: "Dear Victor, I thought you would like to have him back. God bless you! Vera."

A crowd gathered around them.

"It's a dog. He sure can run fast," said one of the guards. "Is he yours?"

"He's mine—back off!" Victor said.

"Calm down, people. It's all right," Tara said from behind the crowd.

Victor walked off with Duke by his side. "Glad to have you with me again," he said in a low tone. The Chesapeake Bay retriever howled softly. The pair continued to the headquarters building, stopping by the exterior faucet on the right side of it. He turned on the tap and gave the canine a complete scrub down. Minutes later, he turned off the tap and the dog shook himself clean. "Now you look presentable," he declared.

The pair entered the building, then walked up the stairs and down the hallways. They passed by various rooms full of technicians and workers at computer workstations busily producing pirated software. In one of the offices was a young man wearing a Hawaiian shirt. Victor recognized him as the chief computer programmer. He stopped by the open door.

"Name's Bradley," said the man, looking up from his computer.

"I'm Victor. Pleased to meet you. Would you look at that!" he said, pointing at the old television in the corner of the room. Bradley turned to the screen.

"GNN special report," said the talking head. "Last night, terrorists assassinated Mr. Omar Hakim, Managing Director of the World Petrol Consortium. Mr. Hakim was returning from a business conference when a missile downed his helicopter. This malicious attack took the life of a greatly respected member of the world corporate community. His death comes as a shock to family members and close associates, as well as the general public. Mr. Maximilian Mephisto, business partner and close friend, expressed his indignation: 'It's outrageous that an esteemed world businessman be assassinated like this. All evidence shows that rebel terrorists are responsible. We must unite in opposition to those who would destroy democracy and civilization.'"

"Sounds to me as if Hakim knew too much," Victor noted.

Bradley nodded. "It looks that way all right."

"I've got something for you." Victor reached inside his jacket, took out the teal mini-disk from Global Police Headquarters, and tossed it to him.

"What's this?"

"All the GPF security codes your heart desires."

"You're kidding! I've been waiting to get my hands on one of these."

"Have at it. See you around, Bradley."

"Thanks. See you later, man."

Victor and Duke continued to the elevator. They took the lift to the fifth floor, walked down the hallway, and entered his quarters. "You must be hungry," he said, smiling. He opened several food packets, emptied them into a bowl, and poured water into an adjacent container.

The dog guzzled the water and voraciously consumed the food.

After a light meal, Victor headed for the door. Duke followed him out of the room and down the stairs; then they went their separate ways as he headed for the arms room, and the dog took to patrolling the streets. He arrived at the arms room, unlocked and opened the door, and viewed the array of weapons inside: assault rifles, handguns, explosives. *I can feel it: the winds of war are gusting.*

SEVENTEEN

"Commander Steele, you need to look at this."

"What is it, Bradley?" Tara said, leaning back in her chair at the Command Headquarters table and pulling up her sweater sleeves to the elbows.

Bradley laid a stack of computer printouts in front of her.

"What are these?" she asked.

"Very important intelligence information."

"Bradley, if this is another one of your WorldGov supply convoy intercepts, I really don't have the time to waste."

"But it's—"

"I know. They'd be valuable to capture: ammunition, food, medicines, gasoline—everything we lack. But the fact is we don't have the fighters or the resources to go after them. I won't risk losing any more people. I will not, understand?"

"This is different," Bradley said, pausing. "You look a little tired."

Tara put a hand on her bandaged forehead. "It's very late in the evening, you know."

"Perhaps this isn't the best time. But the fact of the matter is that it can't wait."

"All right. What is it?"

"It's the mini-disk."

"What mini-disk?"

"The one your . . ."

"Go ahead—everyone knows Victor and I are lovers."

"Well . . ." the computer specialist cleared his throat. "Victor gave me a mini-disk containing the access codes of Global Police Headquarters. With the codes I've been able to get this critical information from their mainframe database."

"Is that right?" she said, thumbing through the stack.

"They've planned another attack against us," Bradley said. Tara looked up from the printouts. "No worries," he said, holding up a hand and grinning.

Tara smiled back, not knowing why. "Pray tell, what exactly is so amusing at this moment?"

"Have a look at page fifty-eight."

Tara turned to the page. The attack plan included the air and ground forces to be employed, weapons to be used, and Global News Network propaganda for public consumption. She read aloud:

"Global Police Force, Top Secret Report. Planned overt operation: WorldGov forces will launch an air-ground assault to liquidate the New York City rebel organization, the Crusaders Rebel Army. Aircraft assigned: one fighter plane squadron. Troopers assigned: one thousand combat troopers plus support personnel. Weapons authorized for use: conventional, microwave, and laser. On the day of attack, GNN news reports must state the following: Our forces are launching this operation to protect democracy and stop rebel terrorists from detonating weapons of mass destruction in the metropolitan area . . ."

The computer specialist chuckled.

Tara's eyes darkened. "I fail to see the humor in this. They'll wipe us out."

"Look toward the bottom of the page," he said, pointing.

She looked down the page. "The coordinates . . ."

"They're not correct, are they?"

"These coordinates are more than one kilometer from our location," she said, smiling. "They've got the wrong locale!"

"That's right."

Tara looked at the page again. "The attack date is only two days from now. We have to warn the residents of that area as soon as possible. Is that all?"

"Not by a long shot. There's a lot more," Bradley said.

"Go on," she said, greatly interested.

"There's a digital audio file—with recordings of secret meetings of the Illuminati front group, the Trident Group, and their leader, Mr. Maximilian Mephisto."

"What? Where?"

"If you look on page twenty-one, it confirms the existence of such a file."

Tara turned to the page and read.

GPF Top Secret Report: A Supreme Bureau of Investigation *special investigation* has determined that Mr. Omar Hakim, Managing Director of the World Petrol Consortium, leads a cabal that undermines the New World Order and the Trident Group. Mr. Hakim and his cabalists, other petrol executives, have been running a petrol smuggling operation with distribution and sales into the black market. The operation also entails credits-laundering and global-tax evasion. Moreover, it was discovered that Mr. Hakim, with blackmail as the likely motive, has been secretly recording Trident Group meetings. These recordings were compiled into a digital audio file, the location of which is yet unknown. Brain-scan Lie Detector tests of various suspects have confirmed the existence of this file. Further information is unavailable as a key suspect had a brain hemorrhage during the interrogation process.

Planned covert operation: The liquidation of Mr. Hakim by way of air attack . . .

Tara looked up from the stack of printouts. "Good work, Bradley."

"Thanks. I've also marked the pages that are most critical."

"That's great, but I'm going to read every word of it."

"Can I be of any further assistance?"

"Sure. Tell Captain George Sebastian to come see me."

"I'll let him know," Bradley said, turning toward the door.

Tara flipped a few pages and continued reading.

GPF Top Secret Report: SBI surveillance and phone tapping have revealed that secret peace negotiations between Region 4's rival quadrants are in progress. There is a strong possibility these negotiations will be successful. And if their war is ended, this will cause financial crises in the arms, petroleum, and banking industries. Such crises may push the world economy into a recession.

Planned covert operations: Planting and detonating explosives at places of worship, marketplaces, and other public gatherings in the warring quadrants. Rival quadrants will suspect and accuse one another for the violence. The targeting of civilians will derail negotiations and ensure the resumption of hostilities . . .

"Commander."

Tara looked up from the papers. "Hello, George. I thought you'd show up right about now."

"I was told to report for duty. How can I be of service?"

"How's Anna?"

"Pregnant. Is that why you called me here?"

Tara laughed. "No, not exactly. Listen, we have discovered they're launching another attack in two days' time."

"Not again—"

"Relax, they've got the wrong coordinates," Tara said, handing him a slip of paper. "That's where they're going to drop the bombs—more than a kilometer from here. So tomorrow morning, take two fighters with you and go warn the residents of that area about the impending attack; they must evacuate immediately. And don't reveal who you are or where the information comes from."

"You can count on me."

"I know I can. Give Anna my best regards."

"You bet," he said, turning for the door.

She flipped a few pages.

GPF Top Secret Report: SBI investigations have concluded that the upcoming world presidential election requires greater control. This is especially true regarding the opposition candidate. His background and psychological profile indicate that he may not be fully supportive of World Government policies. And he has expressed doubts about the Universal Identification System and mandatory VerChipping laws in private conversations with undercover agents. Repeated attempts to bring him into the fold have yielded minimal results. Despite considerable financial backing for the reelection campaign of the current World President, the opposition candidate runs only five percentage points behind in the polls. Therefore, given these factors, he might pose a threat to the New World Order.

Planned covert operations are as follows: (1) To significantly increase the campaign budget of the current World President by funneling millions more credits to his reelection coffers. (2) To conduct a disinformation campaign about the opposition candidate. The revelation of any infraction he may or may not have committed in his life will be fully exploited by the official news network. (3) The cyber-manipulation of the computer voting process to get the desired result.

In the unlikely event that the unsanctioned candidate is elected, the following covert operation will be carried out: Said individual will be detained and administered a Brain-scan Lie Detector test. The lie detector machine will then be switched to its stealth capability, the behavior-modification mode. In this mode it will focus intensive electromagnetic waves on his cerebrum, reforming noncompliant thought patterns as required. Successful completion of the behavior-modification procedure will turn him into a tractable World President.

Tara leaned back in her chair, closing her eyes momentarily. Fourteen hours of work had exhausted her.
"What's up, boss?"

Tara slowly opened her eyes. A man with a black eyepatch over his left eye stood before her, grinning. "Dante—don't you ever sleep?"

"Sleeping is but a futile attempt to enter the parallel universe."

"You're a lousy philosopher."

"So what's your point?"

"My point is your talents should be applied more usefully."

"So apply them usefully. Stop sending me on these routine errands and give me a mission."

"I sense frustration in your voice."

"You sense correctly. Anyway, I thought I might offer you a fresh cup of java!" Dante said, holding up a thermos bottle and two mugs.

Tara laughed. Dante always made her laugh. "I graciously accept."

He sat down across from her and filled the mugs. Then he pulled out his flask, uncapped it and spiked his coffee.

Tara shook her head. "Whatever happened to you, Dante? I've heard that you graduated top of your class at the military flight academy, only to be thrown out of your operational unit for disciplinary reasons."

"The military is only as good as the leaders who direct it," he replied. "It was combat; I disobeyed illegal orders to open fire on civilians. That cost me my career. What of it? Given the choice between my livelihood and my soul, I'll choose my soul any day. Besides, why should I serve the likes of them?"

Tara took a drink of coffee and smiled. "All right, in truth, I can't argue the point. But I will explain why you're not sent on risky missions: The fact is we can't afford to lose you. You're the only pilot we've got. And we may need your skills in the near future."

"Got a flying mission for me?"

"It's a possibility."

"When might that be? When the sun becomes a supernova?"

"Dante—you're an aviator?" Victor asked, leaning in the open doorway.

Dante turned toward the interloper. "I don't like uninvited guests."

"He's never uninvited," Tara said.

"Oh, I see!" Dante nodded. "Well, to answer your question, I was once an aviator."

"Then you're still an aviator," Victor said. "We can't change what we are, only the paths we follow."

"I see we have a sage among us. Would you care for an intellectual joust?"

"I would." Victor grinned, taking a mug from the shelf by the entrance. He walked across the room and sat down at the end of the table. Tara snickered, leaning back in her chair, enjoying the scene.

Dante downed his coffee and then poured mugs all around. "Do you believe in the underdog?" he asked.

"Generally, I don't." Victor took a drink from his mug. "Why not?"

"Because the odds are against him."

"You're such a pessimist. *We're* the underdog. So what? We're going to win."

"What makes you so sure?"

Dante raised an eyebrow, lifted his mug and took a long drink. "I choose not to answer that question at this specific time. Instead, I'll ask the two of you a question."

"Let's hear it," Tara mused, sipping her coffee.

"Okay," Dante said. "Do you think man is superior to technology or is he inferior to his own creations? *That* is the question." He turned to Victor.

"I—I'm really not sure," Victor said, thoughtfully stroking his beard.

"The creator is always superior to his creations," Tara said.

Dante grinned cynically. "If humans are superior to technology, why do robocops, surveillance cameras, and implanted microchips have control over them?"

Tara and Victor exchanged silent glances.

"I'll leave you to contemplate that question," Dante said, pouring the last of the coffee into their mugs. "In the meantime, I'll answer yours: I think we'll win because victory is in our minds, our hearts, our very souls. We'll win all right. I assure you." He finished his coffee, excused himself from the table, and walked out the door.

Victor moved next to Tara and put his arm around her. "Maybe he's right, and we'll win. Maybe he's wrong and we'll be destroyed. But come what may, we must never give up the fight for freedom."

"We never will," she said, resting her head on his shoulder and drifting asleep.

A loud baying sound filled the room. Victor and Tara awoke in a start. The baying repeated itself. "Damn," Victor said, trying to focus on the blurred image of white fangs dripping with saliva. "Duke . . . can't you present yourself politely?" The dog leaped under the table then bit and tugged his pant leg. Victor shook his leg. "Duke! Have you gone mad?"

"I think he's trying to tell you something," Tara said.

"All right, already!" he said, rising from his chair.

The canine ran across the room to the open window, put his front paws on the sill and pointed his nose at the sidewalk below. Victor moved next to him and surveyed the scene. Clusters of people were walking in both directions.

Tara came to his side. "What's the problem?"

"I don't see one," Victor replied.

Duke barked again, looking to his right. Then he spun and sprinted from the room.

Victor and Tara observed the sidewalk. The dog dashed out of the front entrance and ran to the right, weaving between pedestrians toward a lone figure in a hooded overcoat. The figure turned the corner, disappearing from view. Duke sped around the corner after him.

"Something's wrong," Tara said.

"Let's see," Victor said.

They exited the building and waited in front of it. Some minutes later, Duke turned the corner with a piece of cloth hanging from his muzzle. He stopped on the sidewalk in front of them, huffing from the effort. Victor took the cloth from the dog. "It's common synthetic material," he said. "This gives us no clue of that person's identity. And now he's long gone."

"I'd like to know who he is and why Duke was so agitated," Tara said. She spoke into the microphone clipped to her sweater, "Attention, all guards: be vigilant for a lone individual in a hooded overcoat." The guard chiefs acknowledged the order.

"Let's go for breakfast, Vic," she said.

"Sounds good, Tara," he replied.

They went back inside the building to the canteen, filled their plates, and sat down at a table.

Tara and Victor ate quietly for some minutes.

"Victor," she began, "we have obtained information about Mephisto and the Trident Group."

"What sort of information?" he asked.

"There's a digital audio file—a recording of the group's secret meetings. It was recorded by one of the members, the now deceased Mr. Omar Hakim. However, we don't know where it is exactly."

"What else do we know?"

"Bradley hacked into the GPF mainframe database with the codes from the mini-disk and retrieved many documents. I read through all the information about Hakim and the digital file he compiled. The name of Thomas Lambert, a top executive for the World Petrol Consortium, appears repeatedly. He was one of Hakim's closest business associates. If anyone knows the location of the file, he does."

"How important is this file?" Victor asked.

"It is of the utmost importance," Tara replied. "The file fully exposes the corruption of the World Government and the sinister global power elites behind them. When the file is made public, and we declare this land a sovereign nation, the people will rally behind the liberation movement. It's one thing to overthrow a government, yet another to replace it with an alternative supported by the people."

"What do you suggest?"

"We need to get hold of the file. You must find Lambert and take possession of it."

"In what form is the file? Is it on disk?" he asked.

"We don't know, exactly," she replied. "What we do know is that the World Petrol Consortium building is on Long Island, not far from the Belmont Race Track. I'll have Bradley research more information for you. When you receive the details, link up with Captain Sean Flanagan for the mission to find Lambert and the file. Don't take one of the muscle cars. Take one of the hybrids or electrics; it'll be less noticeable."

"Understood. I'll wait for Bradley. In the meantime, I will begin the mission planning."

He finished his meal, gave her a familiar wink, and headed for the arms room.

Terrible high-pitched screeching sounds rattled the windows as fighter planes made their bombing runs. Victor walked to the windows of his room. The starry night lit up with bright flashes, little more than a kilometer in the distance; the subsequent explosions shook the building.

"Enjoying the show?" said a voice from the doorway.

"Bradley—what are you up to at this time of night?"

"Working, of course. It's only midnight. I usually work till the early morning hours," Bradley replied. "Anyway, who can sleep with all this noise?" More explosions shook the building; the lights flickered. "I have some information for you."

"Be my guest." Victor motioned toward his desk.

They sat down across from each other. The lights flickered into darkness.

"Well, that's convenient," Bradley commented.

"Give it a minute," Victor said. "If the lights don't come back on, I'll start the backup generator."

"There's no need for that," Bradley said, striking a match and lighting a thick candle, which he placed on the desk. His face appeared ghostly in the candlelight. More blasts shook the building; the candle's flame blinked several times, then shined once again.

"Do you have all the necessary information?" Victor asked.

"More or less. I don't have everything I would like to give you, but I think it's adequate."

"Go ahead."

"Thomas Lambert: Top executive for the World Petrol Consortium and close business associate of Mr. Omar Hakim. They knew each other well, including their respective families. Hakim did, in fact, keep a digital audio file of the Trident Group meetings. We're quite sure it was registered on a flash drive device. We have also confirmed that Lambert knows all about the digital file as well as its probable location."

"I'll need more than that."

"There's more. Apparently Hakim led a cabal within the petrol consortium, a group of executives in the corporation itself. The group ran a petrol smuggling operation with distribution and sales into the black market, enabling them to keep all the profits. They consisted of no more than a dozen individuals; it's unlikely that Lambert was one of them." Bradley slid a large white envelope across the desk. "Through Lambert's VerChip Identification Number, I was able to obtain this information on him."

Victor pulled Lambert's file from the envelope. He looked through the printouts and photographs. The subject's personal profile and information about his work, vehicle, and residence was included. "This should be adequate," he resolved.

"It's the maximum I could hack from the GPF database."

"Sean and I will act on the information, straight away." Victor rose from his chair and extended his hand. "Thanks, Bradley."

Bradley stood up and shook hands. "Good luck, friend," he said, turning for the door.

The fighter planes made their final bombing runs. The building shook once more, then the screeching sounds disappeared almost instantly. The lights came on again, flickered several times then remained lit at reduced capacity. Victor walked to the windows. Fires burned in the distance, smoke drifted across the night sky, and there was silence again.

EIGHTEEN

Sean drove the silver electric car down the 295 Expressway. Traffic flowed smoothly. "It's a nice day for a drive," he said, stroking his crew cut and adjusting his sunglasses.

"Depends on your viewpoint," Victor said. "We could have selected a vehicle with a less noticeable color."

"That's the whole idea. The local police won't take notice of a shiny silver car."

"The word is the police around here don't want trouble. But if they do, they'll get more than they bargained for," Victor said, reaching inside his leather jacket and drawing his Glock. He charged the weapon and holstered it back inside his jacket. "Did you look at Lambert's file?"

"Sure did. Here it is." Sean handed him a large envelope from the map pocket of the vehicle. "There's not so much to go by. We have photographs, addresses, and some personal information. We know what he looks like and where to find him."

"I understand Lambert's quite the gambler."

"Yeah, most of what he earns goes down the tubes. Hey . . . I think we're being shadowed."

Victor looked casually in his side mirror. A dark sedan paced behind them. "That would be Romano's men."

"Romano? How did he get involved in this?"

"Commander Steele contacted Romano and asked about Lambert. It turns out the Mafia has given him loans, and his payment's overdue. Even more significant, they are also interested in obtaining information about the Trident Group. We have common interests."

"I'm not sure I feel comfortable with the Mafia at my back."

"Relax, Flanagan." Victor smiled at him.

"Ganin, if this is your plan, anything could happen. How can I relax?" Sean replied sarcastically. "Oh, and, Steele told me to give you this," he said, taking a capsule from his inside jacket pocket and tossing it to him.

Victor caught it with cupped hands. "What's this?"

"A cloned SpyChip, which bears the data of your alias, Mr. Miles Ambrose. It's encased in a larger capsule so that you can palm it across any RFID reader."

"That's a magician's trick," Victor noted, stroking his beard.

"Start practicing," Sean said.

They continued on the 295 past Long Island Sound into the Cross Island Parkway. Along the parkway were office buildings mixed in with old neighborhoods where native-born generations continued to live. Some of the old houses looked as though they would catch fire at any moment. Sean took the Belmont Race Track exit and turned into the streets toward their destination. A few minutes later, he pointed at an office building in front of them. "There it is. That's the World Petrol Consortium headquarters in New York."

"It doesn't look so impressive," Victor remarked.

"That's their building in New York. You should see the one in Dubai," Sean said, pulling into a parking space across the street, facing its main entrance.

Victor took out his binoculars and surveyed the building. Then he zoomed into Lambert's office window on the eighth floor.

"See anything?" Sean asked.

"Just a bunch of suits going about their business," he replied.

The hours passed by. Victor glanced at his watch; it was two-thirty in the afternoon. He looked again at the photos in the file. Lambert had a weak jaw, brown eyes, and dark hair. He wore expensive suits with white shirts and power ties.

People began coming out of the building.

Victor raised his binoculars again. "Damn, they all look alike!"

"Look for a guy with greed in his eyes," Sean said.

"Wait, I think it's him."

"Standing by . . ."

"It's Lambert all right."

The man walked to his Mercedes sport coupe parked a few spaces to their front. He entered the vehicle, engaged the ignition and revved the engine.

"We'll never be able to keep up with that," Sean said, turning the key and shifting into drive.

"Do your best. Stay close but not too close," Victor replied.

The Mercedes sped off down the avenue. Sean took off after it, pressing the power pedal for all it was worth. Still, the sleek profile of the sport coupe grew smaller and smaller, disappearing in the distance.

"Lost him already," Victor said.

"Maybe he'll slow down," Sean replied, weaving between vehicles.

"You're wasting your time. He's long gone."

"What do you recommend, smart guy?"

"Let's check out the Belmont Race Track."

"What makes you think he's not headed home?"

"He was in too much of a hurry to be going home. No, there's something else on his mind. Besides, it's the last horse race of the season—his last chance to recoup his credits."

Sean drove through busy streets to the racetrack. He pulled into the parking lot and continued slowly down row after row of parked vehicles, searching for the sport coupe. "By gosh, you're right," he said briskly, pointing at the coupe parked in the row on his left. "Lambert's here."

Victor nodded. "Park as close as you can to it."

Sean parked in one of the few remaining spaces nearby. Then they exited the vehicle, walked to the booths, and stood in line.

"Tickets?" asked the booth attendant.

"Two," Victor replied, palming the falsified chip across the electronic reader.

"Here're your tickets, Mr. Ambrose," said the attendant, sliding them through the slot under the window.

The lobby was bustling with people. Bookies and gamblers shouted to each other across the crowded hall. The ever present robocops surveyed the multitudes.

"Well, which thoroughbred should we bet on?" Sean asked.

"What?" Victor said.

"Which horse should we bet on?"

"Are you out of your mind, Flanagan?"

"Why not? If our horse wins we'll get lots of credits. If not, Ambrose will pay the bill."

"We're here on a mission."

"The credits won't hurt us."

Victor eyed him curiously. "Which horse do you think will win?"

"Zephyr," Sean replied.

"Why do you think he'll win? That horse is a three-to-one underdog."

"I like the name."

Victor wiped his forehead. "All right, but just two hundred credits."

"It's a deal."

"Keep your eyes open for Lambert."

Victor went to one of the booths to place the bet. Some time later, he returned and handed Sean his bet ticket on Zephyr. "See him yet?" he asked.

"No," Sean said. "Let's look inside."

They went into the stands. . . .

"As a regular, he must sit close to the finish line," Victor said, taking out his binoculars and scanning that area for Lambert. A dark-haired man in an expensive suit came into view. "I . . . think it's him."

"You think or you're sure?"

Victor handed Sean the binoculars. "Two o'clock position, about twenty rows down."

Sean peered through the optics; the man turned his head. "That's not him. This guy's younger and slimmer." He searched the rows in a grid pattern. "Got him—one o'clock position, in the front row."

"Positive?" Victor asked.

"Absolutely," Sean said, handing back the binoculars.

They descended to the lower bleachers and took seats nine rows above Lambert.

"Take your seats. Take your seats, ladies and gentlemen. The race is about to begin!" declared the announcer. Lambert leaned forward in his seat, wringing his hands as if his entire life depended on the very moment.

"I'm guessing he's on his last credits," Victor noted.

"Then the Pied Piper's calling on him," Sean said.

The bell rang loudly and the thoroughbreds crashed through the gates.

"They're off!" the announcer blared, speaking in rapid phrases. "Comet takes the lead with Falcon and Zephyr at his hooves, leaving the others in their dust. Falcon is coming from the center; Zephyr's coming from the outside—the challengers are making their move. The margin is three lengths, narrowing to two, one . . ."

"Go! Go!" Sean shouted.

Victor peered through his binoculars, not at the charging horses but at their subject. Lambert was hanging on the horses' every stride. "I think he's rooting for Falcon," he said. The comment went unnoticed by his mesmerized partner. He zoomed to the speeding horses. The jockeys snapped their whips and yelled; the thoroughbreds stretched their legs, straining every muscle, vying for the lead.

"They're coming around the track," said the announcer. "It's Comet, Falcon, and Zephyr, bolting round the bend . . ."

"Go, baby, go!" Sean shouted. Lambert clenched his fists.

"This is it, folks—they're coming down the stretch! Comet, Falcon and Zephyr are just inches from each other, galloping at blinding speed . . . They're neck-and-neck crossing the finish line! Oh, my! It's a photo finish!" The crowd roared in amazement.

"Unbelievable!" Sean exclaimed. Lambert rose from his seat.

"We're waiting for the judge's decision . . ." The crowd silenced. The photo finish appeared on a huge flat screen. Comet's nose was slightly in front of the others. "And the official winner is . . . Comet! It's over, folks. It's all over . . ." People cheered and booed.

"Damn it," Sean said, tearing up his bet ticket and tossing it in the air. Lambert buried his head in his hands.

"Take it easy. The bet's on Ambrose!" Victor grinned at Sean. Then he looked down the stands again. "Where'd he go?"

"Who?"

"Lambert, damn it!"

Sean eyed the empty bleacher seat where Lambert had been.

"Let's go," Victor said, springing to his feet. The two ran toward the aisle, looking in every direction. Lambert was gone. "Back to the parking lot," he shouted. They ran up the stairs, across the lobby and through the doors. Then they paused and scanned the lot for the Mercedes sport coupe.

"There." Sean pointed. The coupe's driver's door was closing shut.

"C'mon, I'll drive!" Victor said.

They sprinted to their electric car. As they jumped into the car, the coupe was exiting the lot with tires spinning. Victor engaged the ignition, threw the shift into drive, and took off in pursuit. As he turned into the street, he sighted the coupe several blocks in front of them. He depressed the pedal nearly to the floor; the vehicle accelerated sluggishly. "Electric cars," he grumbled, "they're even weaker than the hybrids."

"I don't think he knows we're following him," Sean said.

"No, he's too preoccupied."

"Just stay on him."

"I'm trying."

The sport coupe raced around a corner. Victor sped down to the corner, made a sharp turn and accelerated again. There was no sign of the coupe up the street.

"We lost him again," Sean said. "Let's stake out his house. What'd you think?"

"He's not on his way home. I doubt he's in the mood to explain to his family that he blew their nest egg on a horse race."

"What's the course of action then?"

"Give it a minute." Victor drove onto the main drag, slowing the vehicle. "Look for the Mercedes."

They surveyed both sides of the street.

"Bingo," Sean said, pointing at the sport coupe parked outside a high-class nightclub on the right.

Victor parked in the space behind it and shut off the engine. They exited the vehicle, then walked up to the club and entered. The lounge was full of business people socializing and drinking colorful cocktails. Lambert was alone in a corner booth, downing a glass of whiskey.

"You sit next to him, and I'll sit in front of him," Victor said.

"Let's go," Sean replied.

They moved quickly between tables and sat down in the booth with Lambert.

"What the—?" Lambert exclaimed. Sean stuck a gun in his side.

"Yell, and it's curtains for you," Victor said.

"Look, I don't know any more than what I already told you. I don't—"

"Cooperate and you'll live," Sean said, jamming the gun into his side.

"I told you people everything I know, I swear." Lambert shuddered.

He thinks we're Supreme Bureau of Investigation agents, Victor thought. He signaled his partner. "Put the gun away. That won't be necessary."

Sean holstered the weapon back inside his jacket.

Leaning back slightly, Victor said, "We're not SBI agents."

"Who are you then?" Lambert asked.

"Let's just say we represent an organization with certain interests. We want information."

"What kind of information?"

"About Hakim and the Trident Group."

"Why should I talk to—?"

The front doors swung open. Four men in overcoats and three-piece suits walked in and took seats at a table near the booth. They were Romano's men.

Lambert sank in his seat, staring at the Mafia men. "Listen, I've got a family to support."

"You should've thought of that before you accepted the loans."

"All right, all right," Lambert said, looking back to Victor and Sean. "Look, I worked closely with Hakim. I know there was underhanded business."

"Of what nature?" Victor asked, knowing full well the answer to the question. He was only checking the truthfulness of the response.

"There was a petrol smuggling operation with black-market sales, credits-laundering, and global-tax evasion. Specifics, I really don't have."

"Is that so? You're a man who needs the credits. What are you willing to do to get them?"

"It's true, I need the credits. But that doesn't mean I would involve myself in matters at the highest echelons of world politics. That's way out of my league."

"There's a digital audio file—about the Trident Group."

"I don't know anything about that—" Lambert's voice faltered.

"Don't you?" Victor leaned forward in an aggressive posture, then glanced at Romano's men. "You owe them payment, and you haven't got it—right?"

Lambert hesitated. "Yes, that's right."

"Looks like they're here to do a hit. The digital file is on a flash drive. Where is it?"

"I—I really don't know."

"I think you know lots of things," Victor said. "Now here's the deal: You can come clean with us and we'll make some sort of arrangement. Or you can continue stonewalling and we'll leave you to the hit men."

Lambert began sweating profusely. "What kind of arrangement?"

"We might be able to buy you some time."

"Okay. Listen, all I know is that Hakim made recordings of the secret meetings. I don't know anything about the Trident Group. I don't want to know. I'm quite sure the file is somewhere in his office. I say this because I don't believe he would have risked endangering his family by keeping it in his home. SBI agents went through his office like a hurricane. They turned everything upside down, but they didn't find it. Wherever it is, it's well hidden."

"Can you access Hakim's office?"

"I have the keycards to all the offices on my floor."

One of Romano's men rose from his seat and walked toward them. The man sneered as he turned for the restroom. Lambert began trembling.

"Ready to play ball?" Victor asked.

"I'll play ball."

"That's a wise choice. We have a deal then."

Victor went over to the table with Romano's men. They spoke in low voices for a few minutes. Then he came back to the booth.

"I bought you a month to make the payment," he said to Lambert.

"I need more time. I need—"

"You're lucky you got that much time. Usually, they don't bargain." Victor slid a device across the table. It was a small black box with a long thin wire connected to a tiny module on the back of a tie clip.

"What's this?" Lambert asked.

"It's a video spy camera with built-in microphone. The black box is a receiver-transmitter, which you can put in the inside pocket of your suit jacket; the tie clip is a pinhole camera that you can wear instead of your usual clip. It's programmed to stream real-time video to my handheld computer. In other words, I'll see what you see and we can communicate. To activate it, just turn on the switch on the receiver-transmitter."

"So, what do you want me to do?"

"What time do you usually get to work?"

"About seven a.m."

"Tomorrow, get to work by six, before most of the personnel arrive. Enter Hakim's office and activate the spy camera. I'll guide you from there."

"What makes you think we'll find the file when SBI agents failed to do so?"

"The brutality of SBI agents far exceeds their mental capacity." Victor smirked.

Lambert cracked a weak smile. "Okay. We're on for tomorrow morning."

"Very good. We'll be anticipating your communication shortly after six in the morning. Any tricks, and Romano's hit men will do their job. Understand?"

"Clearly."

"What'd say we get out of here?" Sean suggested.

"Let's go," Victor said, coming to his feet.

"Do you think he's true to his word?" Sean asked as he drove the silver electric car down the main drag.

"If not, Romano's men have assured me that he'll disappear and his body won't be found," Victor answered.

"A lot of good that'll do us if we're caught by authorities. I'm sure it will be a comforting thought that Lambert was eliminated while we're being tortured."

Victor glanced at him. "Just be on the alert at all times."

"So where do we go from here?"

"I don't know, exactly. We can head back for the Bronx, but at this time of the afternoon we run a high risk of being pulled over by local police or troopers. We can check into a motel, but there's the risk of being turned in by one of the multitudes of citizen-informants. Or, we can find an empty lot and sleep in the vehicle. What do you think?"

"Sleeping in the car sounds like the safest option."

Sean turned off the main drag into the side streets. The surrounding residential areas were run-down. Global taxation and unemployment had long since driven the homeowners into insolvency.

"There's smoke up ahead." Victor pointed.

Sean slowed the electric car as they passed by fire engines parked on the street. Firefighters were battling flames from burning houses, their blackened faces dripping with sweat, shouting over the din. Several blocks further on, an abandoned factory came into view. He continued down the block and pulled over in front of it.

The old cement structure still stood with its burned out interior, collapsed doors, and shattered windows. "Gone overseas. Globalist traitors!" was scrawled in bold graffiti on its façade. They surveyed the area. The parking lot was empty except for a few abandoned wrecks.

"Seems calm," Sean noted.

"Looks like a good spot," Victor said.

Sean pulled into the lot and parked the car to the rear between two of the wrecks. Victor got out and began pitching fallen leaves on top of the car.

"Ganin," Sean called, exiting the vehicle. "What're you doing?"

"Relax, Flanagan. We need cover; the vehicle has to blend in."

"Knock yourself out!"

Victor continued until the vehicle was camouflaged in the gathering darkness. "We'll guard in shifts. Do you want first or second watch?" he asked.

"I'm wiped out. I'll sleep first and take second watch."

"Okay then. We'll change shifts at one in the morning."

The pair reentered the vehicle and locked the doors, cracking the windows for ventilation. They ate sandwiches and drank bottled water they had brought with them. Then Sean reclined his seat and went to sleep almost immediately. Victor looked up at the stars between scattered leaves on the windshield: they shined brightly, beckoning those who would dare. *How I would like to spread my wings and fly to you.* He looked through his binoculars toward the stars. But they were too far away.

The hours drifted by. . . . An icy wind blew in, the temperature dropped rapidly and autumn snow flurries began to swirl in the air. Victor leaned back on the headrest, observing the glittering snowflakes. The sky was now obscured and a light layer of snow formed on the windshield. He looked at his watch; it was nearly one o'clock in the morning. "Sean." He shook his partner. "Sean, it's your shift."

"Uh . . . all right," said an awakening Sean.

"You're ready then?"

Sean turned, blinking his eyes into focus. "I've got it, Ganin."

Victor closed his eyes, spread his wings, and flew to the stars he had gazed at hours ago.

"Ganin . . . Victor, wake up," Sean said. "It's five-thirty in the morning."

Victor opened his eyes. Darkness still prevailed. The two exited the vehicle and cleared the leaves and snow from the windows with their forearms. The cold air had a bite to it. They reentered the vehicle. Sean engaged the ignition, selected window defrost, and ran the windshield wipers twice to clear off the remaining snow. Then he shifted into gear and drove out of the lot.

"We need to get within five hundred meters of the World Petrol Consortium building," Victor said. "That's the range of the video equipment."

"You got it," Sean replied, driving through the streets toward their destination. The building soon appeared in front of them. He slowed down . . . then pulled into a parking space across the street, facing its main entrance.

Victor glanced at his watch; it was almost six o'clock. He raised his binoculars and zoomed into the lighted office on the eighth floor: Lambert's familiar form moved about the room. He released the optics to the lanyard around his neck. "We're in business," he said, taking out his handheld computer. He placed it on the dashboard mount and initialized it. Then he plugged a pair of lightweight headsets into the computer and put them on. "Lambert—Lambert, can you hear me?" he said into his microphone.

"I'm with you," said Lambert's voice as the screen materialized.

"Listen, first of all, I need you to give me a full view of the office. Turn slowly to your left and right."

The spy camera turned in sweeping motions. Hakim's office lay ransacked from the SBI searches. The desk was overturned. Computers were felled and smashed. Files, documents, envelopes, pens and pencils were scattered about the floor. File cabinet drawers had been pulled out and thrown down. Shattered glass was strewn across the room.

"Lambert," Victor said. "Check out the floor paneling; follow a set pattern."

"All right," Lambert replied. The image vibrated on the screen as he crisscrossed the room, pausing to check for any loose paneling where objects could possibly be hidden.

"Nothing?"

"Nothing at all."

"Feel inside the file cabinet. Check for magnetic stashboxes inside the frame."

The camera jogged sideways. Lambert's sleeved arm reached in the file cabinet and scoured the inside of it. "Nothing," he breathed. "There's nothing. Maybe we're wasting our time."

"Wait. Let's see another full view," Victor said. The camera swept the office again. "The pens . . ."

"What?" Lambert asked.

"The pens on the floor—take them apart."

Lambert's hand reached in front of the camera and picked up one of the pens. He pulled it from both ends. The writing instrument separated, exposing a flash drive.

"Activate it," Victor said.

Lambert initialized his handheld computer, plugged in the device, and clicked the play button. Mephisto's voice sounded sharply.

Victor laughed. "It's on a pen voice-recorder. Hakim used a pen voice-recorder to chronicle the meetings! Check out the rest of them!"

Lambert picked up and pulled apart all of the remaining pens. They were ordinary writing instruments. "It's the only one. What meetings he recorded are on this one," he said, holding up the glossy pen recorder.

"Meet us in the lot off of Elmont Road and Dutch Broadway in half an hour."

"All right then. I'll see you there," Lambert said.

Sean pulled off and drove through the sunlit streets onto the parkway toward the rendezvous point. The morning rush hour traffic had cleared and the fallen snow was melting. He depressed the pedal and accelerated. The white lines on the road pulsed. . . . Red-and-blue lights flashed behind them; a squad car paced several meters from their rear bumper. Victor looked in the side mirror with his hand on the grip of his holstered firearm. The squad changed lanes and sped past them with its lights flashing and siren shrieking.

"Man, they're everywhere," Sean said.

"Just so long as they're not after us," Victor replied, withdrawing his hand.

Sean took the next exit then turned into the streets toward their destination. Some minutes later, he pulled into the lot and parked the electric car facing the entrance.

They waited for the delivery. . . .

"Here he comes," Victor said, observing the approaching Mercedes sport coupe through the windshield. "Lock and load, just in case."

Sean charged his handgun and held it by his side at the ready.

The sport coupe entered the lot and pulled up window-to-window with the electric car. Its driver's window lowered. "There you go," Lambert said, handing over the pen voice-recorder and spy camera.

"Okay," Sean said, taking possession of the items and handing them to his partner. "Wait a minute."

Victor pulled apart the pen recorder, plugged it into his handheld computer, and clicked the play button. Mephisto's voice sounded. "Everything checks out," he said, unplugging the recorder.

"All right, Lambert. Good work," Sean said.

Lambert nodded, raised his window, and drove off.

NINETEEN

Sean drove northbound on the Cross Island Parkway, the electric engine humming at high pitch, heading back to rebel territory. They passed by the poverty-stricken areas. Soon the mansions, commercial centers, and golf courses of the upper-class neighborhoods came into view.

"Play it," Sean said.

"What?" Victor asked.

"Play the pen voice-recorder."

"Inquisitive, aren't you?"

"Why not? Let's hear the recordings."

Victor took out his handheld computer from inside his jacket and initialized it. Then he pulled apart the pen recorder, plugged it into the computer, and clicked the play button.

Mephisto's voice boomed. "The human masses should never be allowed govern themselves. For they are the most destructive species on the planet! Have they not demonstrated their ruinous character, time and time again? They cause nothing but troubles and must be controlled. Only we Illuminati, the superiors, have the wisdom to rule the world!"

"Fast-forward," Sean said as he maneuvered through traffic.

Victor clicked the fast-forward button.

Mephisto's voice sounded again. "Unity, Progress, and Total Security for Mankind. That is the key to the future! Unity in purpose, direction, and thought: The New World Order is our great unifying force, thus the concept of individualism must be abolished. Those who think, feel, or behave outside of the established laws must be liquidated. . . . Progress through technology and productivity: It is imperative that new technologies be implemented as rapidly as possible. And production is most efficient when the masses work at maximum capacity for minimum compensation. Religions, labor unions, and human rights organizations are an obstruction to progress. They, too, must be eliminated. . . . Total Security means total control, which requires the eradication of free will. Global Security Incorporated has given us the ultimate technology to achieve this objective: the VerChip *is* total control . . ."

"There must be fifty hours of recordings in this device," Victor noted.

"The more the better," Sean responded.

Victor fast-forwarded again.

Various voices spoke, followed by Mephisto once again. "History has proven that the inferior masses can be very dangerous. Enraged masses have decapitated kings, hanged dictators, and deposed governments. Even we, the superiors, have to exercise great caution. We must give people the *impression* that they have some control of their lives. Democracy gives us this ability. Invented millenniums ago, it was a system that granted basic rights to all citizens. Many civilizations adopted this concept. But all democracies were eventually corrupted and defeated.

"Globalism is diametrically opposed to democracy. It is a system that rightfully recognizes the superiority of global power elites over the inferior masses. In fact, it has conclusively demonstrated the futility of democratic ideals. Nevertheless, democracy remains a useful tool to control the masses. Through the media and other means, we are able to pass off an *illusion of democracy* to the public . . ."

Light smoke started blowing from the vents. Victor began coughing. He turned off his computer, unplugged the pen recorder and pocketed the items. "What's wrong?" Sean asked. The smoke grew thicker. He too began coughing. He reached to the panel and shut off the ventilation fan. Smoke blew onto the windshield. The engine shuddered briefly, then silenced. "Damn it! The car's died on us!"

"Take the exit ramp—there," Victor said, pointing.

The silver electric car coasted silently, slowing with each passing meter. "Come on! Come on! A few more meters!" Sean said as the vehicle slowed to a crawl approaching the exit ramp. With little momentum to spare, the car entered the ramp and then gained speed in the descent. At the bottom of the grade, he turned right onto the cross street then right again into an empty lot.

They got out of the vehicle. Sean popped the hood open. The engine was smoldering and the batteries had melted. "The engine's shot," he said.

"Totally? Are you sure?" Victor asked.

"Definitely. It needs major repairs."

They looked around them. On the opposite side of the street was a strip of restaurants in front of an expansive golf course. They crossed the street and entered a restaurant that was facing the lot. The establishment was spacious with wide windows, cedar tables, and parquet flooring. The pair took seats at a table by the front windows and looked across the street at their now abandoned car.

"It's only a matter of time before one law agency or another discovers the abandoned vehicle," Victor said.

"Don't sweat it, the license plate is unregistered," Sean replied. "They can't positively identify it on sector-control computers. They'll have to find the vehicle by chance, and that'll take some time."

"What'll it be?" asked the forty-something waitress with painted-on makeup.

"Two regular coffees, please," Sean, without making eye contact.

"Two coffees, coming up," she replied, turning to the adjacent tables.

"You must be coming from the Belmont Race Track," said an old man wearing a blue golf cap and dingy clothes from the table behind them. "Gamblers, I'll bet."

"What's it to you?" Sean asked, turning to face the man. Victor kicked his partner's shin under the table, signaling him not to attract attention.

"Nothin'—just thought you look like the kind of sucker that might've bet against Comet."

"Who're you calling a sucker?"

"So you did! I knew it. I can tell by the look on your face. How much did you lose?"

Sean was visibly irritated. "You don't know anything."

"Oh, I know a losing gambler when I see one. Who'd you bet on? Falcon? Or that even bigger loser, Zephyr?" Another kick from Victor kept Sean from answering. Instead, he turned his back to the man.

"There you go, two regular coffees," said the returning waitress, placing the steaming cups on the table. "Anything else?"

"Nothing for now, thanks," Victor responded.

"Which one was it? Falcon or Zephyr?" the man pressed.

Sean turned again and stared at him. "It was Zephyr."

The old man started laughing.

"How's that so damn funny?" Sean asked.

The man collected himself. "Don't you know the races are fixed?—like everything else in this society."

"Fixed?"

"Yeah, sure. The winner's predetermined. And racetrack profits go straight to WorldGov."

"There was a photo finish."

"A computer-generated image. Anyway, the thoroughbred owners were paid off, the jockeys were paid off, the technicians were paid off. Everybody was paid off. Comet was the designated winner from the very beginning."

Sean sank in his seat, feeling like a dupe.

"I remember when we weren't a region, but a nation," the man continued. "We were a people with a representative government, a distinctive culture, an identity."

"You're a fool, old man!" exclaimed young Sean. Victor nervously sipped his coffee.

"I'm a lot of things, but a fool, I'm not. I was a fool in my youth. Nowadays, no one can deceive me," he said. "Take the World President: It's clear to any *thinking* citizen that he's merely a puppet of the world's elites—a figurehead—presented to the public to give us an illusion of democracy. Most likely his brain was physically or chemically altered, so he could be manipulated. Some say he's not really human, but a cyborg. Maybe he's only a computer image. Whatever the case, it's clear that he doesn't represent the people."

Patrons from the adjacent tables began looking at the arguing parties.

"Look, mister, be careful of what you're saying," Victor said in a low voice.

"Careful? I'm an old man. I got a weak heart; I got the cancer." The man laughed, pulling out a handful of medications from his pockets and scattering them across the table. "I take dozens of these every day. They're the only things keeping me alive. I'll say what I damn well please!"

Some of the patrons were now staring openly at them.

"Is there a problem here?" inquired the waitress, making her rounds.

"There's no problem, sweetheart." Victor gave a false smile.

"If there's a problem, I can call—"

"There's no problem," he repeated, trying to maintain his smile.

"Wake up, citizens!" the man roared, rising from his chair. "Don't you see what they're doing to us? We're afraid to speak in public. We're afraid to speak in our own homes. Have you people ever heard of freedom of speech? Freedom of movement? Human rights? Or are those just ancient concepts they've purged from the history books? Stand up for your rights, damn it!"

Some of the customers began speaking on their mobile phones. Victor gave the signal to Sean. They got up and walked briskly toward the doors.

"Hey! You need to pay for the coffees!" the waitress shouted after them.

Victor stopped and turned toward the register. In his rush, he dropped the falsified VerChip. It fell to the floor with a slight tapping sound that filled the room with silence.

The waitress walked over to Victor, grabbed his hand and ran it across the register's RFID reader. The screen showed blank. "You're not chipped! These guys aren't chipped!" she exclaimed.

"Not chipped? Who's not chipped? That's antisocial!" said a patron.

"Not chipped? That's criminal!" said another customer.

"Terrorists!" screamed a woman sitting at a table by the register.

The people began pointing fingers in their direction. Victor withdrew his hand and dashed out the door with Sean right behind him. "Walk fast but don't run," he said as they rounded the corner and began walking up the golf course. They turned momentarily, looking back at the restaurant.

The old man had exited and was crossing the street. People gathered outside the doors, shaking their fists and yelling after him. Suddenly a low whirring sound came from above. All eyes looked up to see a fast-approaching black helicopter gunship. "Bastards . . ." Victor said with a grimace.

Laser light flashed instantaneously from the pod underneath the gunship. The man disintegrated—a cloud of ashes swirled on the street where he had been just seconds ago. Moments later, a rush of passing vehicles scattered the ashes to the winds. The whirring faded as the gunship disappeared beyond the skyline. The people standing outside the restaurant were cheering.

"He never stood a chance," Sean said.

"Let's move out quickly," Victor said, continuing up the golf course.

An empty golf cart sat next to the eighteenth hole. The caddie stood some distance away. Victor entered the driver's side, turned the key, and signaled his partner. Sean entered the passenger's side. Then Victor shifted into gear, applied the pedal and began driving up the course.

"Hey! Hey, wait!" called the smiling young caddie as they drove by.

"Well, this is a brilliant idea. I'm sure we'll outrun anything with this crate!" Sean said.

"Got a better idea?" Victor asked.

"Not at this particular time."

"Then give me a break, Flanagan!"

To avoid attracting attention, he drove at normal speed across the field. Equipment jostled in the back of the cart as they crossed uneven terrain. They passed by men in twill sweaters, khakis, and checkered hats, swinging clubs that flashed in the sunlight. Others were sipping cocktails and chatting. He pulled alongside the clubhouse and parked under its awning; they hopped out of the cart, remaining under the awning for cover. The whirring sounds returned in overlapping waves.

"I hear several gunships," Victor said. "They're flying at lower altitudes in a visual search pattern. No doubt, they've received information from the citizen-informants at the restaurant. I'm sure they have our physical descriptions. And they know that we're not chipped and can't be tracked electronically."

"That doesn't mean they can't find us optically. So what's the plan?" Sean asked.

"Just a moment," Victor replied, taking out his handheld computer and initializing it. "They're looking for two males fitting our descriptions. We'll have to split up and meet at another location." He selected the computer's tactical map mode. "We're here," he said, pointing at the screen, "just to the south of the Long Island Expressway. We'll meet here—three kilometers to the north by the shore of Little Neck Bay. Note the coordinates. On the way I'll send a secure text message to headquarters. They'll send a car to collect us. Got it?"

"Got it, let's go."

"Not so fast." Victor pocketed his computer and walked to the back of the cart.

The whirring sounds were now passing with increasing frequency as the gunships flew a low-altitude search pattern of the area. The golfers interrupted their games to look skyward.

Victor scoured the back of the cart, retrieving golfing jackets, caps and clubs. He handed one ensemble to his partner. "Put these on, quickly," he said.

They put on the golfing outfits over their leather jackets and slung the clubs casually on their shoulders.

"See you at the bay," Sean said.

"Walk at a normal pace and don't stop for anything or anyone."

"All right, but if I get liquidated I'll never forgive you!"

Victor cracked a half-grin and began trekking northward, diverging from Sean. He continued across the field to the expressway. At the curb, he waited for an opportunity to cross the lanes as countless hybrid and electric vehicles cruised by quietly. A small break in traffic gave him the opportunity. Tossing the golf club aside, he sprinted across to the median between opposing lanes. He paused to catch his breath. Then he took out his handheld computer and sent a situation report to headquarters, requesting a car at the pick-up point. A few minutes later the text response came: "We'll scramble a vehicle. Estimated time of arrival is forty-five minutes from now." He pocketed the computer and waited to cross the remaining lanes. When a brief chance presented itself, he dashed across at full speed and dove onto the grass on the opposite side.

Rising slowly, Victor looked up to the sky. Among the scattered clouds, slicing through the sky, were the black gunships just to the east. Instantaneous flashes struck their victims below. *More liquidations. I hope Sean wasn't one of them.* He began hiking northward again, paralleling the Cross Island Parkway at a distance. A whirring sound appeared within seconds. He turned to see a dark shadow pass over him; there was no laser flash. *Guess it wasn't my time.*

Victor continued across several more fields and crossing roads. The gunships did not return. He came to a tree line at the top of a slope. To his front lay a body of water, glistening in the sunlight; wooden benches were fixed on the shore. He breathed a sigh of relief and descended toward the bay, removing the golfing jacket and cap. The grass rippled under his boots as he walked to one of the benches. He sat down, leaned his head back and closed his eyes momentarily. He could hear waves rolling, wind whistling, and seagulls cawing. . . . *You're drifting—stay alert.*

As Victor opened his eyes, lights flashed in his peripheral vision; he spun, drawing his Glock instinctively. The front end of a car protruded from the tall grass at the bottom of the slope. Its headlights flashed again in sequence. He recognized the signal, holstered his weapon, and walked toward the vehicle. As he came around the driver's side he found himself looking down the barrel of a Colt handgun. "Take it easy," he said, "I'm your pickup."

"You're Ganin?" asked the fighter in the driver's seat.

"It's him," confirmed his partner, leaning from the passenger seat.

"Where's Captain Flanagan?" the driver asked, holstering his firearm.

"I don't know. I wish I did," Victor replied.

"We can't wait for long. Squads and troopers are all over the place around here."

"This is a secluded spot. Just keep your cool. I'll position myself as a sentry until he arrives."

"My orders are clear: half-an-hour waiting time, maximum. If he doesn't show up by then, we have to leave."

"Then you'll have failed to accomplish your mission. I'm not leaving without him."

"We understand the two of you were being tracked. It was even on the news reports. How do you know that he hasn't already been liquidated?" the driver asked.

Victor looked away briefly, then said, "Give him an hour—please."

The fighter eyed him anxiously. "Okay, but not a minute more."

"Fair enough."

Victor moved to the surrounding tree line at the top of the slope. He took out his binoculars and surveyed the area. The field to his front was bordered by an avenue. Aside from the flowing traffic and a few pedestrians walking on the sidewalk, there was no activity. He maintained a constant lookout, periodically scanning with his binoculars, hoping for the best. But as the hour wore on and there was still no sign of Sean, he began to fear the worst. The time wound past an hour. . . .

The car flashed its headlights. "Time's up, let's go!" the driver shouted. Victor raised his binoculars and scanned one last time. Reluctantly, he walked back down the slope toward the vehicle. As he reached for the right rear door handle, there came the sound of rustling leaves. He and the fighters drew their weapons and pointed them in the direction of the noise.

"Where do you think you're going without me?" Sean asked as he descended toward them.

Victor couldn't remember the last time he was so glad to see someone. "We thought you were a goner," he said, holstering his weapon.

"Don't count me out unless the final bell rings!" Sean laughed, tossing the golfing clothes aside.

Sean and Victor entered the back of the vehicle. The car pulled off, hooked a turn, and headed back to the Bronx.

"We've got it, Tara," Victor reported, sliding the pen voice-recorder across the headquarters table.

Tara picked up the device and examined it closely. "Good work . . . very good work," she said, looking back at him. "I'll have Bradley download the contents and send a copy to Romano. That was the deal we made, right?"

"That's right," he affirmed. "Now if you'll excuse me, I'm going to get some rest." A smile came to his lips as he headed for the door.

"Victor," she called, "I'll expect to see you at the council tomorrow."

He paused by the doorway and turned. "I wouldn't miss it for the world."

TWENTY

Tara, Rafael, Dante, Sean, and George were seated at the headquarters table, focusing on the map in front of them. They looked up as Victor walked into the room.

"Welcome to the council," Tara said.

"Thank you, Commander. But you may not like what I have to say," he replied.

"What's that supposed to mean?" Rafael asked.

"The fact is we're surrounded, outnumbered, and outgunned."

"What else is new? Got any good news for a change?"

"Yes, I do: There is a way to victory. But it will be a high-risk mission."

"We are not in a position to assume high-risk missions."

"We're not in a position to wait for their next attack, either. Every day they grow stronger, while we become weaker."

"Do you have a decisive plan?" Tara asked.

"It depends on how many fighters we can put together," Victor replied.

The group looked at one another. "Five hundred, maximum," she said.

Victor sat down at the table. "That's somewhat less than I calculated."

"Calculated for what, exactly?" George inquired.

"The mission to eliminate Mr. Maximilian Mephisto and spark the liberation movement," Victor stated.

"Assuming we rub out Mephisto, what will we do about the *governmental machine*?" Sean asked.

"WorldGov is controlled by a few global power elites. Without their supreme leader, they will be fearful, confused and disorganized. Of course, we will also require supporting operations to destroy VerChip production plants and to take over the Global News Network broadcast studios."

"You once mentioned a Trojan horse?" Tara said to Victor.

"A helicopter air-assault, to take out Mephisto," he replied. "We'll need to land an assault team on the roof of the Global Security Incorporated building, where there's an entrance into his office on the top floor. How this can be done is best left to the discretion of our pilot." He turned to Dante.

Dante took out a redwood pipe from the inside pocket of his leather jacket. He filled it with tobacco, flicked his lighter and drew several times, puffing thick clouds of smoke. George, Sean, and Rafael coughed almost in unison, waving off the smoke. "I need a detailed map of Manhattan," he said.

"There you are," Tara said, sliding a laminated scroll across the table.

Dante spread the map on the table. He bent forward, peering at it, drawing slowly on his pipe. His wavy hair fell about his brow. After a long period of contemplation, he looked up. "It's going to be difficult and extremely dangerous. We will need a very maneuverable chopper armed with smoke rockets. We'll fly in at night, low and slow to avoid radar detection, and then fire rockets at the roof of the building, creating a smoke screen and disorienting the rooftop security agents, some of whom have antiaircraft weapons. Then we'll land the assault team under cover of darkness and smoke." He delineated a course on the map with a grease pencil. "Very difficult indeed. But, by the grace of God, it can be done," he resolved, leaning back in his chair, drawing heavily on his pipe.

"Well, there it is," Victor said with reserved optimism.

"We're still short on personnel and most everything else," Tara reminded them.

Dante pointed the tip of his pipe at her. "If Sergio is my blood, he can lend a hand."

"Your famous uncle only cares about profits," George remarked.

"That's a fact," Sean chimed in.

"Don't sell him short," Dante said.

"All right," Tara said. "Let's begin by procuring the aircraft. We'll deal with the other issues in due time. Dante, Victor; I'll arrange for you to meet with Romano. See if he can get us a flyable chopper. Make a deal, got it?"

"Yes, absolutely," Victor replied.

"You bet," Dante said.

"Very well then. The plan is confirmed," Tara stated. "That concludes today's council."

Several days later, Tara came to see Victor in the arms room. Her bandages were removed and her deep blue eyes sparkled once again. "Hey, you! Have you missed me?" she said, smiling.

They embraced amorously. "I love you, Tara," he said.

"I love you too, Vic. I'm here to see you, but I've also brought you some important news."

"Well, what is it then?" he said, releasing her.

"It's good news. We've contacted Romano and requested a business meeting, without giving any specifics. He's agreed to meet with you and Dante."

"That sounds promising. When and where is the meeting?"

"The two of you are to meet with him in his office in the South Bronx, anytime tomorrow morning."

Victor nodded. "Great. Tomorrow morning it is."

Dante drove the green Chevelle with a melancholy look in his eyes; the windshield wipers swept slowly back and forth. "Damn this cold drizzle," Dante said, rounding the park and turning toward the South Bronx. "You'd think we could get a warm rain shower for a change."

"You'd think so," Victor agreed. He leaned back in his seat, twisted the radio button, and tuned in a music station. . . .

The rain intensified as they pulled in front of Romano's multistory headquarters. As they exited the vehicle, men in overcoats and dripping hats escorted them into the building. They went up a spiral stairway to a pair of mahogany doors guarded by two men with submachine guns. The men opened the doors into the spacious office. The Mafia boss was seated behind his large desk, leaning back in his armchair, blowing smoke rings from his cigar.

"Morning, Uncle Sergio," Dante said from the doorway. Victor nodded respectfully.

"Be my guest," Romano said, motioning toward the two chairs opposite his.

Dante and Victor walked across the room and sat down in the chairs.

"So, what is it this time? A flying Pegasus?" Romano asked sarcastically.

"Not exactly, but you're close," Dante replied. "We need a helicopter."

"A chopper? Is this some kind of a joke?"

"It's no joke, Sergio. We need a four-seat helicopter with a turbine engine, preferably a military type but a standard civilian one will do."

Romano laughed. "Now why would you need a thing like that? I venture to guess you rebels are planning something unpleasant for the authorities!" He sparked his cigar with his metallic lighter, taking several long drags, which filled the room with a bluish-gray haze. His smile faded. "I can get just about anything, but a chopper's real difficult. Besides, where would an outfit like yours come up with the payment?"

Victor looked straight into his eyes. "You and your people's interests are the same as ours, at least in one way: we refuse to be marked like cattle with the VerChip."

Romano's large face drew closer. "My interests are to make profits. I can't do that playing *their* game." He put the cigar between his teeth and leaned back in his armchair.

"With all due respect, Don Romano, I think you're holding out on us."

Romano grinned slightly. He took the cigar from his mouth and pointed it at Victor. "This man knows respect, unlike you, Dante." The captain remained silent, looking back at his partner. Romano took another drag and continued. "Still, that doesn't explain how you're going to pay."

"I suppose glory for the cause isn't enough?" Dante said, eyeing his uncle.

"Not by a long shot, my moralistic nephew. Your principles . . . barred you from our organization, got you thrown out of the military, cost you an eye, and condemned you to the life of an outcast. Isn't that right?" Romano stared at him. Dante looked away quietly.

The mob boss turned to Victor, shaking the cigar in his direction, scattering ashes across the desk. "My illustrious nephew refused to hook up with our organization. So he joined the military instead. He made chopper commander.

Then, during one of the wars, they court-martialed him for disobeying orders to open fire."

"Those were unlawful orders," Dante said through his teeth.

"If that's not enough," Romano continued, "he once fought a guy armed with a blade over the honor of a woman he barely knew. That cost him an eye. Can you believe that?"

Dante was now fuming. He ran his fingers through his hair but remained silent.

Victor stroked his beard, then said, "Don Romano, we're here for business . . . that's all." After a short pause he continued. "Do you have an interest in muscle cars? Like the one parked outside, for example?"

Romano looked through the window, drawing smoke again. "It's a valuable car. But it would take five of those to pay for a chopper."

"We can't spare that many," Dante interjected. He drew glares from both Romano and Victor.

"Don Romano," Victor said quickly, "we are indebted to you already, and your generosity is greatly appreciated. So we'll also promise you this: if we succeed, you'll own the docks of this great city."

Both Romano and Dante started with surprise. The Don withdrew the cigar from his mouth and leaned forward, staring at Victor. "If you're messing with me, that'll be your last mistake."

"I'm on the level, I assure you," he replied, returning the stare.

Romano glanced at Dante, who was too stunned to speak.

"Perhaps you would agree to three cars?" Victor suggested.

The mob boss examined him closely. Then he shook his cigar at him again and said, "You're either courageous or mad!"

"I tend to believe the latter," Dante commented.

Victor proceeded assertively. "Don Romano, we very much need an answer at this time."

The boss squinted at him. "Three cars are acceptable. I'll get you what you want, but I can't guarantee the chopper's condition other than the fact that it'll be flyable."

"It's a deal then," Victor said, extending his hand.

"It's a deal." Romano gave a crushing handshake.

Tara spoke with Sean in the canteen a week later. "Romano just called me on the secure line," she said. "He's procured a helicopter for us."

"Excellent. What do you want me to do, Commander?" Sean asked.

"Round up Victor and Dante without delay and select three of our best muscle cars to exchange for the chopper. Then, with you driving the lead vehicle, take them to this location in the South Bronx," she said, handing him a slip of paper. "Romano's men'll be waiting for you there with further instructions."

"We'll be on the way briefly," he affirmed.

Sean briefed Victor and Dante in the underground garage. "I'll drive the blue Javelin. Victor, you follow me in the black Thunderbird. Dante, you bring up the rear in the green Chevelle," he said, tossing the car keys at them.

They drove the vehicles out in single file, engines rumbling and exhausts puffing smoke, and went on a route parallel to the one they had taken the week before. Victor drove the Thunderbird with ease, following the Javelin at a normal interval. He looked in the rearview mirror. The Chevelle was following so closely that he could see Dante's broad grin.

"If you get any closer, we'll have to call for a tow truck," Victor said into the microphone clipped to his jacket.

"Just testing your nerves," Dante replied with a chuckle.

"Radio silence, gentlemen, we never know who's monitoring," Sean reminded them as they entered the south side of the borough. They slowed down in the narrowing streets, occasionally maneuvering around potholes and ruptured asphalt. A few kilometers further on, midway down a fairly busy street, they pulled alongside the curb at the designated location.

Instead of the usual hit men, two young men in jean jackets and holstered side arms appeared from behind parked cars. One of them leaned into the window of the Javelin. "You're to proceed to this location," he said, handing Sean a note.

Sean unfolded the paper. "All right, what's the—?" Before he could finish his inquiry the men had disappeared. "Okay, gentlemen, we're in for a ride," he breathed into his microphone while inputting the rendezvous point into the vehicle's navigation system. "I have the coordinates. Our destination is halfway to Atlantic City."

The Javelin took off with the Thunderbird and Chevelle following at normal intervals. "Listen up," Sean said as they entered the expressway. "Maintain visual contact with the car in front of you at all times. Do not exceed the speed limit; we don't want to draw unwanted attention. We should arrive by twilight time."

The Javelin accelerated. Victor accelerated after it; as the Thunderbird gained speed, the speedometer needle vibrated off its peg and rattled within the gauge. *Shoot. Now I won't know the exact speed.* In the rearview mirror he could see the Chevelle several car lengths behind him. The wind blew past his window, the sun flickered between lampposts, and clouds streamed by overhead as they maintained the pace.

"We're taking the next exit," Sean announced after nearly an hour of cruising. They decelerated, took the exit ramp and came to a stop at the crossing highway. Then they turned right and followed the highway for several kilometers onto a dirt road. Blowing dust obscured the view.

"Hold steady, I can't see in front of me," Victor warned.

"I can't either," Dante said.

"Holding thirty miles an hour," Sean advised.

Victor estimated the speed according to pressure on the gas pedal.

"Slowing to twenty," Sean said.

The dust began to clear. Victor saw the Javelin's tail lights a few meters in front of him. "I have visual contact," he reported.

"So do I," Dante said.

The vehicles went up a gently rolling hill . . .

"We're almost there," Sean said.

The trio drove over the top of the hill into the misty valley below; through the dusk, they could see a large dark form in the field to their right. They pulled over to the side of the road and stopped.

Several submachine gun-carrying men in overcoats approached them. "Steele's people?" asked one of the men.

"That's right," Sean replied, exiting the Javelin. Victor and Dante exited their respective vehicles.

"Follow me," said the man.

Sean, Victor, and Dante followed the man and his associates, walking into the tall grass and darkening mist of the valley. A great figure appeared before them.

"Don Romano, it's good to see you again," Sean said. Victor and Dante nodded politely.

"The feeling's mutual, *if* everything is in order," Romano said in his deep voice.

Another man came from the road. "Don, the vehicles are legit and in excellent condition."

Romano grinned. "All right. Have a look at the chopper." He motioned toward the dark form in the field behind him.

Dante walked to the helicopter, activating his flashlight and directing the beam from front to back. "An MD 500: fast, highly maneuverable, excellent reliability record. But is this one in airworthy condition?"

"What do you want, first-class transportation?" Romano said. "You got any idea how hard it was to track down one of these?"

"I understand," Dante said. "But I have to check it out before we put our lives on the line flying it." He began a preflight inspection, opening the right front pilot's door and inspecting the flight controls—the cyclic stick (flight control stick between the pilot's knees), collective stick (flight control stick alongside the pilot's left leg), and left and right pedals. He closed the door, then pointed his flashlight at the main rotor system and examined it. Then he inspected the engine compartment, fuselage, and tail rotor. He reversed the procedure on the opposite side. "It looks good," he said, "but I have to start it up before anyone gets on board."

"Suit yourself," Romano said.

Dante strapped himself into the pilot's seat and donned his headset. Then he flipped a switch, lighting the cockpit dome light. "Battery's good!" he declared. "Everyone move back at least thirty feet." Romano, Victor, Sean and company complied, moving a safe distance from the helicopter. He closed the door, flipped a series of switches, adjusted the twist-grip throttle on the collective stick, and engaged the starter switch. The turbine engine spouted smoke into the misty air; slowly, the rotor blades began turning and then wound to idle rpm.

Dante engaged the generator, verified the checklist, and scanned the instrument panel. The gauges were steady except for the oil pressure, which fluctuated between yellow and green markings. Minutes later the oil pressure stabilized in the green range. He twisted the throttle to one-hundred-percent rotor rpm, then gave a thumbs-up.

"You're all right, Don Romano, but we could use more help." Victor slapped him on the back and ran for the chopper.

"I'll bet," Romano said under his breath.

Victor strapped himself into the left front seat next to Dante. Sean jumped into the back, shut the door, and fastened his seatbelt.

Dante moved the cyclic stick to a forward position, applied slight left pedal, and pulled up on the collective stick. The helicopter took off like a cyclone. "It's got power!" he said as they took to the sky. He glanced at his passengers, then realized they hadn't heard him. "Headsets," he shouted, pointing at the headsets hanging above their seats.

Victor reached up, grabbed his headset and put it on.

"Can you hear me now?" Dante asked.

"I can hear you," he replied, adjusting the rotary volume switch on his left earmuff.

"Sean?"

"I'm with you."

"Okay. We're headed northeast. I'm flying low to avoid radar. Look!" Dante pointed to the galaxy of lights in front of them. "That's our city." The passengers marveled at the magnificence of the city, illuminating the night sky. He maneuvered the helicopter, turning to the north and increasing the speed toward the Bronx. "Get Steele on the radio. Tell her we're on the way in and requesting a beacon."

Victor flipped through the radio channels to the secure frequency. "Command Headquarters, this is Ganin, over." The radio crackled. "Command Headquarters, this is Ganin, over," he repeated.

"Ganin—go," Tara's familiar voice responded.

"We're on the way in. We need a beacon."

"Copy that. We'll fire up the beacon."

A radiant barrel fire lit in the streets some ten kilometers in front of them, indicating the landing zone.

"In sight," Dante radioed, lowering the collective stick, beginning a descent. He flew a long approach toward the lighted area, gradually reducing the airspeed as they closed in. As the area became clearly visible, he broke left then turned back to the right, flew a wide circle around the locale, and made a descending turn in to a landing adjacent to the barrel fire. The rotor wash blew sparks into the air. . . .

Dante initiated the shutdown procedure. With the rotor blades winding down, Victor and Sean climbed out onto the street. As the rotors slowed to a stop, rebel workmen quickly towed the chopper into the underground garage of the headquarters building.

TWENTY-ONE

The electrode blew sparks in the underground garage. Victor focused through his dark goggles on the joint he was welding. The rocket pods had to be fixed to the helicopter's exterior mounts at exactly the correct angle. Dante worked in the cockpit above, rigging the red fire-button on the cyclic control stick to wires that led to the pods. Daylight streaked through the narrow windows on the upper walls of the garage.

Suddenly a muffled barking sound came from outside the building. Victor stopped welding for a moment. The sound repeated itself. He dropped the welding gun, took off his goggles, then ran up the stairs and threw the doors open.

Duke was charging toward a lone figure in a hooded overcoat on the opposite side of the street. The figure turned and fired several times from the handgun under his coat. The canine wavered, then surged forward, knocking the man down and ferociously biting into his neck.

Victor sprinted across the street, stopping at the curb. As Duke stood upright, blood dripped from his fangs, and flowed from his chest down his front legs. The canine staggered momentarily, then collapsed—his hazel eyes closing for the last time.

Tara and Sean dashed across the street from headquarters, stopping on either side of Victor. The trio looked down at the scene. It was a mutual killing. The dead man lay several meters from the dog, with blood still spurting from his carotid arteries.

Tara went through the pockets of the man's overcoat and removed their contents. "Business cards, sales receipts, family photos—that's all," she said.

Sean ran a handheld RFID reader across the man's right hand. "It's registering an apparently ciphered VerChip. The chip is unreadable; there's no VerChip Identification Number or accompanying information."

Victor looked at the gun lying on the ground. "A Ruger 9mm handgun, a ciphered VerChip, and no specific documents. It's the standard profile of an undercover SBI agent."

"This is the same suspect Duke pursued previously," Tara said. "This individual was a spy. And the dog sensed that."

Victor turned, looking at her with sorrow in his eyes. He picked up the dog's limp body and walked across the street. One of the fighters pointed toward the graveyard behind the buildings. He continued walking in that direction, staring straight ahead.

The yard was full of dirt piles and makeshift crosses. Shovels were haphazardly dug in the ground. He grasped the handle of one of them and began digging. With each thrust of the shovel, his anger intensified; not only for the loss of his companion, but also for his parents, his priest, and so many fellow citizens who had disappeared forever. When he finished digging, he wrapped Duke's body in a cloth and gently placed it in the hole. Then he filled the hole with the same fervor. On the grave he fixed a plaque and inscribed on it: "Duke. My courageous friend." As he walked away a hard rain fell unnoticed. He entered the building and began trudging up the stairs.

"Victor . . . Victor . . ." Tara called from the bottom of the stairway. He turned, the rain dripping from his hair. "Sorry, Victor, but I need to remind you that tomorrow's the final mission briefing at headquarters."

"Let's get it on," he responded solemnly.

Tara, Victor, Dante, Rafael, Sean, and George stood around the headquarters table.

"The best aerial approach to the Global Security Incorporated building is from the east," Dante said, pointing at the map on the table with the tip of his smoldering pipe. "This gives us maximum cover from the surrounding buildings. If we fly low enough, even if we're momentarily painted by radar, we'll be indistinguishable from, say, a flock of geese."

"It's the season for migratory birds," George remarked.

"Where will the air-assault team enter the building?" Sean asked.

"Here, in the center of the roof," Victor said, pointing at the satellite photo of the GSI building next to the map. "Computer analysis has confirmed that the dark square on the image is a trapdoor entrance into Mephisto's office on the top floor." He paused, then continued. "I assume it's usually locked. However, it's possible that it remains unlocked sometimes, especially in the early morning for coordination of security agents to and from the rooftop. If it's locked, we'll blow it open with a grenade."

"How many agents are there on the rooftop, and how are they armed?" Rafael inquired.

"We don't have the specific intelligence information we would like to have regarding that. But we estimate that between ten and fifteen agents guard the roof at any given time of the day or night," Victor said. "They're most likely armed with standard-issue weapons: assault rifles with night vision scopes, and semiautomatic side arms; three or four of them will have shoulder-launched, heat-seeking antiaircraft missiles." He turned to Dante, who was looking unusually pensive. "Do we have any countermeasures for the missiles?"

"Yeah . . . me," Dante replied, drawing heavily on his pipe. "The one and only advantage we do have is the element of surprise. I intend to use it to the fullest extent. We'll slip in without warning and fire smoke rockets at the roof, disorienting the agents before they have a chance to spot us. If all goes according to plan, they won't even know in which direction to point the missiles."

"Everything sounds all right—in theory," Rafael remarked.

"Be optimistic," Sean said, slapping him on the back.

"What's the breakdown of assignments?" George inquired.

Tara, as was her custom, had remained silent—only listening and observing. "It's like this, gentlemen," she finally spoke. "Victor, Sean, and I will be the chopper assault team. Victor, I want you in the front with Dante, spotting for him. Sean and I will ride in the back." Victor and Sean nodded affirmatively. "Rafael, you're in command of the assault on the VerChip production plants in Soho. George, you're second-in-command."

"What about the takeover of the Global News Network building in Midtown Manhattan?" George asked.

"We haven't sufficient forces," Tara said. "If the Soho assault is successful, depending on casualties, you may redirect your forces to the GNN building. The decision will rest with you at that time."

"How many fighters do we have available for the assault, or should I ask?" Rafael said.

Tara nodded. "As I'm sure you know, we're critically short—"

"No, you're not!" said a booming voice from the entrance. Sergio Romano's imposing figure stood in the doorway, flanked by two burly bodyguards. The floor vibrated as he and his entourage walked to the table. He unbuttoned his overcoat and removed his hat, exposing his thinning hair. "If you people need a hand, well here it is," he stated.

Surprised faces looked at him. Dante eyed his uncle. "What are the terms of this generous offer?"

Don Romano spread his hands in a sweeping motion. "What makes you think I want something?"

"Because you always want something," Dante replied.

"Don Romano, please sit down," Tara requested diplomatically.

"I prefer to stand," he said, tossing a manila envelope across the table.

"What's this?" she inquired, picking up the envelope.

"Call it a gesture of goodwill. My men put it together. It's a first-rate piece of work," Romano said, glancing at his bodyguards on either side of him. Tara opened the envelope, taking out security documents, satellite photos, and blueprints of Global Security Incorporated. "Look, I'll make this brief," he said. "Give us the mission objective, date and time. That's all we require."

Tara looked up from the intelligence information with raised eyebrows. "We don't have the necessary forces to take over the GNN building."

"Is that what you want?"

"Yes, but we must also broadcast the liberation speech," she said, sliding a transcript across the table.

Romano picked up the papers and looked them over. "That's fine with me. Just remember your promise: if you succeed, I gain ownership of the docks."

"You have my word on it. Would you mind taking Captain George Sebastian as part of your team? He'll give the liberation speech."

"I don't mind, so long as he obeys *my* orders."

Tara turned to George. He nodded in agreement. She looked back at Romano and said, "The mission day is a week from tomorrow. The GNN studios must be under our control by early morning. We'll give the go-ahead over the secure line."

"You got it, little lady," Romano said, putting on his hat, flicking its brim and walking toward the door. He turned momentarily. "By the way, if worst comes to worst, I want you to know it's been a pleasure knowing all of you."

"Likewise." Tara smiled as the men walked out the door.

The group analyzed the intelligence information, closely examining Global Security Incorporated security procedures and blueprints of the GSI building and production plants. The attack was planned in detail through the night into the early morning hours.

"Any questions, gentlemen?" Tara finally asked. Everyone remained silent. "All right then. The liberation movement begins before dawn, one week from today."

In the following week, all of the preparations were made. Tara reviewed the plan of attack, resolving any last details and finalizing it. Victor shed his disguise, washing his hair back to its natural sandy color and shaving his face clean. *If I'm going to fight and possibly die, I'll fight and die as myself,* he thought. Dante completed the helicopter's modifications. Rafael and George assembled the best fighters and briefed them. Romano mostly listened to the ticking of his pocket watch, given to him by his grandfather long ago. Everything was readied on schedule and the weather forecast was positive.

*   *   *

The day of reckoning arrived . . .

"It's show time," Tara declared as they assembled in the early morning. Her olive-drab fatigues ruffled in the breeze. The silver cross around her neck glimmered in the moonlight. "God, be with us this day," she whispered, crossing herself.

The garage door opened and workmen towed the helicopter into the street.

Dante strapped himself into the pilot's seat, closed the door, donned his headset, and went through the checklist— setting the flight controls, switches, and buttons for start-up. Then he adjusted the throttle on the collective control stick alongside his left leg, and engaged the starter switch. The exhaust spouted smoke; slowly, the rotors began turning and then wound to idle rpm. Victor pulled back his jacket sleeve and looked at his watch; it was 4:45 a.m. He gazed up at the stars in the sky. They were clear and bright.

"Let's move out!" Tara said, walking toward the helicopter, zipping up her parka and slinging her assault rifle on her shoulder. Victor and Sean, their weapons holstered or slung, walked by her side. Dante grinned as they boarded. Victor strapped himself into the left front seat; Tara and Sean strapped themselves into the back seats. Then they shut the doors and put on their headsets.

Dante twisted the throttle to one-hundred-percent rotor rpm. Then he moved the cyclic stick between his knees to a forward position, applied slight left pedal, and pulled up on the collective stick. The helicopter took off smoothly . . .

The darkness of the desolate streets below contrasted with the gleaming lights of Manhattan to their front. Dante glanced at the airspeed indicator, which showed 60 knots. He was flying low and slow to avoid radar detection. He flew over the 278 Expressway across the South Bronx and then followed the East River. Victor could see ground fog covering the expanse of Central Park to the right. The chopper stayed low, less than two hundred feet above the ground, as they crossed over Roosevelt Island and the Queensboro Bridge. Dante turned toward Lower Manhattan, slowed to 40 knots, and began climbing and weaving between the skyscrapers. People could be seen in those offices that were lit at that time of the morning. In the near distance, the Global Security Incorporated building loomed.

"Approaching target building," Dante announced over the headsets. Tara and Sean leaned forward to look through the windshield. The helicopter pulled to a hover behind the apex of the tallest structure adjacent to the GSI building. Dante moved the cyclic stick slightly to the right. The chopper hovered right and faced the building.

Victor raised his binoculars and scanned the top floor. "Hold her steady. The lights are on . . ." He went to high zoom. "He's there," he said, identifying a foreboding, black-suited figure with slicked-back hair. "It's Mephisto all right. And he's by himself."

Dante moved the cyclic stick back to the left and assumed cover behind the adjacent structure.

"Target positively identified. Weapons check," Tara said, racking the bolt of her AK-47. Victor charged his Uzis and checked the grenades on his belt. Sean charged his assault rifle. Dante glanced at his side arm.

"Thumbs-up all around, Commander," Sean confirmed.

"Mission's on. Let's go!" Tara ordered with sweat trickling down her face.

Dante pulled up on the collective stick. The helicopter rose to an altitude slightly higher than the GSI building. Victor raised his binoculars and scanned the roof of the building. "Steady . . . steady . . ." he said. "We have a dozen security agents on the roof. Four of them are armed with shoulder-launched antiaircraft missiles. They're mostly smoking and joking."

"Then they have no idea what's going to hit them," Tara said. "Fire when ready."

"Target range: four hundred fifty meters," Victor said, reading the markings in his binoculars.

Dante steadied the chopper, then pushed the red fire-button on the cyclic stick. A pair of smoke rockets launched, streaking toward the GSI building. . . .

"We have hits on the northeastern corner of the roof," Victor said. "Adjust fire: fifty meters left, fifty forward."

Dante moved the controls slightly then pushed and held the fire-button. More rocket pairs launched in sequence. Seconds later, they struck the center of the roof.

"The roof is completely covered with smoke," Victor reported, lowering the binoculars.

Dante flew the helicopter toward the building. "Touchdown within a minute," he advised as they approached the landing zone. The chopper slowed and descended into the dense smoke screen. Tara, Victor, and Sean removed their headsets, unbuckled their seatbelts, and opened the doors. The rotor wash cleared some of the smoke as the chopper's skids settled onto the rooftop.

The assault team leaped out with guns blazing. Security agents blindly returned fire. The firefight was brief but intense. Terrible screams cried out within the smoke screen; one of the screams was Sean's. The chopper took off in a whirl of noise and haze. Victor yelled for Tara. "Here! I'm over here!" she shouted back. He made his way through the smoke, searching for her.

He holstered an Uzi; "Tara! Tara!" he called, his hand reaching out.

"I'm here, Vic!" her voice came from the obscurity. They joined hands without seeing each other.

Victor took the lead, running toward the center of the roof as flashes of gunfire lit up the smoke all around them. He tripped on a bump, and they both fell to the tarmac.

"Vic!" she said.

"Up! Get up!" Victor said, feeling for the bump in the dense haze. His hand ran across a large metallic square onto a handle. He pulled it, opening a trapdoor that led down a staircase. "This way—let's go!" he shouted, leaping into the opening.

Victor rushed down the stairs, drawing his Uzis and pointing them at the black-suited figure at the front of the room. Tara followed, closing the door behind her and then descending with her assault rifle trained on the figure. . . .

"So . . . you've finally arrived!" Mephisto said, standing at the head of the conference table. On the wall behind him was the crest of the golden phoenix with the slogan, Unity, Progress, and Total Security for Mankind. Victor and Tara observed him silently. "So, you've finally arrived!" he repeated in a louder voice.

"What do you mean?" Victor asked suspiciously.

"I've been expecting you!" Mephisto stared at his uninvited guests.

"Expecting?" Tara breathed heavily.

"That's right," he said, adjusting his scarlet tie, which matched the carnation on the lapel of his black suit jacket. "Every time I try to advance your miserable kind, a diametrically opposed force appears in one form or another."

"The only force here is the firepower of our weapons," Victor said.

"How incredibly crude," Mephisto said, stepping forward.

"Don't come any closer," Victor warned, aiming twin Uzis at his chest.

"Of course," he replied, stopping some meters in front of them.

"Who are you?" Tara inquired nervously.

"I am the compelling force and the hidden hand. I am your wildest dream and your worst nightmare. I am all the fears you haven't the courage to face." Mephisto smiled assuredly.

"You're a monster who has enslaved humanity," Tara said.

"Freedom? Is that what you want? You cling to the concept of freedom, but this is only an illusion. You delude yourselves with the ideals of liberty, justice, and democracy, but these are only diversions. *We* provide you with the notion that you are somehow in control of your lives."

"We?" Tara inquired.

"We, your superiors, the chosen rulers. We who make the decisions that you are incapable of making for yourselves."

"You speak of the Illuminati? The Trident Group?"

"I speak of life itself! The state of being! Your very existence! You are merely creatures who spend your meaningless lives pursuing selfish interests. You have no concept of the greater cause. No vision of the glorious destiny that awaits the world!"

Victor remained silent as Tara continued her inquiry. "We are human beings. We cannot be marked like cattle."

"Human beings? What is that exactly? Fools! You think of yourselves as higher beings, but you are not. What you are, in fact, is the most dangerous life form. You need to be monitored and controlled."

"You're a sadist!" she said bluntly.

Mephisto fixed his eyes on hers. "Sadist, you say? Who is a sadist? Who killed multitudes in countless massacres, genocides, and wars? Who committed these atrocities? You did—your miserable kind. Who are you to judge? You hypocrites!"

Tara and Victor stood in stunned silence for a moment.

"You must cooperate," said a shaken Tara. "We direct you to make a public declaration denouncing the SpyChip."

"Direct indeed!" Mephisto said, stepping forward. "*I direct you* to yield. I direct you to obey me." His eyes flashed fiercely, pointing a commanding finger at them.

Tara and Victor felt an almost uncontrollable fear. Tara's legs wobbled. Victor began to tremble.

"We will not yield. You must make the declaration," Tara said, struggling to maintain her balance.

Mephisto laughed thunderously as he approached closer and closer. "You came here with demands, but you have not the strength to enforce them. And your pathetic ideals won't save you."

"Halt! Stop right there!" Victor exclaimed in a weakened voice.

Mephisto stopped unconvincingly a few meters from Tara, his right foot in the advancing position. "We know each other already," he said. "Oh, yes we do. Victor and—"

"How do you know my name?" Victor asked.

"Oh, I know your names. I know who you are. And I know everything about you. *I've been watching you!* No one can hide from me. No one can escape me. Victor: When you were orphaned, I was there! When you destroyed the black sedan and its occupants, I was there! When you fought in bloody conflicts and wars, I was there!" Mephisto nodded with satisfaction, shifting his attention to Tara. "And you, Tara: Throughout all your trials and tribulations, particularly the dark times, I was there, too. I'm always there, watching and manipulating, especially wherever there's pain, misery, violence, injustice, and disaster." He took another step forward.

"Stop right there! Stop right there!" Victor shouted, forefingers hairpin on the triggers.

"You see, I am powerful," Mephisto continued. "And mankind is weak. You cannot stop me, for I rule this earth. Resistance is futile."

Tara's AK-47 lowered slightly. Victor's Uzis shook in his hands.

Mephisto stepped forward. Suddenly the silver cross around Tara's neck flashed brightly across his face. His eyes lit with burning anger. He lunged toward her—his teeth morphing into fangs, his hands into claws.

Victor and Tara opened fire on full automatic; their weapons blazed furiously. The bullets struck Mephisto, riveting him violently and hurling him under the conference table. The magazines emptied in a few seconds. They fell backward to the floor, drained of energy.

Some minutes passed by unnoticed. . . .

Victor and Tara rose slowly, staring at each other in a stupor. They moved toward the table, looking left and right, above and below. "There's nobody here! His body isn't here! There's no flesh, no blood—nothing!" Victor exclaimed in disbelief. Tara confirmed his statement with a silent nod.

Mephisto had disappeared without a trace.

EPILOGUE

Tara and Victor rapidly climbed the staircase. The sound of whirling rotor blades vibrated the trapdoor above. Tara pushed the door open, pointing her assault rifle in a sweeping motion as they exited. The rising sun shined through the remaining smoke. "Are you with—?" came a transmission over the radio clipped to her belt. "Are you with me?" said Dante's familiar voice.

Tara drew the radio from her belt, pushed the talk button and spoke into its microphone, "Mission accomplished. We've just exited onto the roof."

"The situation's under control here. My rocket pods are empty but the security agents have their hands up."

"What about Sean?"

"He's wounded, but alive—that's all I know."

Tara and Victor walked through the clearing smoke. The dark elliptical form of the helicopter hovered on the east edge of the building with the sun rising behind it. Security agents stood with their hands in the air on the opposite side of the roof. Tara slung her rifle on her shoulder. A single figure approached them. His face was streaked in red, and blood flowed from his chest, running down his clothes to his boots.

"Sean!" Tara exclaimed.

"We've done it. Mission's accomplished, right?" Sean said, staring blankly.

"Mission's accomplished," Victor affirmed.

Sean collapsed to the ground, motionless. Several bodies of dead and dying security men lay around him. Tara crouched and checked his neck for a pulse. There was none. "He's gone," she said quietly, removing her parka and covering him.

Victor pointed twin Uzis at the remaining security men. "Inside—move it!" he ordered.

The men filed into the trapdoor entrance and down the staircase. Tara rushed to the door, then closed and jammed it shut with her switchblade.

Victor holstered his weapons. Then he took out his binoculars and viewed Soho to the north. The sunlight intensified and the chopper's rotor wash blew across his face. Tara came to his side.

"What does it look like in Soho?" she asked.

"Lots of fire," he replied, viewing the distant flames. "The VerChip factories are burning."

"Steele to Rafael . . . Steele to Rafael . . ." Tara called on her radio.

"I'm here, Steele . . . I'm here," Rafael responded in a faint voice.

"Situation report?"

"The final assault . . . we've taken the objectives . . ."

"Are you all right?"

"I've been hit—" The radio crackled. "I'll be okay . . . heavy casualties . . ."

"Copy that. Complete the mission; burn everything to the ground," Tara said. "Is that clear?"

"Clear . . . Out."

Victor shifted his binoculars to Midtown Manhattan. "The GNN building appears calm," he said, viewing the broadcast building with its towering antennas.

Tara took out her handheld computer and initialized it. George's image appeared on the screen, broadcasting from what was now, the former GNN studios. On the bottom of the screen was the address of the website that disclosed all secret information about WorldGov, NWO, and the Trident Group.

"My fellow citizens," George announced with Romano's men in the background. "We, the citizenry, have liberated New York City. Mr. Maximilian Mephisto has been banished, VerChip production plants are burning, and the media studios are under our control. From this day forward, freedom, justice, and human dignity shall reign in our great city. We are once again a free people. Nevermore will the forces of dictatorship rule over us. I direct my fellow citizens to go to the nearest medical facilities to have their VerChip implants removed. We will serve as an interim government until free elections are held . . ."

Tara turned off her computer. "Everything is under control," she said with a quiet smile on her lips.

They stood silently for a moment, overlooking the city.

"Can you believe this view?" Victor said.

"It's the view of a great and free metropolis," Tara stated as the sun beamed down on them.

"I'm down to minimum fuel," Dante warned over the radio.

The helicopter's skids settled onto the rooftop. Victor and Tara jogged to the chopper, jumped into the back seats, closed the doors and threw on their seatbelts. Dante moved the controls and they took to the sky. Tara leaned back on the headrest, closing her eyes momentarily.

"Tara . . . Tara, are you all right?" Victor asked.

"I'm fine, Victor," she replied, slowly opening her eyes and turning to him. "Everything is going to be just fine."

The liberation movement spread, for the light of freedom gleamed irresistibly. People across the globe rebelled against WorldGov, removed their VerChips, and fought for their rights. The rebellion proved unstoppable: the World Government was overthrown, the New World Order was dismantled, and SpyChip production facilities were destroyed. Then the nations were reinstated with representative governments based on ethical principles.

And Mephisto? It is said his evil spirit escaped to the invisible world. That it blows in the chilling winds of wicked hearts. That it comes to us in many forms, to be accepted or rejected, according to our capacity to be righteous.